DEATH DROP

I0526188

John Klawitter

DEATH DROP

A FICTION4ALL PAPERBACK

© Copyright 2020
John Klawitter

The right of John Klawitter to be identified as author of
this work has been asserted in accordance with the
Copyright, Designs and Patents Act 1988

All Rights Reserved

No reproduction, copy or transmission of the publication
may be made without written permission. No paragraph
of this publication may be reproduced, copied or
transmitted save with the written permission of the
publisher, or in accordance with the provisions of the
Copyright Act 1956 (as amended).

Any person who does any unauthorised act in relation to
this publication may be liable to criminal prosecution
and civil claims for damages.

ISBN 978-1-78695-257-8

Published 2020
Fiction4All
www.fiction4all.com

Author Acknowledgements

This project probably began a long time ago when my Navajo brother, James Curtis Shorty, invited me to go with him from Silver City and the deserts of Southern New Mexico (we were on a geology field trip) to spend a few days on the reservation of his people. That was over a half century ago. I was a college grind, and I didn't go because I was worried about my grades and getting into grad school...but if I had taken that trip with him, I think it could have changed my life forever. Those lands are special, magical, as they say, enchanted. And, in a way, I've been trying to understand just why ever since. A few years later, I did write and direct a short educational documentary on the Navajos in modern times, and Jimmy helped me do that film in and around Monument Valley. There had been some bad feelings about a spaghetti western shot earlier on the reservation, and without Jimmy's help we'd never had gotten it done. And now, all these years later, his patience and his sense of humor, as well as his insights into the joys, the problems and the prospects of the people of the Southwest have been a huge contribution to writing this novel.

Taos, New Mexico, is a unique location, full of history, a rich heritage brought about by a mix of cultures, and lots of surprises. I have to thank Southwestern fine artist Bill Baron, a member of the legendary Taos Artists Group, for his understanding and his sharp and pitiless observations on the human condition.

Also, many thanks to educator, essayist and social commentator Richard Erlich, PhD, for his fine editorial services and his measured opinions that go above and beyond the normal call of duty.

And the last who is, in fact, always the first on my mind and in my heart, my deepest thanks to my best fan and my most honest and intense critic, my wife Lynn Jensen-Klawitter.

Chapter 1

My full given name is Alexia Georgianna the Third. Lexi, for short. I am a massive, shaggy-haired and perfectly formed wolfhound bitch, and I'm a champion. I've trotted the winner's circle with the nice old lady who struggles to keep up with me. I've basked in the warm approval of dog lovers as they clap and cheer from the sidelines; I have been awarded the plaques and golden cups, and I have often felt big heavy medals carefully placed on my massive neck, the round prizes that shine golden under the bright lights.

My owner, a decent old lady named Cory Anderson, is proud of me, and I've been to breeder kennels for that experience of a lifetime, rewarded not once but four times. Joy, joy, joy and…well, this fourth time at Bornton Breeders, I have a problem and I think it is a serious one. The joy is still in the process of having some wonderful puppies, but also something very bad is here as well, something my mom-sense tells me I have to be on guard against.

It isn't the stud dude they assigned to me. Manfred Arthur is young and proud and brave and he comes with top dog lineage, and he is quite up to his job. But after my three earlier breeding bouts, I know what I am doing and – not really bragging here – I have him huffing and puffing and in a bit of a whine before I lovingly wring him dry.

My worry doesn't come from the food, either, and certainly not the kennels, which are in fact quite nice. It is something else.

In the short time I've been at Bornton Breeding Kennels, almost every bitch I see leaves with a sad look on her face. And from what I can tell, that's because in each case one single puppy, the pick of the litter, goes missing before the owner shows up. It might be a day, it might be three or ten days, but that one little special pup is not to be found, and that's not right. We lady dogs know it is too soon to be separated. We all know something at Bornton Kennels is very, very wrong.

I don't need anything more than that to make up my mind. The same bad thing is going to happen to my own new brood. That is, unless I do something about it; and, as it happens, Lady Luck is giving me the perfect opportunity.

Chapter 2

Taos, New Mexico. Two in the afternoon in early December. One of those crisp, clear days with a no-forgiveness chill-your-blood wind hissing through the pines. Jessie Carter is in the driver's seat of her dusty forest green Range Rover, a hand-me-down from Ed, her father. Jessie Carter; short blond hair, thirty-ish, pretty, bright, sensible, college degree in literature (one of the two not-so-sensible thing she'd ever done, might have been better to have gone into hotel management or bookkeeping if she'd wanted something practical, but then she'd have missed Keats and Shelly and Coleridge, and so she was happy with that choice. Chooli, the full-blooded Navajo girl who worked for Jessie's father, was riding along to pick up a load of groceries she'd ordered from Cid's Food Market. They \had stacked the cardboard boxes filled with food way in back and now they were going to pick up Jessie's daughter Billie from middle school.

"You notice, the helpers disappeared when they saw us checking out," Jessie flipped a careless thumb back at Cid's.

"Yeah. Like magic."

"Women as equals." Jessie gave her friend a puckish grin.

"We been liberated. Get to vote now, and everything."

Jessie pulled to a stop at the curb at the Taos Middle School. Chooli slid out of the passenger seat and moved to the middle seat to make room for Jessie's daughter Billie. Chooli was a few years younger than Jessie; she'd come to Carter Cabins in an awkward and foolish time and, under the unusual circumstances, big hearted Ed hired her and she proved to be a hard worker, in charge of the main house kitchen and supervisor over the three Latina sisters who cleaned and made up the guest beds in the main house and the cabins.

"She's usually waiting right here…" Jessie scanned the schoolyard, looking for her daughter.

"Over there." Chooli pointed to the cement apron in front of the school. Billie was easy to spot, the center of attention as she yelled in her highest-pitched pre-teen girl's voice at a boy about her age.

"Will too, dorky dork-brains!"

"Will not, crappy crap-head!"

She was arguing with Jimmy Flagg, both screaming kid curses with half the school watching. When she saw her mom and the Rover, Billie grabbed her book bag and hurried over. She got in the front seat and slammed the door hard so it wouldn't rattle so much.

Jessie got back behind the wheel, shrugged at Chooli and gave her ten year old daughter a questioning look, "Jimmy's not coming with us?"

"No, he is not. He called me a dork!"

"No, you called him that. He called you a crappy crap-head."

"Whatever…"

"What were you arguing about?"

Billie lowered her dark eyebrows and pursed her young lips. With her brown hair and flashing eyes she took after her father, who had died in a racing car accident when she was just a toddler. "Jimmy says we're gonna have to sell Carter Cabins. He says there's a secret plan. His daddy's gonna squeeze us out!"

"It better be a good plan. Believe me, Billie, Jimmy's dad can't squeeze anybody out. He's only an employee. And we're doing okay. And the people who own the lodge Jimmy's daddy works for are in worse shape than we are."

Jimmy's family lived at the Taos Pines Lodge next door, just down the mountain from the Carter Cabins. They were newcomers, at least to the Carter way of looking at things, but so was nearly everyone else. The Carters had owned their big tract of land in the hills above Taos for generations. While it was true that Jimmy's mom and dad, Art and Amy Flagg, had a sweet deal – free rent in a big manager's suite and a nice salary – they didn't own anything. They had moved up from Santa Fe two years before to manage the lodge. Jimmy's mom handled the staff and his dad was general manager, both reporting to some big corporation in Los Angeles. But whatever their son had overheard had to be pure speculation; they were managers, not owners.

"Jimmy says he's going to ride with Miss Paulson."

Chooli smiled and shook her head. "He must really be mad at you. He hates to ride with Miss Paulson."

"Aw, he'll get over it. We're best friends, you know."

"I know. That's the way best friends are."

"Do you have a best friend, Chooli?"

11

The Navajo girl nodded, her dark eyes sparkling, her short clipped black hair close around her face. "Your family is my best friends."

"Well then, you know how it is."

"Yes, I do." Chooli gave her a playful tap on the back of her head.

Chapter 3

That day Church Dickens came in to work early, driving in from his apartment in Santa Monica to the Verhu Financial building in West L.A., not to do actual work, but to get in some light morning exercise before his appointment at the nearby Veterans Hospital. Verhu had a great little workout gym – executive employees only – tucked in one corner of the lobby of the eleven-story building. The room was crammed with weights and machines, and now they'd added something new, a climbing wall.

Church was expecting to be alone, and he did have the place to himself for all of about five minutes. He was doing deep pulls on the rowing machine when Philby walked in: thin, wiry, ancient, a blinking vacant look on his face. Church's boss Alan Philby, the quasi-legendary head of Verhu Financial.

The old man folded his ancient Brooks Brothers suit jacket and carefully placed it on the seat of a stationary bike. He took off his tie. He unlaced his shining Florsheim shoes and lined them up on the floor. He left his suit pants on.

"Hello, Dickens," Philby said as he fell to the floor.

"Hi, Alan." Church ignored the fall; he'd seen this move before.

Old Alan's rigid palms smacked the polished cement surface and he started pushups, counting, "One – Two – Three," until he got to twelve, on the last three pushing with enough energy to clap his hands together.

"Show off," Church said.

Philby ignored the jab. He jumped to his feet, tried to hide that he was panting. "Real men – don't use – machines."

"You ever see that bit on TV with Jack Palance at the Oscars?"

A frown crossed Alan's thin features and he blinked twice. He didn't like not knowing things. "Jack Who? No, what was that?"

"It was in the early 1990s. Jack Palance was really old at the time."

"Old as me?"

"Older, I guess. He was up for Best Supporting Actor – won it, too – takes the stage to pick up his statue and starts doing pushups."

"Anybody can do pushups. I can do a hundred."

"One-handed pushups."

Philby's frown deepened "I don't see you doing any pushups."

"Can't. Docs at the VA won't let me. Maybe someday, they tell me..."

But Philby's mind had wandered back to the Oscars. "Those statues they give the actors ... I bet they ain't real gold."

"You're betting right. They're just gold plated."

Philby was putting his tie back on, having set aside the rest of the dozen warm-up exercises he'd been telling everybody he'd learned in the military in the 1950's. "How do you know that about them statues?"

"I know metals. I have a B.S. in Geology."

"I know BS when I hear it."

14

That sent Dickens' mind searching for some way to avoid confrontation. Annie, Philby's old secretary, says he was supposed to be on meds, but confided he goes off them whenever he feels like it.

Dickens decided the metallic composition of an Oscar probably was a safe topic. "No, seriously, Alan. Last year around Academy Awards time, ABC Nightly News did a report. The Oscar statues are cast in heavy bronze. They plate that with copper, and after that, with nickel – and then that's plated with pure 24 karat gold."

"24 K gold!"

"Yeah, but just a thin layer."

"Oh. Not expensive as it looks, then…"

Philby seemed to lose interest. He picked an imaginary string off his suit jacket. "You like my climbing wall?"

"Not really. It looks dangerous, cramped in here. Fall, you land on a bike."

"Just don't fall."

"I guess…You climb it?"

"Oh, yeah. It's nothing. Kid stuff."

Dickens watched Philby glance at his image in a full-length mirror, straighten his tie and run his hands through his thinning hair. "I thought you did the military Daily Dozen. You still got eleven to go."

"Measure twice, cut once," Philby said. The old man blinked, looking around the empty room like he was seeing it for the first time. Then he headed for the door without another word, leaving the younger man to wonder what any of that was about. Had Philby stopped by just to do a few pushups?

Did he have some other motive? With Philby there was no way to tell.

Church Dickens, who had only worked at Verhu for six months, went back to his rowing exercise. He'd learned a lot about his boss in the last few weeks, and some of it was very disquieting. A random comment by Annie, Alan's former secretary, triggered his initial alarm; after that, some quiet digging turned up evidence that Philby was more than a tottering old fool; he was a serious financial renegade. This was, Dickens had solidly reprimanded himself, important background he should have looked up before he signed on. Back then the opportunity had looked too great to pass up, the chance to make junior partner in a year or two. And now Verhu was on his resume, and there was no way to delete that. Chances were good that old Philby wasn't heading for Happy Times Retirement Village – he was going to jail; Church could end up down the hall in another room with bars on the windows and just one handle on the door.

Chapter 4

Jesse drove from town, heading back to the ski area. The narrow two lane asphalt road had been widened – and even expanded into four lanes in some areas – but as it headed steadily upward in elevation the switchbacks were still the narrow two lanes with steep drop-offs into canyons below.

"Beautiful, this time of day," Chooli said.

"Yeah. But we sure could use some snow."

Chooli had heard that complaint before, particularly the last couple years, and thought back for a moment. "Heavy snow that first season you came to the cabins."

"You remember that, huh?"

"Hard to forget. Your daddy picked me up in a downright blizzard, Jess. I was hitching back to the rez; snowing so hard I was surprised he saw me standing by the road."

"What happened, Chooli?" Billie said.

"You was just a toddler. Me, I was married to the sheriff."

"You was married to Sheriff Joe, Chooli?"

"Yep. He wasn't sheriff, just a deputy back then. And me, I was a child bride, thrown in the trunk of a rusty old Buick and hustled off to Vegas."

"Nooo...." Billie gave her a wide-eyed look of disbelief.

"Oh, yeah. I had a mean old uncle, drunk, and we were living with him and my aunt in a mobile home in Tuba City, sleeping on the floor. Mom's at work, Uncle Tony kidnaps me, shipped me off to Vegas."

Billie looked from Chooli to Jessie, "I don't understand. How did -?"

"Bad things happen to good people," Jessie said. "You couldn't have been more than two or three, Billie. My mom – your grandma - had died of cancer when I was ten, long before you were born. After that the years went by and I grew up and got married and we had you and then a few years later daddy died."

"But I know all that."

"I know, honey. But then the time came when Grandpa Ed got lonely and one night he was sitting around with two of his old high school buddies and they all three declared they were tired of the single life. So they did a really dumb thing. They piled into Grandpa Ed's big old Cadillac convertible and headed for Las Vegas, looking for fun and romance."

Billie gave out a snorting laugh. "No, they didn't..."

"Oh, yeah, they did. And their crazy plan worked – at least it seemed to, at first. I guess they thought they were in one of those madcap adventures like you see in the movies, three free and single buddies in their mid-life crisis driving to Sin City to find true love in all the wrong places. Three single dudes headed out for Vegas that day, but a few days later three couples returned, their wild and crazy plans having succeeded beyond their wildest dreams. And then, as actual life would have it, the dreams changed themselves into nightmares."

Billie, still not believing, shook her head, "Not possible."

Jessie smiled, but there was a sad look on her face as she remembered how the adventure of the three amigos had played out, Grandpa Ed's new bride turning out to be Kate, the mean money-grubber. Joey the cop, Chooli's new husband was a wife-beater, so that wasn't going to work. And the third was some tramp from Sin City, took one look at Taos, stole whatever cash she could lay her hands on and disappeared, probably heading right back for Vegas.

Billie's Great Grandpa Frank was gone and Jessie's dad Ed was getting on in his sixties now, still ornery as ever, still very much in charge of Carter Cabins, though Vegas Kate thought she ran things. Las Vegas Kate, thin face, cigarette in a corner of her wrinkled lips, not aging well, a case of obsessive/compulsive disorder or maybe something worse, never satisfied, always trying to put people and things in their proper place.

Jessie didn't like to hide anything from Billie, but still … what had happened made the grownups she was supposed to look up to seem worse than kids. She paused, wondering how best to go on with the story – after all, Ed was too stubborn to admit his mistake and they all had to live with Kate at the cabins.

But then Billie screamed, "Mom, look out!"

The next moment Jessie heard the hard blat of an air horn, not so much a warning as a shriek of doom. And she saw the rusty-chrome tooth grill of a huge logging truck that crossed into their lane and was heading straight for them.

Chapter 5

That nice bitch hound Belinda Royale (you may have noticed show dog owners tend to give us fancy names) was in the cage across the aisle from me, looking even more sad than usual. I knew her from the shows, had seen here and there. She was white and brown, white with big irregular patches of golden brown all over. A real beauty, if you were into Bassett hounds. She had actually bested me once at the Phoenix show, but we don't hold grudges, at least I don't. In a way it's unfair, her type of hounds have that naturally morose look and judges feel sorry for them, at least that's what we show dogs all think. But as I said before, every bitch at Bornton Breeding Kennels was in a worrisome way, so maybe her expression wasn't anything that unusual.

It was a Friday night, the two young people who worked for Jay Bornton had hurried through their chores and rushed off, intent on being somewhere else. And I was left with Belinda, who was still standing at the front of her cage, standing patiently on her stumpy legs, staring at me. I had been thinking all day, trying to figure out how to get out of here. I was tired and so I moved to settled down on the worn blanket at the back of my cage. And that was when Belinda barked, just once, one short yip. I returned one step to the front of the cage. And she was still staring in my direction with that forlorn hound look. With her short legs, her long brown ears were down near the floor. Her eyes remained on me and she nodded her head, just one quick little nod. She had something to say. I was sure she was trying to tell me something.

I reached out with my left paw, more a comforting gesture to Belinda, a way to say Come on, girl, everything's going to be okay. The pad on the bottom of my foot brushed the wire door of my cage – and the door gave way, moved open an inch or two. The latch that was supposed to secure it hadn't fallen into its slot!

Our cages were raised about a foot above the aisle that separated us into two parallel rows. I pushed my door open and easily stepped down to the tile floor. I was about to slip away into the night when I looked back to see Belinda still staring at me. Oh boy, and here comes the guilt trip! I knew I would still be back in my cage if it wasn't for her. I wondered if I could push up her latch and open her cage door. I was tall enough and there was nobody else around. Seemed to me like it was only fair to give it a try.

Chapter 6

The logging truck was a huge double load parallel rig, one trailer behind the other, and it was capable of crushing Ed Carter's dented old Land Rover and continuing on down the road as if not much had happened. There was no time to think. When it veered across the lane and started toward them, Jessie acted on instinct; instead of breaking, she hit the gas and spun the steering wheel, skidding off the road and clearing the front bumper of the truck by inches. There was a small flat gravel area about the size of a baseball infield. Jessie jerked the wheel and the Rover spun out, three complete circles before it came to a complete stop at the edge of a steep canyon. The truck had gone off the road as well, but didn't stop. It disappeared over the lip of the canyon and was gone.

"Oh, my Gods!" Chooli said.

Billie was more excited than afraid. "Mom! That was incredible! Where did you learn to drive like that?"

"Your daddy taught me. I asked him about his job, and he took me to a race driving school. We never thought some day it might save our lives!" She was quiet for a moment, thinking about it. "At least, I never did…"

The Rover's engine was still running, and the tires were new and things were so quiet and normal it didn't seem possible they'd had such a close call and come through with no real damage. And then they heard an explosion from the floor of canyon a thousand feet below.

"I'll take a look," Chooli said.

"Billie, stay here!" Jessie said, but her daughter had already jumped out of the front seat and run after Chooli. A few seconds was all it took, and they came running back.

"There's smoke from way down there at the bottom! The truck is burning!"

Jessie was already dialing 911, and in a few minutes a highway patrol car showed up, and thirty seconds after that Sheriff Joey's black and white skidded to a stop behind them.

The sheriff hurried over to them while the state troopers were still in their car. "What's happening here?" he said.

Jessie pointed in the direction where the big truck had disappeared. "Big logging truck couldn't keep his side of the road. Got in our lane, zipped on by. Gone over the edge."

"Ain't no logging up here no more."

Jessie shrugged, "I don't know about that, Sheriff Joey. Not our problem."

His frown said he didn't like Jessie's attitude, but when he saw Chooli, his look turned cold as ice. Jessie wasn't worried. There were two state troopers climbing out of their own car, and she figured Joey wasn't going to make a scene with his ex-wife in public, leastwise not with other-cops "public." The sheriff huffed over to the edge of the cliff and looked down. There was a curl of smoke, but the truck itself was over a thousand feet below, somewhere out of sight.

"Jesus H. Christ…" Sheriff Joey said to nobody in particular.

There was nothing anybody could do until they got a crew out there; there was no easy way down the steep canyon wall. Jessie told the troopers how the truck, moving downhill, had crossed into their lane, missed them, and kept on going off the road and over the cliff. Nothing else to it. There were several others who had seen the accident and had pulled over as well. Their eye witness report matched Jessie's. She characterized it as a near miss, gave her identification and phone number and drove away just as a local lady TV reporter and her quaintly moustachioed one-man video crew pulled up in the ABC Action Van.

Chapter 7

I moved through the brush along the roadside, putting distance between me and Bornton Breeding Kennels. No particular hurry; just the opposite, a big dog like me can attract too much attention even when I'm not doing anything special. And, after all, I had no idea where I was going. And there was Belinda, thinking I didn't know she was there, quietly tracking behind me on her short legs. Boy, for a little stump of a dog, that girl could really keep up.

Bel gave me a little woof, that deep voice of hers, and came trotting up to me. She looked back over her shoulder. It was daylight, a good ten hours after we'd slipped away from the kennels. She gave me a little nudge with that white nose of hers and shook her ears; I listened more closely and heard what she heard — and we slipped deeper into the brush until we found a good place behind a roadside clump of tan rocks. Just in time, too, as Jay Bornton's van went roaring on past, trailing a scent of unhappy dog smells that reminded me of her kennel.

Bel tilted her head, giving me that mournful Bassett look. I nodded once; we were teammates. We waited a while and then moved on uphill, staying close to the road and yet trying to use whatever cover we could find along the way, Bel listening all the time and sniffing now and then with that amazing hound nose of hers No one would sneak up on us.

Chapter 8

"Well, Great Grampa Frank would have hated this!" Jessie had their green Range Rover inching forward in the heavy traffic in front of the Taos Pines Lodge. Traffic was heavy as the schools had let out at the same time taxis were arriving from the airport and there was a bus from Santa Fe and the one from Albuquerque as well.

Billie's eyes narrowed as the Rover took them past the dark brown stained shingles fronting the lodge. The big three hotel was touted as state of the art in Western Ways magazine, a sleek and modern ski lodge that had been built as close to the ski lifts as they could get without bumping into Carter land and the Carter Cabins. Not that Billie didn't see it all the time; she was trying to imagine the big lodge not being there. She glared at the building and angrily rubbed an imaginary spot off the passenger side window.

"Jimmy really got to you, huh?" Jessie said. Billie didn't say anything

The Carter land didn't seem like too much from where they were, just a few hundred feet fronting the main road with the big log house in the center and maple and aspens and birch trees all around. The cabins were hidden behind, and then, beyond that stretch, their land widened and ran back for several miles, much of it running uphill away from the main road in a pleasant valley with a small stream fed with runoff from the higher elevations;

and there was a grove of ancient pines — the oldest literally ancient — as the hills steepened.

Ed's dad had saved those pines, and the loggers had been gone from their area for decades, replaced by more trout fishers and trail hikers in the summer and skiers in the winter. And the two Frank Carters – senior and junior - and Junior's son Ed's dreams had mostly come true. Just upslope from the lodge and a snowball throw below the lifts, the rustic Carter Cabins offered a main boarding house with rooms for a dozen guests and six stand-alone rustic-chic log cabin houses, each set near a rocky stream, each with a view better than the last.

The lodge people had been trying to buy them out ever since the new comers had gotten there; the Cabins were on better situated land than the lodge; every time some misfortune or setback came to pass on the Carter family, the absentee lodge owners in Los Angeles sent out somebody to test the Carter resolve with an offer to buy. Ed thought that lately it was the Flagg family who passed on the word to California, but nobody knew for sure. In a town like Taos everybody pretty much knew everybody else's business.

"We're not going to sell, Billie," Jessie said, her voice breaking a lengthy silence. "We've been through lots worse than this."

"Like what, Mom?"

"There was the time Grandpa Ed broke his legs. A mine shaft he was working caved in on him."

"And when Dad died."

"Yes, that time…"

Billie's dad Martin Eber, who'd made his fame if not his fortune — definitely not his fortune! —

racing grand prix cars for Porsche, had died shortly after Billie was born, suddenly taken from them in a fiery auto race in Monaco. Jessie had met him on a trip to Paris after college; he had bought her purple roses and with a delightful tenor burst into operatic lyrics had completely swept her away. After a marriage in a cathedral in Le Mans they'd lived in an apartment in Paris. It was there they'd had Billie, and then just as quick he himself was swept away like it all was all a dream, a love story, a romance movie going great until the terrible, horrible fiery bad ending. No matter, she told herself with a brief shake of her tight blond curls, her lips thinning with the memory. That was then and this was now; Martin had died and that was the first time when the real estate investors from California were right there, sniffing around the cabins, wading in the cold stream behind, working up their offers to buy.

"Not too many bottom feeders around yet this year," Chooli said, thinking along the same lines as Jesse, the way close friends often do.

"They'll be back, if not now, in a month or two. With no snow yet and going on December and this the third bad ski season in a row …."

"I heard Molly's Coffee Shop in Taos sold out to Coffee Bean & Tea Leaf."

"Yeah. Pretty soon the old folks sunning themselves in the plaza near the Hotel La Fonda de Taos will be gossiping who gives up next."

Jessie took one hand off the steering wheel to shield her eyes from the bright sunlight. "Well, it's not going to be us. It's going to be Taos Pines selling out way before Carter Cabins."

"Why you think so?"

"They lost a lot when they built the second set of ski runs. The ones nobody much uses."

"You have to go further to get to there," Billie said. "Jimmy and I don't like them."

"You don't go near Death Drop run, do you?"

"No, Mom. Jimmy's dad won't let him, either."

"It was Grandpa Ed who found the gold," Jessie said, trying to change the subject.

"But that's all gone, Mom."

"Maybe. Nobody knows for sure."

"You can't count on gold, Mom." Her daughter spoke with the same tone of finality as Kate. If Vegas Kate had her way, she'd have done with all her husband's ideas, cabins and gold mines and such foolish nonsense; she'd have had them sell out years ago and move her back to the casinos of Nevada where she believed the action was. Kate was relentless; there had been loud arguments and cold angry whispers between her and Ed ever since she'd arrived at the cabins. The woman from the game room casinos (or chicken ranches, Jessie suspected) had made her true wishes known so many times you could see it coming from the first words out of her mouth. When she started up like she did, the real estate page open on her place at the dinner table and her voice chirping like an annoying sparrow's, Ed would gather up the breakfast or dinner dishes and remember a few stalls in the big barn out back that needed mucking.

Jessie never felt like her mother-in-law. Even as a young girl, she had been happy and even excited they owned their own land and cabins and even their own gold mine. (Even if it was collapsed in with just a short tunnel in the side of a hill remaining, these days totally fenced off with a locked gate.) Jessie still was proud of her dad for starting it up, even though nobody else seemed to care.

"You know the gold mining began when Grandpa Ed found a few shiny little flakes in our creek," Jessie said, smiling at Billie. "One of the locals told him it was fool's gold, and that was true enough – we do have lots of fool's gold on our property – but the next day he caught that same guy panning in that sandy bend in the creek right behind cabin number two. Panning for real gold, and we had lots."

"Granpers told me the story, Mom. About a dozen times. He learned how to pan gold for himself and he followed the tiny specks of gold upstream and that's how he got to the place where he dug the mine in that very hillside where it is today, all chained up and nothing there. And Grandma Kate says he nearly got his silly foolish butt crushed, to boot!"

"Don't use that language, Billie. That gold is still there. Somewhere close to our old mine. We just don't know exactly where."

"I know, Mom. That was before the earthquake – "

Chooli sighed, not liking the conversation. She had the Navajo fear of going underground in mines or caves. "I think maybe Mother Earth was unhappy Ed took her treasures."

"Well, maybe…" Jessie spoke in a neutral way, respectful of her friend's beliefs. "No matter what, if there's any gold left, it's all jumbled up and buried somewhere under the hills back there."

"No, I don't think so, Mom. If it's really there, why didn't Old Grampers just go back and get it?"

"He had to earn a living to support us. This was before Kate the nag came along. That mine tunnel he dug was caved in but you just couldn't keep a Carter down; the very day he could walk he set the mining idea aside and soon as he was able to get around he started drawing up the plans and soon he was building more cabins one by one all on his own. No one was sure where that gold vein might have gone off to and they still don't know to this day, but in Grandpa Ed's mind cabins were a sure thing."

"Yes, the cabins are a real thing," Chooli said.

"Still, that gold … that was one dream my dad never let go. I remember one time he hired a couple of fancy geology professors out from Colorado State to take a look. This was before Kate – "

"And they found nothing." That was Billie, sounding firm as a rock.

"Well, they did find where the original quartz vein came to an end."

"Nothing," Billie said.

Jessie saw Billie wasn't going to change her mind; it looked like Kate had gotten to her. Kids were impressionable; they made up their own minds. Jessie didn't say any more; she thought the world of her dad and what he had accomplished. Ed had been an unstoppable force. Once he saw there was no way to get to that gold that still might be in the ground, he cashed in most of his stored up little sacks of the shiny metal and bought logs and timber from the last mill still open, and then he set out to build the cabins that over the years had accumulated in value and were really more like fancy little log homes, great vacation getaways, their source of income.

Early on, most folk in the area thought Ed had lost it and joked behind his back, he was just like Noah building a big dumb ark with no water in sight. But over the years, they had to change their tune — a bit. Then they grudgingly said he was just plain lucky, because skiing had become popular and there the Carter Cabins were available for rent at a great price, right next to the ski lift.

And in the new good times – with all the hikers and bikers and trout fishers and skiers invading the local mountains – the sheriff had come nosing around, saying he was concerned about liability and safety. That was when good old wife beater sheriff Joey Johnson came out to their place arguing about public safety even if it was private land, and soon after that the old Carter mine got its ten foot high cyclone fence and double-locked gate.

And now the local gawkers were saying the Carters would have to sell out to Taos Pines Lodge? No way was that going to happen. This was their place, their personal history, the homestead four generations of Carters staked out as their own.

Chapter 9

Ruger Dickens had skin the color of mahogany and curly black locks, while his twin brother Church looked like a Viking with straight blond hair. Their differences were not entirely unexpected although it was a rare DNA play left over from great, great grandma Mabel Archer-Dickens' amorous adventures with the hired help on what remained of the Dickens Virginia tobacco plantation, while Captain Moab Dickens kept up the family tradition of running guns, modest artillery pieces, explosives, whiskey, and other sundry goods to and from Ireland and other places with troubles, and a market for the wherewithal to make more trouble, or to drown their troubles in one drug or other. Black-and-white twins were said to blossom in less than one in every thousand sets of twins born with similar hanky-panky in their ancestry. Back in her day, Mabel's son was born white or at least high yellow, as they said, and her husband Captain Moab was inclined to forgive and forget, having himself now and then traded passage for cabin affections with (mostly) Irish lasses and Latina señoritas, themselves desperate to escape the violence, famine, and poverty of their native lands — to which more fastidious souls might suggest he had contributed his wee bit, and grown rich on. "Judge not that ye be not judged ...."

Aside from color, Church and Ruger Dickens were like as twins could be in weight, height, build, education, mannerisms, and even thinking. Born into old family money, they went to the best schools, grew up in a big old house on what was left of the original plantation, traveled, had great lives. But then Ruger took over the family trust fund with considerable success while Church – happy to be freed of the responsibility – joined the army, was involved in many firefights and nearly died in Afghanistan, came back, got a law degree and spent time to repair the maimed lower section of his spine.

Church had dropped off his cherished eleven year old Porsche for repairs; Ruger, in Los Angeles from back east, was glad to drive him around in a rented yellow Mustang convertible with a big black stripe painted front to back, including a black patch on the fabric roof.

"So you like this car because of your affection for bumblebees," Church said.

"No. I like it because the rental guy swore it can go one hundred and sixty."

"Glad it's only a few blocks to the VA."

"You going to be all right? I can wait for you."

"You don't want that. This is the army. They have schedules, but they never keep them."

"You sure?"

"I'll just take a cab or Uber from there to my office. It's not far."

Ruger pulled up to the hospital entrance. He got out and lifted a big black wheelchair out of the back seat.

Church settled in the chair and gave his brother a friendly salute. "By the way, we're going to buy in on a ski resort in New Mexico."

"Huh. I didn't know they had skiing. How much?" Ruger said

"In the northern part they have really good skiing. Pennies on the dollar."

"I like it."

"Thought you would."

"I especially like the skiing part. Next best thing to sky diving."

Ruger held out a brochure with a picture of a happy couple falling out the door of a light plane. Church studied it, a frown on his face. "Serious now, Rugs – I might need some major flimflam over at work. Electricity down and out for fifteen minutes or so."

"Wooh. You lawless scamp. When?"

"Tuesday. One oh five in the afternoon."

"Black out?"

"Total."

"Cell phones, too?"

"Not necessary. Just the building."

"I guess I can do that. It's all in knowing who to pay to pull the right switch. Let me know when it's a go." Ruger got back in the driver's seat. Church knew his brother was thinking of that classic old move, leaping in over the side of the closed door, getting in without opening it, but had changed his mind, probably because of his freshly pressed slacks and dark navy sports jacket. Church also knew that when he got out of the hospital his brother and the bumblebee rental would be back where it was, waiting for him.

Chapter 10

A few minutes later, Church met Jesus Christ. Church had slapped the square brushed chrome auto-entry panel next to the entrance and was wheeling in through the wide front doors of the VA hospital and there was the Lord and Savior to greet him. At least it was a guy who looked so like Jesus – with the beard and the soft brown eyes – that the orange sunburst tie-dyed t-shirt and worn jeans he had on seemed out of place. Church was thinking he should have been in an ivory colored robe and carrying a staff or a book of wisdom. But at least the enterprising fellow had the Birkenstocks right.

"Help a Vet," Jesus said, holding out a worn black fedora.

"You really do look like Jesus," Church said.

"Curse of my life." The man raised his shirt, showing an ugly puncture scar with stitches that ran in three directions the entire length of his upper belly. "But I didn't get this hanging on no cross."

"Shrap, huh?"

"Proximity blast. Mortar round from our own guys. Baghdad. Took out half my stomach. They call it friendly fire."

"Sounds better than unfriendly, I guess." Church reached in his pocket and came up with a ten-dollar bill. "It's all I got."

"I'll take it." Jesus snatched the money before Church could drop it in the hat. That was all right; he was going to give it to Jesus anyway, ten bucks

36

for a little good luck, not a bad deal … if it worked at all.

Jesus straightened, gave him a look, a little more interested, "Hey, I know you – you're that Dickens guy!"

"How do you know that?"

"Saw your picture in WSJ. Verhu Financial Hires Crippled Vet."

"You read the Wall Street Journal?"

"Sure. Got to keep track for my portfolio."

"I suppose it's too late to get my ten-spot back?"

"Bless you, my son," Jesus said. "And remember, it is tax deductible."

"Thanks for the tip." Dickens said as he wheeled himself away.

Church saw it was an average day at the hospital; a vast and impersonal place, long beige hallways leading to sometimes frightening, sometimes strange, sometimes dangerous encounters with medical magicians and therapeutic wizards — or inspired sadists— some of the encounters physically or mentally beneficial, others not so much.

He was a veteran with an honorable discharge and had been an out-patient at various VA hospitals and rehab centers for the past half dozen years. His strong arms pushed the wheels on his wheel chair through a long and nearly deserted hallway toward his release appointment. He tried for calm, but the words kept ticking over in his mind: This was his last time! Last time! Last time! He was heading for his goodbye check-out. He could hardly believe it had been so long; he had invested six years and countless gym hours to his own rehabilitation, and very much wanted to believe this was indeed his very last appointment, that from now on he would exercise and rebuild on his own. How could they stop him? They couldn't! He looked forward to leaving the wheelchair life behind, hopefully forever. He took in a deep breath and picked up his pace as he rolled by walls decorated army style with long rows of identical wreaths, somber in their dark green pine with two brown pine cones and a red bow on each for a spot of color. That's the army for you. He was thinking frivolous thoughts; Put the Christmas Season in a uniform and get it to march in step. Put those wreaths on wheels on a jeep. Get the Generals tasseled caps like Santa.

He locked one side of his wheelchair brakes and the wheels did a little screech as his chair skidded to a neat, curving halt in front of the nurses station.

"Whoa there, Stallion!" Doc Jane eyed him, not unfriendly but with that wary look she reserved for veterans who might or might not be right in the head. Doctor Jane Monroe, Captain U.S. Army. Married, three kids. Stayed in shape running 10 K's and half marathons. Husband already retired, waiting for her in Hawaii. Three more years and she'd be out, 20 years served, 80% pay, not bad, not bad at all.

"You sent the bad, unhealthy delicious donuts, didn't you, Church." Accusing, but friendly.

"Guilty as charged," he said.

"Well, you're late. We ate 'em all up."

"Wanna see a wheelie?" Church couldn't stop grinning.

She had taken him to bed a time or two, professional curiosity, at least in part, she told herself. It had been an accident, sort of; she was ten years older and neither of them expected anything like that to happen, and maybe that was it, they weren't expecting the moment when it first hit them. They had both been lonely and she saw he was wondering if he still could, and they were caught off guard, and after that initial encounter they both were discrete and if anybody else knew, they weren't saying anything.

"Gift for you," she said, handing him a loosely wrapped sack. He opened it and found the widest back brace he'd ever seen. It was of some webby elastic and hand stitched with the words ARMY CHAMP. "It's something we've been working on in our spare time."

He strapped it on. "Woow. Comfortable. You should get a patent."

He had surprised her, professionally speaking, and himself personally, that everything about him in the love-making department had still worked so well. The surgeons had plucked plenty of metal out of his lower back area and sometimes with a back wound – well, you never knew. Still, especially on his own, he was going to have to be careful about everything from picking up a bag of groceries to good old-fashioned rolling around in the sack, because if he wasn't careful, then there was the chance he could blow out his spine and that would mean a wheelchair for life, dead below the waist.

He signed the release papers and finally there was nothing more to do. She handed him his second gift: a new set of crutches. We'll keep the ones you practiced on new set of crutches. You can use these nice new ones. Without fail."

He grinned as he saluted.

"Without fail," he said. "And thanks for the special belt."

"Park your wheelchair over there, Church. And get the hell out of here."

She was going to miss him.

Chapter 11

It was Belinda's fault, really. We'd been cutting through back yards, me mostly over and Bel under or around fences, and though I have a pretty good nose, she can sniff out a barbeque rib or even a hot dog a mile away. We were making our way uphill when she took lead and in no time at all there was this great little swimming pond and some young humans giggling around, wearing no clothes to speak of and not paying any attention to those burgers waiting to be cooked and you know we hadn't eaten since we made our escape the night before so before we knew it, Bel and I were gobbling those raw paddies, not even paying attention to the buns. But heaven only lasted for a moment and then we had to scoot out of there because a fat bald man wearing a vest and a too-tight bathing suit stretched under his big belly came charging at us with a wooden stick, yelling all kinds of things in human-speak. I didn't know the words, but his intentions were clear. I growled him in woof-speak and that stopped him long enough so Bel could squirm under the fence. I jumped over and took off after her with that jiggle-tummy madman waving his stick in the air and stomping right after us.

Chapter 12

As she drove past the Taos Pines Lodge, Jessie slowed the Rover behind a tour bus that was letting off passengers. She laid on the horn and was able to get around the bus and then they were moving nearly parallel to the cabins, approaching the road that ran alongside the main house. She clicked the turn signal for a right turn – and slammed the brakes hard – locked her knee and practically stood on the pedal – as a huge shaggy grey dog and a short brown one with big ears bolted pell-mell across the road directly in front of them.

"Wooh!" Billie and Chooli said in the same moment.

The Land Rover skidded to a halt, and lucky thing, too, as a chubby man waving a baseball bat darted in front of them. He was a sight to behold in his olive vest covered with sports pins and ribbons and his tight yellow speedo swim suit, and he was chasing after the dogs without a thought for his own safety. Jesse stopped the Rover inches shy of knocking him to the asphalt. The man was in a red-faced rage, out of his mind and mad at the world, and for a moment it looked like he might use his bat to bash in the front hood on the Rover as well, some sort of get-back at the world for doing him wrong. They knew him, of course. It was their neighbor, Nate Morley, who lived across the street, an aging party boy, notorious in his own way from Santa Fe to Gallup, divorced, coasting through his middle years, casting a wide net to find his third wife, looking for a pretty young thing to share bits of his vast fortune inherited from Morley for More, the chain of supermarkets his dad had left him after a heart attack took the old man away while he was stacking a banana display in the fresh produce department of one of their stores. Jessie put the Rover in park and jumped out, and Chooli joined her while Billie stared in wonder. It certainly had been a wild ride from school. Her pal Jimmy was going to be sick with envy.

Jessie stepped in front of the man. "What the hell are you doing chasing some dogs with a baseball bat? You can go to jail!"

Nate snarled at her, looking more like an angry piglet than a wild boar. "These thieving mutts stole burgers right off my plate, right next my grill in my back yard! Wild dogs roamin' the neighborhood, and I got important guests coming! I'll kill 'em!"

"You'll do nothing of the sort!"

Jessie knew Nate's important guests were foolish young girls in bikinis he'd imported from town, kids barely of age, trying to understand hip-hop lyrics while they hung out by the heated pool behind his house; but she wasn't going to say anything about that.

"Come on, Nate, it's just hamburgers. It's just a couple of stray dogs, probably been hanging out around the garbage cans."

Jessie moved closer to the man, so close she was inside the arc of his bat and he wouldn't be tempted to take a swing at her and if he did she could handle him. Afraid for Jessie, Chooli reached out and grabbed Nate's wrist. Billie gasped from the safety of her seat in the car. She knew her mother

43

was fearless; all the more reason she was worried for her. She watched with wide eyes as Jessie grabbed this crazy fat man who weighed twice what she did, grabbed him by his shirt front and gave him a big shake.

"Nate! Listen sharp! Listen to me! You've got a party, important guests to take care of. Go to our place right now. Go into the main house. Talk to Kate. She'll get you some steaks."

Some of the wild look drained from his eyes.

"What? You sure?"

Billie relaxed a little. Her mom had this; she was talking to Nate like he was a baby.

"Yes. Come on, Nate, forget the dogs!" Chooli said. "We will take care of this for you."

Jessie let go of his shirt and straightened it out with a few pats. "My step-mom is at the main house, just over there. You know Kate. You go over there, Nathan Morley. Tell Kate I said Filet Mignon. We have a half a steer in the freezer, way more than we need."

"But they're frozen…"

"Nate, seriously now, you have a microwave. Defrost takes two minutes."

"Well, I don't know…"

While they were talking, the lanky wire-haired dog crept behind Jessie and looked around her, not afraid but looking on in an intelligent and curious way, looking to size up these new developments. She was a really big dog. Her head came up nearly to Jessie' shoulders. And after a moment the short legged one peeped out from behind her as well. Nate took a step back and made a warning gesture with his bat, a tan wooden one that had a lot of signatures scrawled on it, but the shaggy grey creature and the little brown one didn't flinch, safe behind their new protector.

"Nathan Morley, get out of here before I change the deal and you get Ball Park Franks."

"Well, okay, all right Jessie Carter. I get the steaks. Deal."

"You got a deal, pal."

"See this bat? It's got Willie Mays signature on it. I'd hate to break it on a couple of stray dogs."

"Yeah, us too," Chooli said. "Then we'd have to break you."

Nate tucked the bat under his arm and held out his hand but Jessie patted his shoulder instead and gave him a little shove, started him shuffling off in the right direction. He leered, looking back over his shoulder. "Hey, why don't you ladies get rid of the kid and join us."

"No thanks, Nate," Jessie said. "The kid is with us."

Billie had come from her seat in the Rover and was staring at the two dogs, who in turn were eyeing her from the safe spot behind Jessie and Chooli.

"Wow, mom. This dog is bigger than me."

"I know, hon. I'm thinking she's an Irish Wolfhound. We saw one on TV, last year at the Westminster Dog Show. Come on, Wolfie." Jessie opened the rear door and the dog jumped in like she belonged there.

"Wait a minute," Chooli said, lifting the other one and setting her next to the bigger dog.

Billie stared at the two dogs. "But Kate told me no more pets."

45

"Kate does not tell us what to do."

"But Mom, what if Wolfie is dangerous?"

"She look dangerous to you?"

"No. I guess not…"

The huge dog gave Jessie a furry kiss on her cheek, followed by a rascally grin. And Jessie threw her arms around the gentle giant and hugged her while Chooli gave the Bassett hound a scratch behind her ears and the dog shook her long, floppy ears and responded with a deep throated little woof of pleasure.

"See, Billie? We're all pals already."

Chapter 13

When Church came out the front entrance to the VA Hospital, Ruger was leaning against the bumblebee Mustang talking to two smart young ladies in army uniforms.

"Told you. There he is now," Ruger said. "My brother Church."

"And you're the handsome one," the 1st lieutenant with the short red hair smiled her fetching smile and gave him an appraising look. "You told us that, too."

"Well, it's all a matter of taste."

"It's a tie," the 1st lieutenant with the short honey blond hair said. "But we can't just go to lunch just like that."

"Call in sick."

"Can't. Can't. Can't. And won't. Sorry." Actually, they did look like they wished they could.

"What's up?" Church said.

"Ladies got meetings. Can't do brunch with us."

"Next time," Church said. He set his crutches carefully in the back seat and made a point of hoisting himself over the car door and into the front seat.

"Hey," Ruger said, "I invented that move."

"No, I think the Fonz did."

"Who is the Fonz?" the redhead lieutenant asked.

"Those who forget the past are doomed to repeat it," Ruger said.

"Happy Days." Church gave the ladies a casual salute and Ruger got a chance to rumble his bumblebee car off smartly.

"Wanna go sky diving?" As he drove east along Wilshire, Ruger reached in the back seat and handed his brother a flyer for some place out on the desert where you could sail down until you hit the ground without landing on anything but sand and sagebrush.

Let Gravity Take The Wheel! the headline said.

"Sounds like a kick, but some people have to go to work. We used to be pretty good at that cliff diving thing, but then I remember you gave it up."

"Kindergarten stuff. With this, you wear a suit, sort of like a flying squirrel."

"Squirrels don't have wings."

"Some do. You jump out of a plane, you get to dive a very long way on your squirrel wings, before you pull the ripcord."

"What about the aerodynamics?", Church said.

"About the same at the end. Just have to open the chute before you hit the sand."

"Sounds lovely." But Church was remembering the past. "Remember we jumped off that cliff in Mexico?"

"You did. I gave up after the waterfall in Kauai. Busted ribs hurt more than you think."

"So you gave it up and now you jump out of airplanes?"

"Gotta confess I missed the adrenaline rush." Ruger shrugged and flashed his brother a smile. "God is my co-pilot. We're the Dickens boys. Give us a high place and we jump off it."

48

"Yeah, I guess…" Church was thinking about the questionable reasons he had re-upped for his fated last tour in the high dry cliffs of Afghanistan, a crusty young army dude looking for adventure in his life and not seeing the potential for disaster until it was too late.

Chapter 14

Fresh-faced apprentice financial advisor Harvey Fineman was going to be late again. He'd worked half the night reviewing the Taos Ski Resort financials for Church Dickens, slept late and then his mom called from upstairs and he had to make her some tea and boil an egg soft the way she liked it and by that time, well, it was late and then Grandma Sharon called from her apartment that was next stairs up from Mom and nobody said no to Grandma Sharon. Harvey grabbed his brief case and took the steps up three at a time.

He knocked and entered at the soft sound of his grandmother's voice. It was like time travel, to be suddenly in that room of pearl pink light soft on old photos of family long past. He had to fight his feelings, being with her there were times when he actually set aside his grand notions of piling up a fortune, what he wanted to do in those moments was write a novel rich with the family heritage and the human emotions he felt all around him. He shook it off, visibly shaking his head. Maybe first make the money and then write the book.

"Harvey," Grandma Sharon said. "This girl you're seeing."

"Right. Janet. She's a nice girl, Grandma."

"She's not — ."

"No, Grandma. She is a nice Jewish girl. Goldberg. Janet Goldberg, and —"

She interrupted him, held up a hand for silence. "You know I'm not getting any younger, Harvey."

"Yes, Grandma."

He had some idea where this was going, but he was very late for work. He could feel he was starting to get twitchy. Calm. Be calm, he told himself.

"You sure you love this girl? A love like thunder and lightning, a love true as true can be?"

"Well … I think so."

"Huh. I suppose that will have to do. Harvey, I'm running out of time. Days, maybe a month or two."

"Oh, no, Grandma. You got lots of time left yet and –"

"No I don't," she said. "Here." She reached toward him with a shaky hand, her fingers holding a small velvet box. He opened it and there was an old fashioned ornate silvery ring mounted with a very big, very clear, very glittery stone. Harvey knew it was the ring her husband Sumner had placed on her finger long, long ago, the ring Sumner's grandmother had given him.

Chapter 15

It was late morning a few days after Church Dickens traded in his wheelchair at the VA hospital. He was looking sharp in what he thought of as his lawyer's costume, a blue striped tie and a dark grey Joseph A. Banks suit newly re-tailored to fit his broad shoulders and waist line made thicker with his back brace. He leaned his crutches against an empty chair and warily lowered himself into a seat; the Coffee Café was across from the gym, in the lobby of the Verhu Building. The early morning crush was gone and the cavernous lobby was nearly deserted except for a group of interns across the room taking an early break. A waitress came by and he ordered a hot Venti Latte and a blueberry scone, not warmed.

It looked like Celeste was late again; no, not really late, he saw her at the other end of the open lobby; short dark hair, white skin, flame red lipstick, wearing a short, too-tight navy-blue skirt with a matching too-tight silk blouse stretched across her breasts, flirting in her bright and quick-glance way with three well-dressed young fellows, part of the crop of new graduates hoping to make their name and fortune at Verhu Financial and, if it was in the cards, to score with sweet, hot Celeste. Church's on-again, off-again Celeste. Now, Dickens was telling himself, be a man about this, it's off again, permanently off again, never to be back on again. They were trying to be friends and colleagues, at least he was, but there were bad feelings – she wanted it clear that she was leaving him, not the other way around – and there were times when venom leaked into everyday chit chat, and sometimes into business.

She saw him in the same moment, said something to her pack of admirers and moved across the lobby to his table as his coffee showed up. She nodded at the crutches.

"Hey, Limpy-boy, I thought you were through with all that. No more gimp, you said."

He shrugged, not liking any of the nicknames she thought up for him. Wheelie-boy. Crutched Crusader. Church the lurch. Sure, there was a time they were close, but things were different now, and none of it had sounded funny to him in the first place, not ever. Without missing a beat she'd pulled away from near-intimacy to cool contempt, lightly disguised. Now that Verhu had an empty spot for a senior partner, Celeste believed they were rivals, no holds barred. Still, she was trying to work him so nobody knew. Staying just close enough to keep an eye on him, not too close, just another discard on her big friends-without-benefits pile. He told himself he didn't mind how she played her game; but the petty meanness, he minded.

"No more wheelchairs," he said.

"Well, I guess that's something…"

"You don't seem too happy…"

"I got a crap load of research to do on some financials out in New Mexico."

"Yeah, Celeste. Taos Pines Lodge. We're all working on it."

"Well, go work on something else. I got this one in the bag."

53

She snatched his latte and took a sip.

"Hey, that's mine."

"We're friends, Church."

"Right. What's yours is yours and what's mine is yours."

"Something like that. You can get another one, sweet baby Crutches-boy. — You coming up?"

She meant up to Verhu Financial, their workplace sprawled on the floors from the middle of the building to the vacant penthouse.

"Well, now I've got to get my coffee first."

"Boo hoo. Poor boy."

She started for the bank of elevators with his Venti Latte. Praise Jesus she didn't like scones. Church had been hoping she would sit down for a bit, but that wasn't going to happen. She had one of his old laptops and he'd like to get it back. He called after her.

"Hey, how about my computer?"

She tossed her shiny black hair cut in that brisk Sassoon look, "I thought you gave that one to me."

"I don't remember it that way."

"I'll see if I can find it."

Church knew that laptop was gone forever. She'd probably sold it on eBay. He was thinking Death of a sort-of relationship. She walks off with an old laptop? And once upon a time you were thinking of tying the knot with her? She didn't look at all pretty when she frowned. But then, who does? Forget it. Why was he even thinking about this? It was over between them.

Still, he would have liked a little quiet time with her, no accusations or arguments or disagreements, just two adults agreeing it was officially quits. But she kept avoiding serious moments with him, almost as if she wanted and at the same time didn't want to admit the breakup they both knew was there.

Chapter 16

Dickens lurched to his feet, got his crutches stable under him, his idea to start after Celeste. He wasn't sure what he would say; the next moment a voice interrupted him and then one of his crutches caught in a chair leg and he nearly found himself on the floor.

"She just dissed you bad, man," Harvey said. He held out a hand and steadied Church until he got the rubber tip end of his crutch un-trapped from the chair. Harvey Fineman, his assigned part-time assistant. Harvey worked hard, was really smart, and Dickens and he had become unlikely friends: the thoroughly Californicated army vet with a Masters in East-Asian Studies from UCal Berkeley who'd aced his way through Stanford Law, and the kid with the newly-minted Economics degree from some place he'd escaped to, for a while, that was "back east."

"I can see that, Harvey. You got my report ready?"

"Did Lincoln wear a tall hat?"

"Really tall, I think."

They made their way to the café register. Harvey slid a single sheet of paper across the glass counter in Dickens's direction and pretended interest in buying some mints. He had a thing about bad breath, something about the chewing gum commercials where they warn you to be ready, you never know when you're going to meet the girl of your dreams on a bus or in a crowded Starbucks.

Dickens scanned Harvey's brief and nodded his approval, "Good work, Harv. Really good. Confirms everything we suspected. Taos Pines is way, way, way overextended."

"Well, I'm pretty sure that's why we're interested in the first place, Dicks. I'm thinking maybe Verhu Financial takes out the second ski runs and builds a mess of condos.

"Wooh. You could be right, Harv; but if you're gonna take over a business and cut it up and sell the pieces like body parts you should want to know the parts are healthy. And I don't think these are healthy."

"Not a problem for the little worker ants like you and me. You know everybody upstairs is working on this thing."

"I figured. Celeste just said she was."

"Celeste is a predatory animal, Dicks. Right out of Alien, the movie."

"You think so?"

"Everybody knows so."

"I think she thinks she's too good for me."

"Hey, if there's any chance she's letting you off the leash, I say, Run! Oh ... make that, get away, fast!"

Harvey gave him a savvy wink and turned his attention to the waitress behind the counter, "Ten dollars on the Jumbo, Miss. Hey Dicks, look; lottery's up to $350 million. You should get in on this."

"You ever take a course in statistics, big spender?" Dickens pointed to a two dollar scratcher, "I'll throw my money away on one of those. And a Venti Latte to go, please."

The waitress poured him a paper cup and put a lid on it. "I saw vampire girl swiped your cup. Refill's free. Two bucks for the scratcher."

"You call her vampire girl?" Harvey said.

The waitress shrugged and gave them a conspiratorial grin. "Sometimes just bitch."

Harvey was still pondering Dickens's relationship with Celeste. "I am surprised, though; I thought you were a gone goose, you and Celeste joined at the hip, never to be parted until she sucked you dry."

"That's brutal, Harv, really brutal. Where's your human compassion? Anyway, that time is passed … for sure. Between you and me, I think she's just tired of being seen with a gimp."

"Or maybe she thinks you got no more to teach her."

"Could be," Church said.

"How you feel about that?"

"If you love somebody, when they want to fly you have to set 'em free."

"Where's that from?"

"My Auntie Jane was a hippie."

Dickens saw, from the look on Harvey's face, he didn't agree with the love bead philosophy. Or maybe he didn't know about it. Harvey was a young guy, life for him started in the decade before the end of the last millennium. "Well, at least there's work," Dickens said. "You ready for whatever Philby throws at us?"

"Yes, but thank the powers that be, we don't report direct to him. We're doing him a favor, 'cause he asked."

"No, we work for him, all right," Dickens said. " Maybe not directly, but he's the only living senior partner we see around here."

"Can't argue you that. You saw, I worked up the numbers, but ..."

"But what, Fineman, my man? You know it's worse than hopeless. I come out same as you. Or even worse: If you're only looking at the financials, Taos Pines Lodge is a lost cause and Verhu is nuts to get more involved. They were okay until they overextended, but the weather hasn't been their friend. I say Verhu should dump them."

"Old Phil's not stupid. Maybe he's got some other plan. Rumor is, he's got friends who've invested a lot of money there. Verhu Financial is in pretty deep, too, I bet. Once you're all in, what you gonna do?"

Dickens shifted his weight on his crutches, trying to find a more comfortable position. He was starting to see, if you owned Verhu, there wasn't one. "Okay, we agree: TPL is fatally overextended. Numbers don't lie — 'cept on the Lottery, where by faith and hope alone do we invest."

"True on TPL, but I gotta tell you, Old Wise One, what we say doesn't matter. Philby is just going to bury our findings. Wanna bet?"

"Nope. You win that one."

The waitress gave Harvey a slip with his twenty dollars' worth of lottery numbers and handed Dickens a new coffee cup and a two dollar scratcher that said HOT SHOT.

"Good luck, sirs," she said.

Harvey could hardly contain his good humor as they made their way across the lobby, "Yeah! Good luck with your big investment, you Hot Shooter, you!"

"Hey, scratchers been good to me." He didn't say how good, and Harvey, not believing him for a second, didn't realize he was being set up.

Chapter 17

They waited for the elevator; Dickens leaned against the wall, enjoying the cool marble surface as he straightened his back. He heard something crack in there, not a good sign.

Harvey heard it, too. "Maybe you got rid of your wheels too soon?"

"That's what they said at the VA."

"But you talked them out of it."

"It's been what, a year rehab in DC and five years out here? Rehab all the time I'm in law school. Harvey, I have to get better on my own. And the time is now."

"Who said that?"

"George Allen. Football coach. Serious, man, it's now or never. There's a risk, but …"

"What risk?"

"If I fall wrong I'm paralyzed. Maybe permanent from the waist down."

"Wooh. Go get your wheels back, superman."

"Nope. Can't."

"Won't, you mean."

"Same thing, boy wonder."

The elevator doors opened and Thurgood Wilson got off, carrying a cardboard box with a few romance detective novels and a wilting aspidistra. He was in his late 50s, short, chubby, bald and crying. The Verhu company's chief financial officer.

"Thur, say it isn't so!" Harvey said, taking in what must have happened.

"It is so, Harvey. Philby fired me yesterday."

"Why?"

"He hires me away from the job of a lifetime at Wells Fargo. I give him the ten best years of my life. And he dumps me like an empty Pizza Hut box!"

"There's got to be some mistake," Dickens said.

"Yeah. The mistake was mine. I told him he had to get rid of Bella." Bella, Alan Philby's ancient twin engine DC-3, parked in its own exclusive hangar at the Santa Monica airport. "I am right. The numbers don't lie. But he went ballistic. I thought he was going to kill me!"

"I guess there is such a thing as being too honest."

Dickens and Harvey looked at each other, thinking the same thought. Thurgood was a good worker, and he really knew his job, but the entire financial world was in a bit of a crunch, and at his age the best opening he was likely to find was greeter at Wal-Mart.

"Good luck, Thurgood," they said as one voice. A weak smile and a huge sniff and a brave nod and the chubby little accountant shuffled off. Too late, the elevator doors closed and they would have to wait for the next one.

As they stood in the lobby, Harvey shuffled his feet and looked nervous. He finally made his mind up about something. He stared at Church, an intense John Lennon look through his wire-rim glasses.

"What is it, Harv?"

"You know gemmologists, right?"

"I know one or two. It goes with the territory."

"Look, I – uhh, here."

Harvey took the small velvet box out of his jacket pocket, and opened it, the very large and clear solitaire glittering in the bright lobby light.

"My grandma gave it to me. I gotta get it insured, but I don't know how much."

"Wooh. Big stone."

"She said it's a diamond."

"How's she know that?"

"That's what my grandpa told her."

"Well, it is a diamond."

"Wow! Should I put it in a bank vault?"

"Probably not. It's a Herkimer diamond. Big one."

"But if it's a big diamond shouldn't I…"

"A Herkimer diamond. What you've got there is a chunk of the finest, clearest, brightest quartz known to mankind. A hundred years ago it was known as the common man's diamond."

"Quartz? You mean like glass?"

"Quartz. Silicon dioxide. A semi-precious stone. It's a good specimen and the setting's nice. Probably worth five hundred bucks."

"This, what I have here, the diamond my beloved grandmother gave me, is not a real diamond? You sure?"

"One hundred percent sure. If you want, I'll Google the keywords for you, print you out some pages from reliable sites."

"Yeah, could you?" Harvey closed the box and handed it to Church, disappointment all over his face.

"Come on, Harv. Don't be a glum Gus. As a family heirloom it's priceless."

"I guess there's that ...."

They got on an elevator and the doors started to close but at the last second a hand whapped them open and Alan Philby got in — that most senior of the senior partners at the firm, and the only one they'd ever actually seen. A disapproving fellow with his lips set in a downward curve, wide blinking eyes and an expression carved in his wrinkled old face like he'd practiced frowning since the cradle, "Couldn't hold the elevator for me, huh?" He set down his briefcase and did some arm exercises, pushing left hand down on right, then the right down on the left, a fitness regimen dubbed Dynamic Tension that Charles Atlas had made popular in the Great Depression when people didn't have weights or stationary bikes. Philby stared at them while he did his exercises, wide-eyed as a grade school kid. He blinked, shaking his head as if that somehow cleared his vision of a distorted world, still waiting for an answer to his surly question about holding the elevator door open.

"We didn't see you, Mr. Philby," Harvey said. Dickens didn't say anything.

Philby's gaze narrowed. "Church, do you have my numbers?"

"Yes, Alan, I do. Harvey did a terrific breakout, too. My secretary should be in-mailing them to you right about now. But they're not good. Taos Pines Lodge's financial credibility is melting faster than ice cubes in hell.'

"In fact it's already melted, a puddle on the pavement," Harvey said. He grinned as he spoke, not a wise choice because Philby, a lot sharper than he looked, saw him do it. The older man's face went bright red and looked like it might explode off the top of his wrinkled neck. He jabbed at Harvey with two fingers, stiff to his checkered tie. "God DAMN it, I'm not asking for commentary from the junior peanut gallery! I know what I'm doing!"

He turned on Dickens, his jabbing fingers ready – but Church's reflexes went automatic and he easily brushed the angry gesture aside. This only outraged Philby more; with his characteristic blinking head nod, he seemed oddly demented and unstable, if only for the moment. He took a deep, shuddering breath.

"Just the numbers out of the two of you," Philby said. "Just the numbers." A bell dinged at five, and he started to get off.

"Don't forget your briefcase, Alan," Dickens said. Philby snatched it and walked away without looking back or saying another word.

Chapter 18

As the old man moved down the hall Harvey dared a pouty-face at his backside. "Told you so, my dear Mister Dickens. That man is crazy, and he doesn't listen to us."

"There goes a really bad person, Harvey."

" Yeah. Mean old fart."

"Worse. Don't underestimate him. I say get your resume out there."

"Is yours?"

"Harvey, I'm so short-term I'm already history."

The doors closed but the elevator wasn't moving. They were alone; Dickens hesitated, thinking before he spoke again. He was silent, eyeing Harvey but saying nothing.

"What?" Harvey said.

"Maybe you should know: TPL is restructuring again. There's a whole new stock offering. Don't get caught with your pants down."

"You couldn't tell me this before? Not that it matters. I don't have any Taos Pines Lodge stock. No stock at all, in fact. I got college debt, is what I got."

"No, I couldn't tell you. Nobody's supposed to know."

"Another offering? That stock is so watered down … when?"

"Next week. Tuesday, I'm pretty sure."

"And you know this how?"

"They're offering old stockholders three for one. I own some TPL."

"You do?"

"Sure. I buy in on whatever Verhu is going for. You know, a few shares. Anonymous, just another sucker investor. It's the only way to know what's going on around here. You should, too."

"Sure – like, I got money for that."

"You would if you didn't play Jumbo Lotto. Twenty bucks will buy you a couple shares."

"Yeah, yeah …. Dicks, why doesn't anybody tell us about stuff like this?"

"Philby trusts no one. And you've seen a little of the books."

"Wasn't supposed to. But Thur let me take a quick peek."

"That might have been what got him fired."

"Maybe …." The wheels were turning in Harvey's quick mind. "But … if we're going under anyway, what's Philby's play with the lodge stock?"

"I don't know, but there's got to be something in it for him. Verhu is really stretched, Harv, and – just my opinion – but I believe Philby himself is way over on the shady side. He's devious, to say the least, and a few years from now you won't want Verhu on your rez. I say get ready. Or better, get out."

"Ready for what?"

"Well, right now, shady business that could get you in trouble. I'm thinking the shell game, but with our investors' stocks."

"But, but I'm not gonna – no, I only got a few little clients, a few relatives. Small potatoes. I can't be involved in crooked stuff. I won't."

"Good for you, but get ready to get booted if you don't play along. He's gonna need every dime, and he might come asking."

"But Church … I get caught, it's my ass."

"We, Harv. Our asses. But you think Philby cares? Verhu needs cash. Needs it bad, and right now. Philby's gonna dilute that TPL stock – and he'll be counting on us troopers to do anything and everything to keep that offer from tanking. The shark doesn't discuss the morality of a tuna sandwich; to him it's just a meal."

"Wow, all of a sudden I get philosophy. Impressive. You think he'll get caught?"

"Who's going to turn him in? We'll get word from on high that any client requests to sell are to be delayed a day or two until he can shuffle the deck and right things. And worse for me, Alan himself will order me to buy when it starts to tank, which it probably will."

"What will it take to hold the fort?"

"Seven or eight figures at least. And that's just temporary."

"You get caught, how much jail time is that?"

Dickens grinned. "I might get out for my retirement party." He thought of something else. "I'm guessing anything you and me and the rest of us peasants can't cover, he'll pass it on to the other four crooks and they'll cover it."

"The other partners? Do they even exist? Why would they contribute? You're the one telling me, TPL is a loser."

"If they exist, they have at least as much to lose as Alan."

The firm had five senior partners, and they were all rich, not counting Philby. They all had offices on the penthouse floor, but they never went there, at least nobody ever saw them. Philby had his main offices on five, but his big private office was on ten, and the penthouse was on eleven. The partners all lived on other continents, the absentee overlords of Verhu Financial. Of course they could juggle funds. Verhu had its own offshore accounts on the Isle of Man and a private bank somewhere in Europe and another in India, and that made it easier. But why go through all the trouble? Why take such a risk for a ski resort that was running in the red going on three years? Dickens didn't have an answer, but it had activated his serious interest. And with what he now suspected of Philby, he felt he no longer owed loyalty to Verhu. Alan Philby was, at the least, a big time financial weasel and it was only a matter of time before he got caught juggling his books.

Harvey eyed Dickens, who had gone quiet.

"It's not like they're actually stealing, Dicks ..." Harvey said. His voice trailed off and then after a moment he sang in a quiet voice, as if singing a lullaby to calm himself, "It's a Holly Golly Christmas, It's the best time of the year."

"Harvey, you have a terrible singing voice."

"I don't believe in Christmas, either .... Dickens, old buddy, I see we have a big huge major problem here. At least I do: What do I do when Alan tells me I have to switch around my few lowly

69

clients' accounts to cover some tiny corner of their stinking bet? I have a life to live."

"I don't think it will get to you. Not this time. Philby will ask me first; he'll want to keep the pack of crooks small as possible."

"And what will you do? "

"Well, like we're saying, if the price starts to fall, he'll want me to buy in and stabilize it."

"And?"

"I'm not going to jail for Philby, and what he doesn't know won't hurt him."

"But – ?"

"Harvey, the computer is an amazing accomplice. No problems with morality, either."

Dickens liked Harvey and might have said more, but they would never know as the elevator gave a lurch and they were on their way to their floor.

Chapter 19

That afternoon Dickens walked to a nearby park and called Ruger.

"What's up, Bright Bro?" Bright for white.

"You still in town, Mo Bro?" Mo for mahogany.

"On my way back to DC. Had lunch with those two nifty lieutenants. We missed you."

"I bet you did. Ruger, I need short-term back up from the family trust. For the ski resort. Not even borrow. Just as security."

"Sure. How much?"

"Ah…quite a bit."

"Six figures?"

"Seven. Maybe eight."

"Oh, ho! Insider trading. The fast track to riches. I like it. Just don't get caught, Brighty."

"Actually, the part I'm doing is legal, everything almost totally above board… except maybe for your nefarious electrical adventures about which I do not want to know."

"I'm having electrical adventures?"

"I need that power outage." Two months before, Dickens had employed Ruger in an experiment, to see if there was any way the Verhu building could experience a power blackout. Apparently, there was a way. Expensive and risky, but maybe worth it.

"Money can buy you anything," Ruger said.

"No. Money can't buy you love." Dickens filled his brother in on the details of what he needed, and Ruger said he would call back if there were any problems. "But? What's that I hear in your voice … something more? Me suspects you're not telling me something, bro."

"Well … I'm not sure, Ruggs. The part that has me worried is Alan Philby personally. I don't know enough about him, and he's radiating some bad vibes. Something's very wrong with that old dude."

"You're sure we want this?"

"No pain, no gain, bro. Imagine yourself out there in Taos, New Mexico, snowboarding off Death Drop ridge."

"Wooh. Take the Death Drop! Okay, I'm there for that! But wait – you're sure now? This is a solid go for Tuesday?"

"Yep. Next Tuesday. The whole Verhu Building. About ten-oh-six A.M. East Coast time."

"No problem. I bribe our big muck pal at the power department, like last time. Costs ten grand. That okay?"

"Yep. But make sure just the Verhu building. Don't mess with the rest of the grid. Cedars-Sinai is right around the corner."

"Right. West Hollywood. Only Verhu on San Vicente. We got that handled. You sure you don't want dead cell phones? Cost another twenty-five hundred."

Dickens was about to say no but then he had a second thought. "Could you make them unreliable? I mean, make them cut on and off, create a little more uncertainty…"

"I can do that. What's your service?"

"TracFone."

"How about I keep you clear, everybody else intermittent, like on a few seconds, off a few, back on again?

"Okay. But the whole thing no more than ten minutes. If I need more, I'll be in deeper shit than you can imagine.

"Okay," Ruger said. "Let me tell you what happened with the army ladies."

"Ménage a trois, I'm sure. No sordid details, please."

There was a soft chuckle and Dickens smiled at his cell phone. That was his brother for you.

Chapter 20

If you counted Kate (and there was no way to ignore her), three generations of Carter women were working in the study they had turned into their office. Jessie's step-mother, Ed's second wife Kate, was annoying everybody by hanging lit strings of red gift stocking bulbs while Jessie worked her desktop computer and Billie was at a small desk nearby writing an essay on The Meaning of Christmas.

"Whatcha doing, hun, that's so important?" Kate said. She liked to keep her eye on her daughter-in-law/

Jessie had been doing her best to work with Kate's strings of Christmas lights blinking in her face, and she hated it when Kate called her 'hun' or 'honey', or for that matter, anything familiar. She gritted her teeth and tried for pleasant. "I'm looking for lost wolfhounds and Basset hounds in Northern New Mexico. It shouldn't take long." And it didn't; barely a minute later she spoke again. "Ah-hah!"

"You got something, babe?"

"Listen to this: 'Grey Irish Wolfhound. Alexia Georgianna the Third', no less... and get this, 'an ex-grand champion, best in show' – Billie, I was telling you, we saw this dog on TV! 'If found, please call the following number. Reward.' "

Billie looked up from her small desk. "Aw, Mom, no … we don't get to keep Wolfie?"

"Not Wolfie, hon. Alexia. Lexi, for short. And we have to return her to her owner. Wait. There's more. Here's an article from the Taos newspaper. Her owner is an old person, a widow, a Mrs. Cory Anderson. Says she lost her loving husband two years ago, hard to keep up with such a big dog, but she manages. At least she did. She recently had a heart attack."

Kate lit up a cigarette from her pack of Kools and took a big drag, the disapproval on her face making her look about ten years older than her real age. "I'm telling you – you best get back to her right away, hon. A big dog like that is more than you can handle."

Jessie could read between the lines. Her mother-in-law meant Dump the fleabag mutt before the old lady kicks the bucket. She ignored Kate and went back to her research, and ten minutes later ran across a Twitter announcement: "Bornton Breeding Kennels looking for two dogs. REWARD".

"Dial that number," Kate said. "Kill two birds with one stone." She reached for Jessie's phone. "Here. I'll do it myself."

"No thanks. I'll handle it myself." Contacting the kennel was probably the easiest thing to do, but Jessie didn't want to give Kate the satisfaction. "I think I'll call this Mrs. Cory Anderson."

"What the hell would you do that for, hun?"

"Two championship dogs go missing from the same kennel. Makes me wonder why."

"Good thinking, Mom," Billie said.

Chapter 21

The Monday after he'd signed off at the VA hospital, Dickens swung awkwardly on his crutches past his secretary's desk.

"Hey, Annie, Channel 7 says it's supposed to rain."

"Yeah, and my mother is a virgin. What do they know?"

"No, really. Today sprinkles. Tomorrow maybe more."

"I say we all move to Seattle," Annie said.

"What's Seattle got?"

"The Seahawks. And lotsa rain."

Church Dickens liked grumpy Annie, and not just because she was Alan's old secretary. He was thinking again how much she reminded him of Francis McDormand in Fargo, that movie about Minnesota … and Three Billboards Outside Ebbing, Missouri. Francis McDormand wasn't somebody like Meryl Streep, always playing different people; she always played the same grouchy lady, probably somebody who was close to herself, to who she was in real life, a plain faced, tough, smart and loyal person. Church felt Annie was like that. And a survivor, for sure. She'd had a long history with Philby, who had fired her over what seemed like some little nothing, some excuse to get rid of her. Church had seen it going down and had rescued her before she could get out the door and he still believed he was lucky he had her now working for him. She worked hard, he suspected she had a lingering love-hate relationship with her ex-boss, and she knew where the bodies were buried at Verhu. And that was a very good thing for Church, who was having his continuing doubts about why he ever signed on as a financial and legal advisor at the place. Maybe some of the old family taste for skullduggery lurked in his genes and leaped out at the scent of Alan Philby.

"Whoo hoo, look at you, no more wheelchair," Annie said. "By the way, Celeste called. Your date's off for tonight."

"Yeah, I figured. It wasn't really a date date."

"You were going to propose, weren't you?"

"Actually, just the opposite. She's been putting me off because I want my stuff back and I think she knows it."

"Wow! The boy finally shows some common sense." Annie looked him over a second time, "Then that velvet box in your hand isn't an engagement ring?"

"Well, it is. Just not mine. Harvey's grandma gave it to him. My bad, I forgot all about it. Could you to do a little research on it for me? I'll put it in my desk drawer. Just Google Herkimer diamonds, print me off whatever you find that looks reliable so I can give it to Harvey. We'll talk later."

"Okay …."

Both of them decided at the same moment not to say anything more. Annie was pleased her boss was seeing the light about gold digger Celeste; the woman had hurt him more than he wanted to admit. It was Annie's opinion that office romances never worked out anyway; she'd had plenty of experience in that direction. Say no more, she told herself.

That's what good secretaries do; they give their boss a little space. Let it go, let it go, and God bless him.

Dickens went to his own cluttered office to handle his emails. He leaned his crutches against a built-in glass front cabinet that held rows of dark green and brown covered law books propped up with rock sample bookends, red-brown agate and glittering geode clusters of purple amethyst and giant pink quartz crystals holding up books on oil exploration and mining and land use. Dickens found there were three notes on his desk that could use attention, clients asking advice about land acquisitions, and one questioning an opportunity to buy in on a recent bond offering, a silver mine that needed cash to divert an underground stream that threatened to flood their enterprise out of business. All three client requests looking for his expert advice.

He didn't like the silver mine opportunity and he said so. He had been in mines and caves as an undergrad student. He'd once been in a fluoride mine, pretty purple crystals of fluorspar, located 200 feet directly under the Ohio river. They kept the mine open with three massive pumps, two running all the time, and there were plug doors that could be shut to save part of the mine should new stream of water suddenly blast its way out of a wall, a ceiling, or the floor. Creepy even thinking about working down there.

Chapter 22

"We just gotta get rid of that damn dog," Kate said.

"We? Why, Kate? You have a real reason?" Jessie didn't like her mother-in-law's tone, the implication was that Jessie couldn't take care of anything, much less a big mutt. Kate was really saying Jessie had more than enough on her plate with the responsibility of taking care of Billie and helping Ed to keep Carter Cabins going, seeing as that she was a woman alone. Jessie knew the rest of Kate's comments by heart; it was her standard patter – she was really saying that just about everything else about Jessie's life was on hold since her European husband died – probably his own fault – in that horrible racing car crash, and it was foolish to get mixed up with a road racing car driver in the first place.

Jessie did agree about returning Alexia, but for different reasons: The obvious right and only thing to do for both dog and owner was to put through a call to Lexi's owners and to give the dog back as soon as possible. The rest of Kate's running commentary was just white noise, the blather from a bitter, middle-aged woman who couldn't resist poking into her step-daughter's life. For the hundredth time Jessie wondered what power Kate had to keep her father from booting her out the door. Nevada chicken-ranch secrets, she told herself. But even as she thought like that, she had to admit she was only guessing about Kate's past, and she told herself she was just being mean.

Jessie picked up the land-line house phone and made the call to Lexi's owner, but a maid answered and, while the maid said they were grateful that Jessie had called, she began to speak of complications. There were whispered conversations back and forth on the far end of the line, the maid speaking to someone else, Jessie figured out she was probably talking to Mrs. Anderson, Lexi's owner. And after a pause, the old lady herself did come on the line, her tone friendly but with the reserve of an upper class English accent.

"She is such a special dog. The Colonel would have been so pleased you found her – he died a short time ago, but Alexi Georgiana was his all-time favorite and they were very close."

"I'm sorry to hear he passed …."

"Oh, his end was a long time coming, my dear. Long time coming. Lexi was originally intended to be a service dog, for the Royal Services military, actually. But we left all that behind when we brexited Britain for New Mexico. Better climate, you know. Doctor's orders. The Colonel had bad lungs. We started showing Alexandra at events and that blossomed into quite a career!"

"We're happy we found him. My father is on standby, and he will be happy to drive her to your place."

"One moment, dear," Mrs. Anderson said. There was a pause and Jessie heard a muffled conversation in the background before the old woman came back on the line.

"My heart attack … was more serious than I had imagined …. Is there any way?... can you possibly find a way to take care of Alexia … just a month or so until I can straighten things out around here, get myself going again? … We'll pay you of course …,"

"Yes, we'd be glad to help. Lexi found the right place, actually. This is Carter Cabins. We love dogs, and we have plenty of space."

"That is very good news, indeed. My lawyer will call … and arrange things …. Thank you. Thank you so much, and I so look forward to seeing Alexia soon."

Ten minutes later Jessie's phone rang; a deep throated woman introduced herself. "I am Sarah Morganfeld, and I am representing Mrs. Cory Anderson's interests."

"Yes. She said you'd call."

"Is Alexia safe with you? Do you have room for her? Are you willing and able to care for her for some weeks or even months as Mrs. Anderson requests, that is, until she recovers?"

"Yes to everything. Here at Carter Cabins we are used to caring for guests' pets, and we have plenty of room."

"Just one more thing," Ms. Morganfeld said.

"What might that be?"

"Alexia Georgianna is almost certainly pregnant."

"What?"

"She is an older dog, as wolfhounds go, but Mrs. Anderson loves that dog and was hoping for one last litter. Alexia was at the breeder's when she went missing along with another dog. That happened ten days ago. The breeder, a certain Mr. Jay Bornton, claimed the dogs gnawed through the latches securing the doors on their cages, though there is some doubt as to that."

"What shall we do?"

"Well, Mr. Jay Bornton claims he needs to examine the dogs. Insurance, he says. We will agree, but I will insist on being present. He is not a pleasant man – somewhat arrogant, if I must say – and we do not trust him."

"What shall we do about the other dog?"

"Good lord! You have her, too? The Basset hound?"

"Yes, Belinda Royale. Is something wrong?"

"No, no. That is wonderful news! Her owners had to leave for Portugal. Death in the family, they said. They left her in our custody. That's why we were so twice so disturbed — two dogs, both ours, both go missing."

"Let's set up a meeting with him when you are sure to be there. I can handle it at our place," Jessie said. "They'll both be safe here until then."

"I'll give you Mr. Bornton's number. Set up any time tomorrow or the next day should be fine with us. But don't trust that Jay Bornton. I would not have taken any animals there had I known this might happen."

Chapter 23

Jessie had barely hung up the phone when her dad Ed came in the study. He'd been grooming the dog and couldn't contain his excitement. "I think Wolfie is pregnant!"

"Granpa, she's not Wolfie," Billie said. "She's Lexi. And we know she's pregnant. Actually both dogs are pregnant."

"How could you possibly know that?"

Kate nodded toward Jessie. "Smarty Pants Jessie here found the owner. Both them damn trouble-making dogs escaped from a breeding kennel in Santa Fe. Your daughter is calling the breeder right now, hopeful we can get rid of the mutts."

*

"Yes, what is it?" Jay Bornton of Bornton Kennels came on the line sounding abrupt and surly.

Jessie sighed, wondering to herself why all the people like Kate didn't marry all the people like Jay Bornton; that way they could take it out on each other.

"We have found Alexia Georgianna the wolfhound."

"Huh. That's what you say. How do you know that? I've had a dozen calls just today. People are so greedy. You are really truly positive it's the same dog? There is no reward, you know, if it's just any dog. Who is this, anyway?"

Jessie tried to keep her cool. Of late, particularly because of her stepmother, she'd been re-reading her philosophy books from college, wise thoughts that had helped her recover after her husband's death, and now were useful to hold back her own impulsive urges to snap back when her mother-in-law acted selfish or foolish. And then there was kick boxing. That was the other discipline she had followed through high school and at New Mexico U. Of course you didn't kick box your own step-mother, no matter how tempting that might be. She took a deep breath and tried to mute the sarcasm in her voice. "Mister Jay Bornton: How many huge grey Irish Wolfhounds and champion Basset hounds do you think are running around the hills outside Taos?"

A failure for Meditation 101. She'd failed to connect in a pleasant way; Jay's voice came back at her full of snarky righteousness. "I don't think you know what you are talking about."

She had thought he'd probably be pleased they'd found his runaway boarder. She put her hand over the phone and looked at her dad. "The breeder sounds not very happy."

Ed knew that look. They'd always been close; she wanted his advice.

"Probably got his insurance payment already," he said in a soft voice, not wanting to be overheard.

Jay suddenly spoke up from his end of the line, sounding like he'd just thought of something and speaking in a take-charge voice, too quick and smooth. "I'll come right over and pick up the dogs."

She put her hand over the phone again and looked at her dad, "He wants to come right now and take both dogs. I don't trust him."

"Yeah, I bet he wants the puppies, Mom!" Billie said. "Don't let him!"

Ed nodded, "I think Billie's right. Go with your instincts, Jessie. We've got all the room in the world here."

She smiled and spoke to the breeder with a firm edge to her voice. "No, you can't take the dogs. We've agreed to board both dogs here for Mrs. Anderson."

" No! That's not going to work on this end! I have a contract to board the dogs! I insist on seeing them. How do I know you're taking proper care of her?"

"That's not actually your call. You don't own the dogs, and you let them run away and get lost."

"So you say. No, absolutely not. I'll come right over and pick them up."

"No, you will not. You can come see them. I'll find out a time that's good for Mrs. Anderson. You'll have to work your schedule around when she can be here."

He muttered Cheeky Bitch! And then he yelled, "You do that!"

And he clicked off the connection.

Chapter 24

Tuesday the weather in Los Angeles decided it would follow the sexy Channel 5 weathergirl's prediction and provide a few brief rain squalls. When it was built a few decades before, the Verhu Building had started out as a form follows function design, a square block of a building, but somewhere along the way the architect had decided to protect the windows from Southern California's intense sunlight glare with chunky curls of bas relief cement that descended in a stiff waterfall design from the top of the building on down to the pavement below. The addition did prevent glare; it also made the interior gloomy on overcast winter days — or what passed for winter days in LA — like this one.

By noon Dickens hadn't heard from Philby so he took the elevator down to the gym and did a light workout, concentrating on his abs and doing 15 minutes on a treadmill that had handrails. By the time he got back to his office Alan had called three times with, Annie said, an increasing neediness in his voice. Even what we might call irritation, she added, grinning as she referred to Alan as Old Blinky.

"Huh," Dickens said. "I'll get back to him in a few minutes." He got on his personal cell phone and called his brother Ruger. He had no moral reservations about what he was planning to do. It didn't bother him at all to take from a crook, and from the little he'd seen the federal regulators would be so astonished if they ever got around to digging into Verhu that they would overlook this one minor transgression. Well, probably — and hopefully, by that time, he'd be long gone from Verhu.

"Hey Bro, can you activate our project?"

"How soon?"

"How about now?"

"Hang on." Church heard some clicks over the phone; Ruger working his keyboard in his office in Virginia, across the Potomac from D.C.

"Five. Four. Three. Two. One. Okay, you're a go."

It didn't happen all at once. The lights started to flicker in the Verhu building. Protests were heard as computers went out. Then Church's office, an interior one with no windows, went nearly pitch black.

"Very dramatic. Thank you," Church said. He hung up and called Philby's office. Alan came on the line with the first ring, clearing his throat with a cough, his voice weak and scratchy. "Christ! Where you been?"

"Hello to you, too, Alan. Gym workout. Doctor's orders. Didn't see you down there. Why do you ask? Is something up?"

"Dickens, I told you the new TPL offering was hot today! You're supposed to be on standby!"

"As I well am. By the way, I saw Jesus the other day."

"Yeah? What'd he tell you, Dickens?"

"That greed is good."

There was a pause, Philby probably wondering if Church had lost his marbles and audibly grinding his teeth. "I think I agree with the Savior, Alan. But you didn't read your mail; if you had, you'd know I resigned as of late last week. Sent you an email, and a registered letter, to boot. Your secretary, what's-her-name, Lenora with the purple lips, should have gotten it; I did get a receipt."

"What?! Don't be ridiculous! You can't resign. You are a vital part of my organization! Get on the TPL thing right now! We'll talk more later!"

"Calm down, Alan. Okay, I'll get involved, do this one last favor for you 'cause we're work out buddies. Give me a little time to see what's up."

"Now! Now! Now!" Alan's voice gave way to another coughing fit.

Dickens had to hold the phone away from his ear. "Not to worry, Alan," he said. He clicked off Philby and lined up three cell phones on his desk with the monitors facing him in a small glowing semicircle. He opened the Verhu trading link, the standard trading monitor and his own private trading account, and then went to the door. "Annie, I'm not to be disturbed."

"Not even for Old Blinky?"

" 'Specially not. I'm locking the door."

Annie nodded and smiled to herself. She liked it when things got exciting, and no matter what happened it was no skin off her nose. She'd switched allegiance from unfaithful creaky-bones Alan to Church Dickens. In spite of Alan's wicked ways, she could never completely give up on him, for old times' sake when they were young – well, middle-aged and foolish – but she was increasingly sure that Alan had gone beyond wheeling and dealing and was approaching lines she would not cross — and so she had entered a new and strong loyalty to Dickens.

She had no problem switching her loyalty - No harm, no foul. Dickens had saved her when she was out of a job, and he'd helped her make some terrific moves with her personal finances – if she could help Dickens in any way she would, and Old Blinky didn't have to know what might not hurt him, anyway, and if it did ... well only if he was on the wrong side of those lines.

She didn't completely understand her new boss with his secretive ways, but she trusted his instincts and she liked his wit, and his coolness under pressure; he was certainly fun to watch as he went about his wheeling and dealing. Alan was trending more and more in the panic mode these days as senility moved in on him like a cold front from Alaska. On the other hand, Dickens never cracked. Once when the market was down she asked him how he could be so cool and he'd said It's only money, baby. She liked that. Now she smiled, locked her desk drawer and picked up her purse. "I think I'll go on coffee break."

He nodded and grinned back, two kids about to pull a prank on their older siblings. "Good idea. Maybe take your emergency flashlight – the lights are flickering. And bring me back a latte in twenty minutes or so. Oh, and Annie, maybe use the stairs, just in case the elevators get stuck."

By the time he glanced over at TPL, their new stock offering was down four from the opening price.

Chapter 25

TPL slid another point and Dickens' three phones started beeping, clanging, and hooting. He clicked on his voice recorder. He'd guessed right; it was Alan Philby – who else? – and the old guy was running out of control. "Christ Sake, Dickens! God Damn it! What are you doing?"

"What do you mean, Alan? You did say buy, didn't you? Ahh, you're starting to cut out on me. I can't hear you."

"It's not – you -ing idiot! – buy more!"

"Alan, you've got five partners loaded with dough –"

"Christ, Dickens, we're -ready all in!"

"Okay, Alan, I'll go out on the limb for you. But if this goes south, you have to protect me."

"Of course, I will - ing protect you!"

Church clicked off with Alan but did nothing else. As he watched his little monitors the TPL stock went into absolute collapse. Down ten. Down eleven. Down twelve and a half. Fifteen. Twenty three.

Someone was pounding on his door.

"Church! Church Dickens! Dickens, goddamn it, you bastard! Open this door at once!" It was Celeste, the shrill in her voice telling him Old Blinky had cursed at her and sent her running to his office.

Still, Dickens did nothing. He watched the screens with a satisfied smile on his lips as the worth of the Taos Pines Lodge stock slid below a dollar, now nearly worthless. And then, when it was at pennies a share, he clicked into the personal account Ruger had backed up for him and put in a series of big orders, everything that was available on the open market, but staggered so the price didn't skyrocket all at once. He held his breath, fascinated, as his orders started to go through. Held a second breath. Then a third. And then the confirmations started coming in. TPL wobbled, stabilized, and then climbed back over a dollar. Okay, his last orders were filled. Price up to two dollars. Four. Seven. Slowing, but still, up to nine. Ten. Twelve. Fifteen.

Celeste outside his door muttered a last hoarse "Damn it to hell!" and went away. Dickens couldn't care less. The stock was still inching up, looked like it might stabilize within ten percent of its old price. Not bad for a few minutes work. He was thinking amused thoughts to distract himself: Maybe he should write a book, How to Make A Couple Million In Under An Hour, or better, Don't Bother Stealing Anything Small.

Once he was sure Celeste was gone he unlocked the door and sat in the comfort of his Herman Miller steel mesh chair. It sure made his back feel better. That Herman was a genius! The lights flickered and came back on. Church Dickens and his bro were big shareholders – probably the major stockholders – in a fancy ski resort in Taos, New Mexico. And he hadn't needed to tap Ruger's funds. He called his brother and kicked back the guarantee. There would be a minimum for the bother, but with TPL now back near its old offering, a five-figure charge was peanuts considering the outcome.

Annie came back and handed him his latte and a paper bag. "I got you one of those blueberry scones you're addicted to."

"Annie, you're a marvel," he said.

Church Dickens took in a deep breath and sat at his desk. He sipped his latte and took a bite of his blueberry scone, cold and crumbly the way he liked them. He could feel the heart beat in his chest slowing back down to something like normal. He had displaced Verhu Financial as the dominant investor in a ski resort in Northern New Mexico. He wasn't sure exactly how much he and Ruger controlled. Certainly more than Verhu. Ruger would get the numbers at some point.

"It's no big deal," he said to nobody in particular. And he was right, in one sense. Taos Pines Lodge, Inc. was so overextended they could go bankrupt at any time; then the stock would be nearly worthless. That was the gamble … still, there was the land. The land itself was always at the back of Dickens' mind. He had a feeling maybe the real estate was what this was all about. Like Harvey said, maybe that was Old Blinky's plan all along, boot the stock for cash, level the sky lodge, or maybe sell it off to some enterprising sucker, and build condos.

Whether that was true or not, Church knew it was high time to talk to Annie and to start clearing out his office. In the past year he'd given her advice that had secured her retirement. She had followed through as planned and they'd gotten a little lucky to boot, and her new nest egg could now buy her a two-bedroom condo in the Bahamas near – or maybe actually on – a sunlit beach where she would be warm and comfortable for the rest of her life.

Chapter 26

The next morning in the lobby of the Verhu building, the commissary server brought Church Dickens his hot latte – and a deviation from his blueberry scone, a celebratory slice of banana nut bread he'd amazed her by ordering.

At the same moment Alan, who people had rarely seen fraternizing with the hired help, dropped heavily into the seat across the table from Dickens. Alan looked wearily around the room, blinking like a man who had no idea where he was.

"We lost control of TPL," he said.

"I did everything I could." Dickens looked the old man over; clean grey shirt, maroon tie, gold cuff links, grey slacks, expensive dark blue sport jacket folded neatly on the chair next to him. "Let me get you a drink. Latte?" Dickens gestured the server to wait.

"Maybe plain black. To go."

"Donut or something?"

"Apple fritter, maybe..."

"On my tab," Dickens said.

"Even after splurging on the banana bread!?" this from the server with a nod to Dickens (he was thinking it would only be proper to leave her a big tip).

Philby stared at him, wide-eyed, and his blinking slowing down. "So what happened, Dickens? What was that flickery light stuff? For Christ sake, my phones were out! And please, for Christ's sake, don't tell me a goddamn Act of God."

He wasn't fooling Dickens, who saw the mind working behind the old man's flustering façade. "Your firm built the building, Alan. Hell, you should know."

"Just how do you know that?" Philby pushed his mean button, glared across the table at Dickens.

"Alan, I am your real estate guy. At least, one of your real estate guys."

"Yeah, yeah," Philby growled, waving a dismissing hand. "Look, Church, I know you're thinking of leaving the firm, but stick around a while so we can clean things up. Give me a couple weeks. You owe me that."

This was something new. It put Dickens on guard. "How do you figure I owe you?"

"Come on, guy, be real: Here I take a chance on a crippled vet with no experience in the real financial world; I think you owe me a lots more than I'm getting."

The coffee came, along with a paper bag with Philby's apple fritter and another with Church's banana nut bread.

"I'll think about it," Dickens said.

Philby, hoping for more than a maybe, jerked to his feet and stood swaying over him like an angry old bear.

"That's all loyalty buys me in this modern day and age? Two weeks out of your busy life! That's all I'm asking."

"Alan. Seriously. I'll think about it. Don't forget your fritter." He should have just said no and gotten on out of there. In his imagination, Church was seeing himself as some sort of a silly young fool, maybe Sponge Bob trying to play with the young jelly fish with the Mean Jelly Dad about to strike.

Philby snorted, a glop of yellow snot appearing at the tip of one nostril. He rubbed one arm across his face, and folded his jacket neatly to cover the wet streak on the sleeve of his shirt. He picked up his cup of black coffee and headed for the elevators.

"Don't forget your fritter, Philby." But Alan kept walking without looking back. Dickens was once again seeing the old man as crazy dangerous. It would be smart to move faster than he'd planned, get totally away from Verhu. Get on his crutches and hobble on out of there as fast as he could move. No going-away party with Harvey and Celeste and his pals at the VA. It was time for his next assignment, his new tour of duty, whatever and wherever that might be; since he was out of the military, now he got to decide for himself.

Philby had probably figured out what he'd done – not how he'd done it, but the basic strokes, and made a couple of good guesses. Now somebody other than Verhu controlled TPL, and it had to be Dickens. Who else could it be?

Still, the lack of real fire coming from Philby didn't ring true; it was odd, and Church didn't like odd; since his army days he had come to think life was combat, and tours of duty in war zones had made him aware of the importance of things out of the ordinary. Time to get out of Verhu...now!

Dickens wasn't going to do anything for Philby that put his resignation in legal jeopardy, and in his mind he moved his timetable up from days to hours. He wondered if he could fly direct from LAX to

Taos or if he'd have to go to someplace in between like Phoenix.

His gaze shifted to the paper bag on the table in front of him. He was guessing Annie would probably like a glazed apple fritter.

Chapter 27

Jay Bornton had hoped he wouldn't have any cell phone reception on the ridge he'd found above the road that led past Taos Pines Lodge and Carter Cabins, but when it rang he had to put down his old Bushnell sports binocs and of course he was immediately annoyed that he'd answered without looking at the number on his screen because it was Tammy, his ex-wife, the one person in the world he most didn't want to talk to.

"You're behind again, Jay." It was that whiney, exasperated tone of hers that bothered him more than anything. He bit his lip and managed to count to three before he answered.

"I know, honey, I know. But with the twins in private schools, I just can't keep up. I can't!"

"You have to keep up, Jay. If we don't pay the tuition they'll boot our kids out of school. You don't want that, do you."

He pinched one arm to keep himself from shouting. "No, I don't want that. Neither of us wants that. This isn't my fault! You wanted three kids! I wanted one! You wanted private schools that we can't afford!"

Her voice came across on the phone with a hard edge of finality. "That was then, and this is now - and I'll expect your check made out to me in the mail before the end of the week."

"Yes. It will be there. Made out to you. In the mail. Arrive by Saturday." There went his weekend in San Francisco. He clicked off the phone, but before he could pick up his binocs a gun barrel poked him in the ribs.

"What you doing sittin' up here on our property, son?"

It was Jessie Carter's dad, grizzly old Ed Carter.

"Come on, Ed, you know me. It's Jay Bornton. I'm just out here getting away from town."

"Yeah. Sure. Bird watching."

"No, I'm looking for a couple of dogs escaped from my kennels."

"What sort of dogs?"

Jay took a rumpled flyer from his pocket. The headline said MISSING DOGS, and it had fuzzy black and white pictures of a grinning Irish Wolfhound and a short hound with big ears.

"Dogs seems happy they got away. Maybe you weren't feedin' 'em right."

"Hey, Ed, you just think what you want, I'm responsible. I gotta find these dogs."

"Let's quit foolin' around, Jay. I heard you talking on the phone to my daughter. You know we been keeping those creatures safe for their rightful owners."

"It's my job to make sure, Ed. That old lady could sue me for everything I own."

"You're telling me that's why you're hanging out up here in the icy cold breeze with it looking like snow and all? I'd say it looks like you're trying to steal a couple dogs."

"Ed, this ain't your property. That's your fence line right over there. I can do what I want here."

"Look, Jay. From right here with them binocs around your neck you can see my barn and the back end of most of my cabins. It's like you're spying on me. I don't like it."

"You can't just tell me what to do, Ed Carter. I could get the sheriff – "

Something hardened in Ed's gaze that made Jay hesitate before he opened his mouth to say anything more. The Carters had been in Taos so long they thought they owned the whole damn place. Oh Christ, what a day, what a day! First Tammy yapping at him, and now this! He sighed and slowly got to his feet so Ed wouldn't do anything stupid. He gave a wave of dismissal and walked away across the rocky, snowless ground, heading down slope toward the lodge parking lot where he'd left his van. He didn't look back or say another word. And that was probably his best move so far.

Chapter 28

Bel nudged me in the side with her big wet nose but I already knew what she was trying to warn me about; the scent of that vile puppy-stealing breeder's smell was in the air, heavy like skunk spray or bad gas. Bel and I knew his greedy desire to get our pups had not gone away; he was watching us from a distance, and just waiting for a chance to pounce on us and drag us away. And then take our pups. For what purpose? What reason? Greed, or fame on the show circuit. Whatever, it wasn't good, and it wasn't his right. If he ever came for our pups I was ready to show him how we wolfhounds got our name. I looked over at Bel; short, stout tough little Bel, her belly nearly dragging to the ground with her pregnancy – I would go for the evil man's throat and Bel could trip him up at the ankles. We were ready and alert. I felt confident, knowing we had a plan to defend ourselves.

Chapter 29

Church Dickens finished his coffee in time for what he was sure would be his last afternoon staff meeting. To say he had a staff was something of a joke, but blinky old Philby insisted he hold weekly meetings and that Celeste be allowed to attend, to give a feminine viewpoint, the way he put it. It was a weak cover and it wasn't fooling anyone. Celeste was the old man's spy.

She showed up early, announced herself with their running gag that wasn't nearly as funny as it had been some months before, "Make partner yet, Dicksie-boy?"

"Nope. Just the opposite; I'm looking for the escape hatch, Cel. You?"

"Not yet. Getting close, though." Old Alan dangled the bait of a junior partnership in front of everyone higher up on the food chain than the mail boy. Dickens wasn't going to let the subject drop this time because he was so short-time he didn't really have anything to lose: "No, you're not. Nobody is getting close. To tell the truth, Celeste, I don't think there are any junior partners. You ever see one?"

She wasn't expecting anything from him but idle banter, and that set her back for a moment. "Well – no…"

"Back when I still believed maybe the old fart wasn't nuts I offered to bring him just over ten million in new client accounts. He said, 'Let me think about that.' That was months ago."

She gave him her cool appraisal, "You don't have ten million in new clients."

Dickens gave her a vague shrug that could mean anything, thinking she was the last person he would confide anything about his business. He smiled and dismissed the subject with a wave of his hand. "Philby doesn't know that."

"So what's your theory? Why didn't he jump on your proposal?"

"It's just my opinion, Cel, but Alan Philby has got some serious secrets. New partners – even junior partners – get to look at the books. I don't think Alan wants that."

"More of this again! You've somehow convinced yourself Verhu isn't solid. Or maybe you're just trying to get your biggest rival to go away."

"You think what you want, Cel."

She made a scoffing sound with her lips, "Nice try, Churchie-boy. I gotta go to the can. Don't start the meeting without me."

"How could we?" he said.

His real staff consisted of Harvey part-time and himself, with Annie to take notes; Church walked down the corridor to re-warm the remaining bottom third of his latte in the office microwave. He returned to sit behind his desk, nervously counting the minutes until he could make his way down the elevator and out of the Verhu building for the last time.

Harvey showed up and took a seat across the desk from Church. Annie took the remaining chair. There wasn't much to talk about; Church figured

103

five minutes and they'd be done. But that's when Celeste returned.

"Celeste. Sorry, meeting's over."

"Maybe it was but now it isn't. Mr. Philby's coming. He'll be right here." She made a shoo-fly gesture with one hand toward Harvey, "Where's your manners, creepy boy?"

Church cut her off, "No, Celeste. Harvey, this is our meeting. Cel, as our guest you get to sit on the floor, if you must stay. Or how about on that slab of Mexican onyx over there." He pointed to a big yellow rock that came to a point on top.

"Ha ha, very amusing," she said, a pouting, pinched look on her face. Now that Church's blinders were off, there she was, the hidden Ms. Russo, pretty in her sleek way, but an ambitious climber. An amoral predator. Predator, like the movie. Wow, did that word fit. It looked like she was about to make another run at ousting Harvey when Philby showed up, and Harvey ended the standoff by giving the older man his seat and standing next to Celeste.

"The subject is Taos Pines Lodge," Philby said. His bloodshot eyeballs were magnified behind his reading glasses. He looked innocent and vulnerable, like an old grade school teacher who was losing his marbles with a classroom of unruly kids. "There was supposed to be a stockholders' vote on debt restructuring, but it's been delayed."

No mention of the disastrous stock offering or the rollercoaster ride it had taken. He couldn't change the annual stockholders meeting, but Philby, who was at least temporarily still the Chairman of the Board of Directors of TPL, could hold or delay special stockholders meetings at his own discretion. Dickens wondered what alternative universe the old man was living in. But he said nothing, hoping he wasn't looking too openly skeptical.

Philby rolled out a modified topo map he'd brought in under one arm and tried to flatten the curled ends on Church's desk. Dickens helped him hold down the map with several chunks of tiger's eye and a half-river rock he had once split open to reveal a specimen of ancient fossil fern that was inside. Alan grunted a few words that might have been a thank you. The map had more detail than most, including geologic sub structures, but it also had a clear plastic overlay showing elevation lines.

"Here we have the projected view of the Taos Pines Project," Philby said, "The area in shaded blue on the overlay is confirmed and approved by local zoning and ready for funding."

"Oh, Condos," Harvey said, pleased his guess had been right. "Lots of condos."

"That's right. A major development."

Dickens didn't say anything. He doubted this new reveal from the moment it left Philby's lips. Condo development took the kind of money Verhu didn't have. Still, the sloping angles were right, they probably could build there, at least on most of it. Dickens pointed to a second area even bigger than the blue colored one Philby had pointed out. "What about that shaded red area next to it?"

"Well, that's the circumstance."

"Alan, what do you mean, the circumstance?"

Alan blinked at him, his expression saying the answer should have been obvious. "The Carter family owns that land. We want it. Need it, actually, to make the whole project work out right for us."

Dickens shook his head in disbelief. "And we have the financing to pay for it?"

Philby had started to shake his head no; but before he could say anything Celeste cut in with an impatient edge to her voice. "Of course we do! And Mr. Philby wants you to go out there and get it! And at a reasonable price!"

Dickens looked from Philby to Celeste and back again. "Wait. That's not my assignment."

"It is now," Philby said, a note of finality to his voice.

"Don't worry, Churchie-boy," Celeste said, "I'll handle your little department until you get back."

Dickens frowned. "Well, that's not going to happen for sure."

Philby rolled up his map, in his haste doing a bad job of it. "You better figure out where your loyalties lie, Mister Dickens. You tried to resign and walk away from your responsibilities a few days ago…"

He faltered, seeming to mix his thoughts, but Celeste was right there to continue for him. "…and now you question the financial resources of the major league firm that gave you – a maimed army vet – the opportunity of a lifetime!"

She scored with that one; Church heard his own voice rising in anger, "I don't need your opinion or your help, Celeste. And I don't see how your input will be needed in my department. This is the computer age. If I have to go, I'll handle my work load from the road. Nobody will even know I'm not here."

"Oh, you have to go, all right," Celeste said. "Put your law degree to good use."

Church got control of himself; he didn't bother to answer; after all, he told himself, it was only Philby's flunky talking, and then he had the thought it might be a good idea to play along with Alan's idea. He was no longer officially with the company, and the pay check didn't matter, if it came to that. Keep your friends close and your enemies closer. Now that he and Ruger were major stockholders in TPL, he might be able to find out what Alan's plans for the ski lodge actually were. He turned to Annie. "Celeste is not to use – is not to even enter – my office while I'm gone."

"Oh, right – like I would," Celeste said.

"Right. Just as if," he said. He looked at Philby, "Understood?"

The senior partner's face reddened and he pretended he didn't see the power struggle going on. He had a brief coughing fit and stood there uncomfortably, trying to make obvious that he wanted to leave, but Church stood in his way and stared at him until he nodded in agreement.

"Of course. We'll have to work it out," the old man said, hunching his shoulders and pushing his way around Dickens to make his exit.

Celeste bit her lip and stormed out of the cramped little room, stomping after Philby without saying another word.

Chapter 30

Later that evening Church was still in his office when Annie poked her head in the door, purse slung over her shoulder and on her way to the elevator.

"Night, boss. You staying late?"

He looked up from his computer screen. "I was hoping this would be my last day ever at Verhu."

"I thought you weren't certain about that."

"Well, I wasn't. And now I've got this Taos assignment, I'm even less sure what to do. I can't figure out Alan's game. My bad: I should have done more digging before I signed on here. Did you know there's nothing on Alan Philby on Bing or Google or anywhere? Nothing. At least I can't find it. He's a man without a past."

Annie hesitated a moment.

"Did you try Phillip Alan Philby?"

"No, I didn't know that one."

"He hates 'Phil Philby'. So he dropped the first Phil."

"Wooh. Lame try, that."

"Night, boss. Don't stay too late."

A few minutes later Harvey dropped by Dickens' office, "Hey, I passed Annie by the elevator. You staying late, huh? How'd it go today, Hot Shooter? Anybody from the Security Commission after your ass yet?"

"Hi, Harv. No, I haven't been arrested so far, but the night is young."

"What are you doing?"

"Trying to dig up any dirt I can find on Old Blinky."

"Hey, I'm a good digger; let me help."

"Why not?"

Harvey pulled his laptop from his backpack and plugged in on the other side of Church's desk.

"Annie says Chicago," Dickens said. "He came from Chicago before LA. And his full real name is Phillip Alan Philby."

Harvey's fingers were flying. "Phillip Alan Philby. Huh. Huh. Huh. Article from twenty five years ago. Chicago Sun-Times. Korean vet. Guy's wife dies. He was a cop, made detective. Grief stricken. Decides to go back to school. Northwestern. Gets a degree in finance. Huh. Huh. Huh. Forms an investment company. Goes broke. Loses his inheritance from his dead wife."

"Wow, that's a lot ... Philby was a cop?" Church thought for a moment and then nodded. "I guess that makes a kind of sense; sort of the way he is. Did you know he carries?"

"Carries what?"

"Philby wears a leg holster. With a small revolver in it. Probably a .32 caliber."

"That's nuts! He's just a semi-senile old fart."

"No, he isn't. Not entirely. His mind may be going, but he's a spry old bastard. And he stays in shape, too."

"But – a gun?"

"Well, he is an ex-cop, Harvey. I caught a glimpse of it in a meeting when he fell asleep. It's a small hide-out. Left leg."

"Why would he carry a gun?"

"Early stage dementia? I don't know. How did his wife die?"

"Home robbery."

"Shot with a small automatic?"

"No, Dicks. Life's never that simple. She was bludgeoned to death with a lead pipe."

"Was she rich?"

"Oh, yeah. She was a Coleson. Chicago high society. Old money."

"Keep digging, Harv."

An hour later Dickens pulled up an article from a Milwaukee newspaper. "Hey, Phillip Alan Philby was a member of the Old Slammer Bammers."

"What the heck is that?"

"It's an old soldiers club. Or was twenty years ago. Korea War Vets. Held their annual reunion in Wisconsin, side trip to the picturesque Dells. Says here Philby was in the 5th DDU...Detonation & Demolition Unit..."

"Wow. Bomb squad."

Church gave a soft whistle of appreciation. "Yeah. Our Old Blinky knows guns and bombs...Philip Alan Philby is way more than he seems. He's dangerous."

"That's a little melodramatic, don't you think?"

"My friend, once you've been in a war zone, life is full of unexpected possibilities."

"Yeah, I guess..."

They ordered carry outs, mushu pork and egg rolls, and kept at it. It was nearly midnight when Harvey found another article, this one from a New York newspaper. "Philby and Beane, Financial Partners."

"And?" Dickens gave him the look that said There's gotta be more.

"Close to fifteen years ago. They were being investigated for fraud. Beane mysteriously disappears on a fishing trip in the Bahamas."

Dickens was once again feeling what he thought of as a really bad dread about Philby, the sort of dark premonition he hadn't felt since just before his team had been ambushed in the hills north of Kabul. "Where was Philby at the time?"

"Doesn't say." Harvey unplugged his laptop and replaced it in his backpack. "People die around this guy. I think I'm going to take your advice; get my resume out there. You watch your back in Taos, Hot Shooter."

"Same-same for you here in L.A., Harvey Fineman, fact digger extraordinaire."

They left it like that for the night. But while Dickens packed his things and caught a plane for New Mexico, over the next few days Harvey continued digging for anything he could find on Philby. That proved to be surprisingly little return for the effort, and worse … in the end it might have gone better for him if he'd left Southern California right away with his pal the Hot Shooter.

Chapter 31

A few days later Dickens was parked in front of the Taos Pines Lodge and thinking through how best to keep his balance while wrestling his luggage out of the trunk of his rental when he spotted an argument going on a short way up the hill on the road ahead of him. An angry young woman was shouting at the top of her lungs at a man who was struggling to drag a big grey dog and a short brown-and-white one into a black van. The van said Bornton Breeders, Inc. in big yellow letters on its windowless sides. The bigger dog, a huge, shaggy thing, clearly didn't want to go up the ramp into the van, and the woman was trying to hold it back by the collar while at the same time talking into a cell phone. The smaller dog had managed to tangle her leash in the man's legs, and he looked like he might go down. Dickens grabbed his knobby wooden cane (supposedly once owned by his ancestor, old Moab Dickens the sea captain) from the passenger seat and limped toward them as fast as he could manage. "Hey! What's going on?"

"None of your business!" the man said.

"This man is trying to steal my dogs!"

"They ain't her dogs! She's a liar! I am Jay Bornton. These animals escaped from my kennel! I have every right to take them!"

Church found himself on the pretty woman's side. Maybe, he would think later, maybe because he was a guy and she was really good looking, call it the pretty blond option. Whatever, he took in the situation like he'd come on a firefight, and he liked her and just like that there were two sides and he was on hers. "I don't know, Mister Bornton from Santa Fe. This is Taos and I personally wouldn't want to be caught aiding and abetting in a robbery if you actually were stealing these dogs. Can we see some papers saying you have rights to this – he took a closer look at the bigger dog, saw it was nearly the size of a small pony – err, this rather large creature?"

"Just who the hell is we, mister?"

The pleasant look disappeared from Church's face and he raised his cane like a jousting staff. "We is the guy who's going to kick your ass in another second or two."

Jessie saw that, for a change, she was going to have to be the peacemaker. "No, wait - I'm Jessie Carter. Carter Cabins. This – this person came onto our property without our permission, brought his own leashes and now he's trying to walk out with these dogs!"

"I have every right!"

"Mister, I don't think you do," Church said. "What you're doing is trespassing. And you're not showing any papers … so this is possible canine theft, and I'm a very reliable witness. A lawyer, in point of fact."

Dickens spoke with a quiet confidence; there was something about him that made the fiery breeder move back a step. And in that moment Dickens took the leashes from Bornton, untangled the one from around the man's leg and handed them to Jessie.

"Mr. Bornton, if that is your name, exactly why are you here in the first place?" he said.

"None of your business."

"It is now."

"I am supposed to have a meeting with this lady, to identify and take possession of these dogs. They are valuable pure breeds, and – "

"You showed up early," Jessie said. "And tried to steal the dogs!"

"Not at all. I am here because I have to identify them. For insurance purposes."

"And have you identified these dogs to your satisfaction, with absolute certainty?" Dickens said.

"Well, yes. They are the two dogs in question. They escaped from my kennel. They are my responsibility. I should be able to take them back to my kennel where they are being legally boarded. I have to take them. To make things right."

"No, you don't! I called the owner," Jessie said. "She is already on their way – with her lawyer. They'll be right here. In fact, here they are, coming right now."

The men looked up to see two women pulling behind them in an old silver Cadillac. A middle aged woman who turned out to be a Ms. Molly Morganfeld, Esq. got out of the driver's seat and handed Jessie her business card. She helped an elderly woman from the car. This was Mrs. Cory Anderson and she eagerly hobbled over to the huge grey dog, who was so happy to see her she caused a scene and nearly knocked the old lady to the sidewalk. The irony was that Dickens was in the right place and kept her from falling to the ground, the crippled vet helping the aged infirm lady.

114

Ms. Morganfeld declared she was Mrs. Anderson's lawyer and, in the next moment settled her stern gaze on Jay Bornton. "Jessie Carter is boarding these dogs, Jay. We have determined you cannot be trusted to keep them safe. We feel you have broken our contract through gross negligence. There is no longer any obligation to you. That said, what is your problem here?"

But the breeder wasn't going to give up without a fight. "Ms. Morganfeld. We agreed on this: I came here to identify the dogs. I have to make sure they are healthy. And ... and, I'm here to reinstate my claim to first pick of the new litters."

"Mr. Bornton. You can see these are the right dogs. You can see they are both healthy. But our absolute and final no to the rest: And this is the first we've heard about any claim to any of the puppies. That is totally absurd!"

"Not just any puppies; pick of the litter." Jay gave her a stubborn look.

Mrs. Anderson frowned and shook her head. "No. I did not sign anything like that."

"It's standard practice. Part of my breeding fee. I would have had you sign the contract but you were too sick."

Church stood back and kept his silence; Morganfeld looked like a tough cookie who could handle things, but it was old Cory Anderson who spoke up. "Jay, I say shame, shame on you! You think you can cheat a rickety old lady, do you? I never heard of such wicked scheming in my life!"

"Get out of here, Dog Thief!" Jessie said. "Or we'll call the sheriff!"

"Better beat it," Dickens said. "While you still can."

"You haven't heard the end of this!" With that, the breeder glared his red-faced anger, and shook his finger at each of them in turn. But they were too many for him, and he had no choice but to retreat to his van and drive away.

They all inspected the barn together, with Dickens tagging along because it seemed like a good idea to him. The old lady decided the barn was a very good place; in back of the main cabin, well maintained and clean, with plenty of room for two dog's living quarters with the Carters. Mrs. Anderson declared everything entirely satisfactory, and they agreed on a price; Carter Cabins would board and care for the dogs indefinitely, until her owner was feeling in better health.

Jessie and Dickens watched as the lawyer helped her client into the Cadillac and carefully drove away.

"Thank you for your help. But just who are you?" Jessie said.

"Church Dickens, from Los Angeles. I was just about to check in at the lodge."

She smiled, liking something about him. "And you thought to rescue a helpless woman in distress."

"No. I had to come over before you kicked that Bornton guy's butt."

"Me?" Her smile broadened and she gave him an innocent look.

"Karate 101. You were winding up, about to take him out. I know that move."

"Kick-boxing. I did have a few lessons. When I was in college." She looked him over, approving what she saw, a well-built man maybe half past thirty, no wedding ring, light blond hair and a firm jaw, walking with a cane but trying to move without it. "You told Jay Bornton you were a lawyer."

"I did pass the bar in a few states, but I'm more of a financial advisor. I specialize in land acquisitions."

"They're getting a lot of guys like you over at the lodge these days."

"Like me, huh?" He passed her a wry smile, but didn't say anything more. He didn't have to; human chemistry is like that. Without really thinking about it, they were on the same page, at peace in a new discovery, where have you been all my life?

They were standing there, nothing special, life going on by the way it should, maybe just looking for an excuse to have a few more moments together. She had an idea, Why not offer him a cabin? Carter Cabins could use the business, and even sweeter to swipe a guest from the lodge. "Why don't you rent one of our cabins?" she said. "I'll do you a way better rate than you'll get over there."

"You got Wi-Fi?"

"Oh, yeah! Ours is lots better than theirs. We're higher up the hill. And we serve home cooked breakfast in the main house."

"Hey, home cooked breakfast – okay, you got a deal.". He held out his hand and she took it. For a moment she didn't want to let go, and it seemed like he didn't, either.

Chapter 32

Celeste knew Saturdays were not a good day for snooping around the office. Sometimes Annie came in to clean up loose ends from Dickens' work week. Celeste wondered if that was just Church's secretary's way to pick up a little extra time and a half, but still, she didn't want to run into her. She also figured Sundays were a much better day to get in a good snoop. Annie was a church-going Baptist who everybody knew (because she told them) sang in the choir and Sunday was God's Day. Very little chance Annie would show up in the office on a Sunday.

That was why God's day found Celeste taking the empty elevator up to the deserted Verhu Financial offices and sitting in the comfort of Annie's expensive and classy Herman Miller chair, enjoying the cool metal-mesh back, wondering for a moment at her insane desire to roll Annie's chair down to her office and switch it for her own worn leather number. She was sure Churchie-boy had bought that chair for Annie – the firm would never have popped for it. She took her iPhone from her purse and snapped a picture of Annie's cluttered desktop (so she could put things back where they were) and then methodically set about looking for the keys to Dickens' office. It wasn't that she really had a plan, or that she was out to destroy the poor old gimpy fellow. No, of course not. It was just that he was in the way. The thing that stuck in her mind, the thing of interest to her: Church Dickens was abnormally successful at the firm. He had a knack for getting in and out of markets at the right time, and maybe that was all there was to it. Maybe it was just confidence. When you're confident, Lady Luck is on your side. Some traders were sure that was all you really needed to beat the market. But if that were true, wouldn't Mister Lucky be overconfident at least some of the time?

The outcome between the two of them was obvious to her from the start: She was going to get her promotion to junior partner and she would leave Church Dickens in the dust. As for the rest of it, well, she would soon be Philby's personal assistant, the rising young star at Verhu Financial.

Old fart Alan was always threatening to fire everybody, but to her knowledge he never had let anybody go...well, there had been that one accounting guy, but he'd deserved it, poking around into Philby's private affairs. That was comforting and worrisome at the same time. One or two employees had told her they were leaving Verhu for greener pastures; though she found that hard to believe. One other thing: nobody was taking Church Dickens' resignation seriously. Everywhere she went, there really was an Old Boys Club, and it pissed her off mightily. Realistically, if she couldn't get Dickens fired, there was a chance he might make partner before her, just because he was a guy, and the pack males stuck together. So she was leaving nothing to chance; she'd given up her Sunday to come in and check out his office, to learn what she'd missed when they were together: who his clients were, what made him tick, how he thought about things and made his decisions —all his secrets,. That was the only way she could see to cut him down to size.

She'd dated him for a few months, nothing serious, keeping it loose and casual (like she would ever get serious with a gimp?), but that effort on her part had proved so totally not worth the effort she had put into it; the gimpster was so common – so ordinary, open and disgustingly honest and predictable – that he bored her to tears, and she'd pushed him away as soon as she realized what a loser he was. Time for a short cut. Everybody had secrets, and she was going to dig into his. And, no big surprise, the key to his office door was in full view right in the front of the top drawer in Annie's desk. Annie, a nice decent church-going girl like you, how could you be so stupid?

Chapter 33

I knew that my stay – in the big red barn that smelled of absent dogs and the three horses who snuffed and shuffled around in nearby stalls – would not be for very long. It was okay for now and I could be patient, but I was used to living in my own room in the big old Victorian house with my Cory, the kind old lady who took a big part in my life after the Colonel, the gruff man with the bushy moustache, started to fail until the time he fell over on one of our walks and didn't get up again.

The barn was a new experience for Bel and me, a different sort of place, big and drafty but with plenty of blankets and a thick bed pad underneath. At night owls flew in the opening to the hay loft and settled in the overhead rafters and then flapped back out into the chill air, and there were times we both came alert to the distant howl of wolves and the closer, more insistent, high pitched yip-yap talk of the coyotes. And, of course, we both kept our ears and noses alert for the puppy thief.

One morning Billie and her grandpa, the old greybeard man named Ed, came to the stall where we were staying and led us to a clean apron of concrete. Billie sprayed us with a hose and scrubbed us with foamy soap and then Ed rinsed us with the hose and they patted us dry with towels and combed our fur to get a few burrs out from when we'd escaped the kennels.

After that, as I had expected, they coaxed us to come with them and led us into the big house where the people we thought of as Greybeard Ed's pack lived. There was a long hallway with doors on either side, and then a big room with a lot of tables and chairs and the smell of something like beef stew.

What startled me a little was when the female who I thought was the alpha-bitch – her name was Kate – began yelling and pointing at us and then towards the door. This was when things got complicated: There was another man there, eating his breakfast, and he stood up to try and calm Kate, but she pushed him aside with a huffing gesture and marched out of the room.

That was how I got involved. When Kate roughly pushed her way past the man who had stood up, he had seemed so strong, but then he went off balance. I knew it was a weakness, something in his back, and he was going to fall and hurt himself. But I was standing right next to him, and I wasn't going to let any bad possibilities happen.

The man, whose name I only later learned was Church, reached out for me and I stood there strong as a big tree as his arm went around my broad shoulders and I steadied him and he did not fall to the hard tile floor where I was sure he would have hurt himself. He looked down at me and our eyes met for the briefest moment and he said words I knew meant thank you. This man knew woof-speak. He was a dog person, and that was how in less time than it takes to tell it a bond was forged; Church Dickens became my new special human person. In short, I adopted him.

Chapter 34

It was about that time Church Dickens realized how much he missed his army dog and asked Ed if Lexi could come live in one of the spare bedrooms in his cabin as long as she was staying at Carter Cabins, and Ed agreed. And Jessie said she was going to take in Bel to live with her. Kate didn't say anything, but her face looked like it was about to explode, and she left the room in a big huff.

Dickens and his new wolfhound friend were in the same dining room a few days later. Lexi sat on the floor next to him and watched while he worked his laptop. Dickens looked at the wolfhound. He reached over and scratched the dog's ears.

"Bet you're hoping I'm a sloppy eater."

Lexi gave him a goofy grin, like she knew what he was saying. Kate frowned as she brought Dickens his plate of ham and scrambled eggs. "No feeding the dog," she said.

"You're Jessie's mom, right?" Dickens said.

"Well, sort of. She doesn't think so. I'm Ed's second wife. Jessie's step-mom. Whatcha doin', hun?"

"Working on my next million dollars."

"You have to be kidding." She looked him over. He had such a nice, quiet way and was so agreeable, she almost could forgive him for this Lexi business going on. Kate had seen a lot of the world in the Vegas years before she'd married Ed, and she was a person of strong convictions, a survivor on her own terms; the world was not a nice place, and she was certain that people with millions – with that kind of money – didn't talk about it all open and friendly like the way he did.

"I'm day trading," he said.

"What's that, hun?

"Here, take a look." He turned the computer monitor so she could see, and out of all the neat rows of numbers and letters he pointed to the letter T. "See that. It's the stock symbol for AT&T. I invested in it at 5 this morning. Now it's three hours later and I'm going to sell it."

"You're playing with other people's money, right?"

"Sometimes."

"Well, that looks to me like a god-almighty waste of time."

"You could be right. I bought in at twenty two dollars and fifty cents a share. Now I'm going to sell."

"You bought it and now you're gonna sell it."

"Right. If it holds another half minute I'll dump it at twenty two-seventy. You follow?"

"Course I do, hun. Looks like you made twenty cents."

He folded his laptop and put his plate on top of it. "You have to add in the number of shares. That would be twenty times one hundred and eighty two thousand five hundred. Hey, these eggs look good. You put cheese on 'em."

Kate had started to walk back to the kitchen area but that stopped her short. She took another moment, calculating. He could see money meant a lot to her, but the look on her face and the quick little shake of her head told him she didn't believe him. "You made them some thousands of dollars since five this morning? And that's your hobby?"

"Well, there's taxes and overhead. And nobody wins all the time."

"Okay. Let's play your game: What's the most you ever lost?"

He paused, thinking about it. "The most I ever lost...I'd have to say it was my heart to the wrong person."

She frowned, the look on her thin face turning sour. "No, don't play slickster wordsmith stuff with me, hon; I mean money."

"I can't remember off the top of my head..."

"Like most gamblers."

"...maybe sixty-five thousand and change."

"Not in one morning?"

"No. It took eight hours...that was a really bad day; I was on the wrong side when that oil rig mess happened in the Gulf of Mexico. I bailed but I had to fight it all the way."

"And you lost sixty-five thousand dollars real money."

"Hey, I got lucky. It could have been a quarter million."

"A quarter million..." She walked away, shaking her head. Some people were so full of malarkey you couldn't believe a word came out of their mouths. She went back to the kitchen to smoke a Kools and push Chooli the Navajo girl to get a move on her lazy butt washing the dishes. Dickens watched her go and then clicked his laptop back to the screen he'd been studying before she had come nosing around. The Carters had owned their land for generations, and there had to be more than he was

125

finding on the internet, or why was Philby interested? He was going to have to broaden his search. The scrambled eggs smelled good. He clicked off his laptop, picked up his knife and fork and started in on his breakfast.

***

Later that morning Dickens was on the Taos County Clerk's site, scrolling through the public records, looking for any recent land activity. Anything, anything, anything. And there it was, in plain view, a three month old application to change zoning on the Taos Pines Lodge property. The request was to change from business/general to suburban/condos. So maybe Alan was telling the truth. Or maybe it was all just a cover story. Still, if it was subterfuge, the blinky old crook was going through a lot of trouble just to hide his intentions. There was even a red APPROVAL stamp, so the project was officially a go, at least as far as the county was concerned. For a lawyer from Los Angeles, used to working with lot sizes generally less than a half-acre, these were large chunks of land. The application had been submitted in October and it had been approved within the past few days.

Church's eyes narrowed when he saw it had been signed by Alan Philby of Verhu Financial. Alan had been in Taos and hadn't said anything about it, kept it a secret. He'd made a big deal about being on vacation in Paris, he'd talked it up around the office, one of those trips of a lifetime. What was he hiding? And most unexpected of all, the application clearly included the big tract of Carter Cabins land in addition to the TPL land – and under Alan Philby's signature was another. One other person had signed the application on the same date and time: Katherine Carter, Carter Cabins, Inc.

Chapter 35

Harvey Fineman had a fetish about keeping his desk and his business papers neat. This was not what might be expected of him, considering his suits were worn three or four days in a row and his shirt collars were rumpled, his tie loosened or missing entirely, and his curly dark red hair was generally in need of a cut and a comb.

But the women in Harvey's family – his mother and his grandma – had taught him right: cleanliness is next to Godliness (as the goyim say), and since Harvey didn't think he was going to get near God in any other way, at least he could keep his desktop clean. That is why, early one morning when he showed up for work, he knew instantly someone had been sifting through his papers. A closer look revealed the file he'd built on Alan Philby was missing. And the note on his desk from old Alan himself, telling Harvey he was being let go, confirmed who had taken it. The note read:

Harvey - We are restructuring and you
are fired. Get your stuff out of the building
today. Pick up your check in my office after
six tonight. Sorry. Alan P.

Chapter 36

Jay Bornton wasn't a woodsman at all, and he didn't pretend to be. So this time when Ed Carter caught him half way up the trail to Death Drop but clearly on Carter land, he simply threw up his hands. "I give up, Ed. Please don't shoot me. Or if you're gonna do me in, make it quick."

Ed, sitting on his favorite red, off-road, all-terrain ATV, the one customized with a yellow flame paint design that looked a little like a dragon, shook his head.

"Lucky you, I didn't bring my rifle today. Just a pistol so I don't get bushwhacked on my own property." He reached into a pouch and pulled out an old army issue .45.

"Yeah. My lucky day. Jesus, that thing is dangerous-looking."

"You can't be looking for them lost dogs no more, Jay. What you doing out here on my land?"

"Ed, you know those dogs was in my safe keeping –"

"So you're still looking to get yourself hung as a dog thief."

"Come on, Ed. They don't hang people for stealing dogs."

"That is right. I would just shoot you before we got to court. You know, Oops, there goes another hunting accident."

"No, you wouldn't – "

Ed raised the .45 and pointed it in Jay's face. "What the hell's wrong with you, Jay? You know this here is private land."

Jay couldn't say the real reason he was on the path back to Ed's old gold mine, that being a blinky, ancient looking old fellow he'd never seen before had spotted him coming back down the hill from one of his scouting missions and offered him a hundred bucks to snap a couple of pictures of that old fenced off place he said looked like a mine opening. If he had mentioned that, Jay figured Ed would have shot him for sure. But he wasn't really a good liar, either. He fumbled for words, but nothing came out and thankfully Ed lost patience with him. "I don't want to hear any more of your excuses. Get yourself gone right about now, Jay, or I will put a hole in you."

As Jay picked up his pace, walking swiftly in the direction of the fence that would put him back on Taos Pine Lodge land, the dog breeder found he was beside himself, shaking with rage. But he also knew he wasn't going to do anything stupid. That round black hole in the business end of Ed's old army automatic was a sobering image that wasn't going to accept any more of his lying excuses.

Chapter 37

It was another fresh, clear and bright-blue sky morning at Carter Cabins; Dickens was finishing his breakfast when he got Harvey's text:

ALAN KNOWS WE'RE DIGGING UP HIS PAST. HE FIRED ME.

Dickens immediately texted back: GET OUT NOW.

Harvey texted back: GO WHERE?

Dickens: COME WORK WITH ME. TAOS AWAITS YOU W/ OPEN ARMS.

Harvey: JEWISH CITY BOY ON A HORSE?

Dickens: A HORSE IS A 4 LEGGED BIKE.

Harvey: I'LL COME IN A COUPLE DAYS. I NEED MY PAYCHECK

Dickens: NO. I'LL GIVE YOU YOUR SALARY. GET OUT NOW!!!!

Harvey: I CAN'T TAKE YOUR MONEY. VERHU OWES ME. THEY WILL PAY.

Harvey sat in his small, windowless cubicle with a growing fear in the pit of his stomach; Dickens was like an older brother to him, and Harvey valued his opinion. But he was conflicted; there was a month's wages at stake and he had car payments to make on his pet, his putt-along avocado green Nissan Cube. He procrastinated while he loaded up the few boxes of his stuff and carried them out of the building and to the parking lot across the street where he'd parked the Cube when he couldn't find free street parking. And then he procrastinated some more, mulling Dickens's warning and his options over a burger and a beer at a nearby watering hole. And then he made up his mind, screwed up his courage, and started back across the street. He entered the Verhu building and strode purposefully toward the elevators. Both his great-grandparents had gotten clubbed on picket lines; he could as least have the guts to pick up his hard earned and rightfully owned pay check.

Chapter 38

Jessica drove a small green tractor into the barn with the front scoop carrying a two hundred pound bag of carrots. Ed was in one of the stalls, struggling to comb out the burrs on a large grey gelding's thick winter coat. The horse gave her a friendly whinny. Jessica jumped off the tractor and came over to see what Ed was doing.

"Dad, it's Lotus! Where did you find him?"

"Came back on his own. Probably figured you had a shipment of carrots coming. Horses have a way of knowing, you know."

"He'd gonna have to share. Lexi loves carrots too, you know."

"And that big dog eats as much as a horse, nearly"

Jessie had worked open the top of the carrot bag and handed one to Lotus. She looked into the empty stall where Lexi had slept until their new boarder took her in. "Big Dog didn't stay out here long."

"She's really taken a liking to that Dickens fellow. And you're one to talk, you got the hound in your room."

"I think Dickens is a good guy. He's been around dogs."

A cheery voice called out from the barn door, "Hey, the carrot delivery is in!" It was Billie, backpack showing she was just home from school. "And Lotus! Wow, that horse has great timing."

133

Billie went to the tractor and got a handful of carrots.

"Just one, Billie," Jessie warned. "She's already had one."

Billie selected the biggest one and fed it to Lotus. "Where's Lexi?"

"Church Dickens took her for a walk," Ed said.

"Not too far, I hope. That man is not strong as he looks, or he thinks he is."

"Just to the pasture, back side of the barn." Ed smiled at his daughter. "I think you're worried about him."

"Oh, he can take care of himself," Jessie said. "I have enough on my mind, worrying about you."

"He's a good man, Jessie. And, you know, I think he likes you."

"Come on now, Dad, stop it. There's nothing between us." But she blushed and started to walk away.

"Ain't you gonna put the carrots in the bin?"

"Billie can do it."

Billie grinned, delighted little-imp enthusiasm written all over her. "I get to drive the tractor!"

She climbed in the seat and after a few experimental tweaks looked over at Ed.

"It's that little lever thing next to the end," he said, gesturing with one hand.

She tried it and the front bucket moved up a few inches. She paused, something on her mind. "Why doesn't Mom like Mister Dickens?"

"She likes him, sweetheart, she just don't know it yet."

"Why?"

"Your mamma got hurt real bad when your daddy died so sudden like he done."

"Is she stuck that way forever?"

"Well, we hope not."

"I like Mister Dickens, Grampers."

"Me too, Billie."

"Lexi likes him, too. Dogs know, you know."

"Yes, they do, Billie. Yes, they do."

Chapter 39

Harvey felt a little silly, like he was acting the part of a paranoid fellow in a murder mystery movie. Still, at that moment it seemed like a smart idea only go up to one floor under Philby's office and then get off the elevator and quietly take the stairs up from there; Harvey was getting off when he realized how quiet the building was; and now his mind was going a mile a minute: crazy old Alan Philby was an ex-cop. He would hear the elevator noise and know somebody was coming, even if it didn't stop on the same floor. So Harvey waited five minutes, sitting in the stairwell. When he finally opened the door on Philby's floor and made his way down the long hall, he could see there wasn't another person on the entire floor. Well, it was late. He tried to calm his jitters with the thought, nothing much wrong about that, it was just late. And it helped his courage to rerun in his mind his family's stories of standing up to the Bosses in times past. Trying to walk as silently as a kung fu master, he passed Purple-lip Lenora's desk and stopped outside Alan's open doorway. Lenora, Philby's hot new secretary. Everybody he gossiped with in the office called out her lips because of the smoldering purple matte lipstick she wore. Called her that behind her back, of course. She wasn't from what remained of the Verhu secretarial pool. She'd approached Alan in the lobby and handed him her hand-written resume and, word was, he'd taken one lecherous look at that zaftig body of hers and hired her on the spot.

Harvey was being so careful he tripped on a rug edge and had to steady himself on Lenora's desk. A little purple glass rose that said Disneyland on the stem tinkled in a vase, and then there was that awful silence again.

Philby's office was dark and deserted, but there was a light coming from a small inner office conference room behind it. And Harvey heard the soothing sounds of instrumental music, Coast FM 101 on low volume. That got his imagination working. Wow, talk about a baited trap! Still, come on, maybe he was just being foolish. He really, really needed his pay check, and, just maybe to prove to himself he had some of the courage of his ancestors.

Genuinely carefully this time, he moved across Alan's office and took a quick look in the conference room. What he saw reassured him.

There the old guy was, feet up on his desk, head back and tie loosened, snoring like a drunk. From the look of it, that inner conference room was Alan Philby's Taos Central: All sorts of old reference books were piled on his desk and there were maps everywhere, rolls stacked in corners and pinned to the walls; Southwestern States maps. New Mexico and Arizona road maps. Beige, brown and green topography maps with the elevation lines on them.

Harvey's curiosity got the best of him. This was the last thing he expected, historical research – any kind of research – from crazy old Philby! Curiosity aroused, he picked up the nearest book, a thick and heavy volume, The Complete History of the Southwestern United States. Printed in 1935. What the hell was this?

Harvey spotted his check; there it was, right there on the conference room table, right next to Alan's hand. Too good to be true!

Still, Harvey held back. "Too good to be true" could mean just what it said. . He didn't believe in luck, his extended family had never had much, what with Europe and the Holocaust and all, and the sweatshops for the lucky ones who came to magic America earlier…and not trusting in luck or the universe made him cautious. He paused just inside the doorway, wondering what he was missing. And then he saw it; the small blackish butt of a pistol poking out from the handkerchief next to Alan's hand.

Saw it too late; Alan's eyes opened, his blinking, his wide-eyed stare huge behind his reading glasses, his big eyes looking in Harvey's direction and his fingers reaching for that gun butt. Harvey's check fluttered off the table onto the floor.

"Pick up your money," Alan said. "You earned it. Pick it up and get out of here before I shoot you." As he spoke he lifted the gun in his hand and the ugly snout of the small pistol was moving to point straight at Harvey's chest. Harvey took a couple steps closer and then stood frozen fifteen feet away. Too close, too close! The gun went off, a loud sound in the office, the bullet hitting Harvey high up on his right shoulder, spinning him around and knocking him back, two or three feet toward the doorway.

"No!" Harvey said. "People don't just shoot people!"

Maybe they didn't among the righteous, but Alan was a cop who'd gone criminal and, very unrighteously squinting at Harvey over his reading glasses, aimed his little revolver to take another shot.

Alan, groggy with sleep, hadn't seen the exact spot where he'd hit his target. That wasn't the problem, it was his stupid reading glasses! He pulled them off, tossed them on the desk in front of him. He jerked up from his chair; he would make sure with a second shot – a heart shot, center left on the chest, just like on the paper targets he'd practiced on at the academy, and some non-paper targets on the street, in the long ago and far away time of his cop duty.

And the stupid fool Harvey was still standing there, holding out that damn book in front of him like it could ward off bullets! Stupid, stupid idiot! He deserved to die!

Alan held the small gun in both hands. No way he could miss. Pulled off his second shot. And the bullet hit the book Harvey was holding, hit it dead center and knocked him backwards out of the doorway. And then the kid was on his feet and sprinting back the way he'd come. Damn it! Alan crabbed around the desk, lost a few precious seconds as he stumbled over his own briefcase, rushed out into the hallway and fired after his fleeing target. He got off three quick shots blam, blam, blam! before the click told him his pistol was empty, but shots rushed like that went wild, and then his fleeing target was out the stairway exit, the steel door slamming shut behind him, his retreating footsteps echoing as he took the metal steps down two and three at a time.

Alan gave out an exasperated puff of energy. He leaned against the door frame, dizzy from his sudden movements; it was unwise leaping to his feet like that, considering his age and his heart and everything. His gaze narrowed and he saw spots of blood on the floor in the hallway. That was something; he'd winged young Harvey, but Jesus, he was getting too old for this crap! Alan's practiced eye scanned the scene. Not a little blood, not a lot. Got him with that first shot for sure, but no way to know how good. Still, Philby shuffled fast as he could to the unreliable elevators, got lucky as one opened right away; he limped in, hit the button with the star on it and took it down to the lobby.

The night guard saw him coming off the elevator, an old man in a desperate hurry, half limping, half loping, rushing into the lobby, disheveled looking and revolver in one hand, the weapon not quite hidden at his side.

"Hey, Mister!"

"No, not me!" Alan said. "Thief in my office! There he goes!"

But there was nobody there. Harvey was gone. It took fifty bucks to quiet the night guard, and another two hours to clean the blood spots from the floor outside his office. The bullet holes in the walls … well, they were really small and high and sort-of out of the way and if anybody said anything he would just have to say he didn't know how they got there. Probably termites, or something like that.

Chapter 40

Harvey hunkered low in the driver's seat of his Cube. He had parked it on a dark sidestreet just off Wilshire Avenue in the mid-Wilshire district, a few miles away from the Verhu building. He stayed down until the two L.A. cops who were worrying him left Kim's Donut Shop.

He was in bad shape; he was quivering from head to toe. He had no experience with physical shock, didn't know how bad he was. He felt an overwhelming cold, ice to his bones, and he had terrible shivers. Was he going to die? How soon? Do people just die like this? He should have listened to Dicks, forget the money, just get away from Old Blinky. He was too young. He had a whole life to live! He didn't want to die! Get a grip, Harv, old fellow, get a grip!

From where he was parked under some thick Mulberry trees, he could see across Wilshire Boulevard to the deserted strip mall parking lot. Going too slow and joking around, the cops went to their squad car and he had to wait while they sat there for ten minutes before they slowly drove off. Even then, Harvey waited another few minutes before he drove across Wilshire. He awkwardly stutter-stopped his Cube into an empty parking space and half walked, half staggered into the MED 24 next to Kim's.

***

His bloody shirt alarmed the on-duty doctor, an East Indian man in a soiled white jacket, and the doctor instinctively reached for his phone.

"No," Harvey said. "Please. Doc, please. I'd have to run. No phone."

"No, Mister Sir, No Mister Sir, I must call the authorities, it is a rule."

"No cops," Harvey said. "The police come, you get no money." He reached in his pocket for a tangled mess of paper money and began to lay twenty dollar bills on the table in front of him.

A half hour later, against doctor's orders, a patched-up Harvey walked like a zombie back to his SUV and promptly fell asleep. He still had a bullet somewhere inside his shoulder, but the medical man couldn't find the exact location and had refused to keep on digging around in there..

Harvey woke at midnight, drank a can of Red Bull with two of Kim's donuts with white frosting and colored sprinkles on top and headed his Cube for the 210 East. He was feeling dizzy and lightheaded. With a little luck, he told himself, next stop New Mexico.

Chapter 41

Church was working on his trunk exercises on a grassy spot behind the cabin he was renting while Billie played catch-the-stick with Lexi. Church was on his back, arching his butt upwards when Ed drove by on his all-terrain vehicle.

"Watch out, you're gonna hurt yourself," Ed said.

"Could happen." Dickens sat up and took a breather. They both watched Billie playing with the dog. "Ed, how soon is Lexi going to have her babies?"

"Her litter," Ed corrected him. "Maybe three weeks. Maybe sooner. Hard to tell."

"I think I saw that breeder's black van in town."

"Yep. I've seen him, too. He better not come around here anymore. I'm getting sick of him. I know he wants to steal Lexi and Bel back. Wants at least to get the puppies. Jessie says she'll shoot him on sight."

"Not really…?"

"Says she will. Don't underestimate my daughter."

"I promise I won't." Dickens studied the older man. "You had leg problems, right?"

"Ain't that a fact. Still do. Doc Heberty said I'd never walk again."

"Well, we have that in common. Docs told me the same thing at the VA."

"Yeah, it's your back, I hear. Me, I got my legs crushed when the roof on my mine came caving in."

"What was that like?"

"Well, I was younger then. There was a warning, a mild shake – an earthquake, you know, maybe 4.5 or a 5 – this growling sort of noise, but not enough time to do anything." He paused, thinking back to those moments, him underground and the earth shaking. "I was so close to the entrance, I could see the sweet fresh air, not that far away. We all call it a mine, but that gold was right there, not very far in and it wasn't a very long tunnel. I had some sort of premonition and when the ceiling came down I was diving for the entrance. Might have made it, too, but a wood support beam came down on my legs, trapped me solid. If my dad hadn't found me, I'd have been a goner, been there forever."

"So the gold was right near the side of the hill? Was it in sedimentary soil?"

Ed hesitated. "I don't know I should be talking about that with you."

"Cause I'm a slickster from Los Angeles?"

"Well, maybe." Ed kicked the throwing stick back over to Billie, who threw it over Lexi's head. "You work for the lodge people."

"Not anymore. It's complicated. I own lots of lodge stock, so, in a way, they work for me. But most of the actual lodge employees don't even know I exist."

"That is complicated."

"Well, I did work for Verhu Financial; that is the company that owned most of Taos Pines Lodge. I did some research, I started to wonder about the

144

guy I worked for, I quit, made some moves, went out on my own."

"None of my affair, Mister Dickens – that's what my granddaughter Billie calls you – but what you still doing around here?"

"Well, that's a good question, Ed. Fool that I was, I invested some of my family money in Taos Pines Lodge. I know, stupid, huh?"

"You probably had your reasons."

"Well, I did get a good deal." Dickens shrugged and grinned. He looked at Ed and then out across the grassy pasture to a rusty barbed wire fence. "You know, Ed, it is clear that the lodge property lies right alongside your property. I'm hoping that we can be good neighbors."

"That's true," Ed said. "And I hope so, too."

"And from what I see, toward the back end of your property that mine entrance of yours is close to the property line."

"Well, yeah, but the tunnel, what there's left of it, doesn't go in your direction."

"I see that, too." Church nodded his agreement. But if we suppose there's still gold there... gold doesn't know about property lines."

"Okay. I'll tell you what I know about it. The gold I found was in a gravel sort of a deposit. I mean, it was up against more solid stuff and that's where it stopped."

"That's maybe why your tunnel caved in. Sediments can be unstable, you go digging into them like you did."

"Yeah, but..."

"Ed, is your mine at the back end of your property?"

145

"No, not really. Back half, I'd say."

"I'll tell you what I think if you keep me in the loop."

"What loop?"

"Your loop, if you find out anybody has been snooping around on your property."

"Why would they do that?"

"How often do you get out back there where it's all slopes, like next to where the lodge put in their new ski runs?"

Ed nodded, thinking it over. "Not often enough, I guess. You think maybe I should take a run or two out there sooner rather than later?"

"Might be worth the effort."

Chapter 42

Lenora-of-the-hot-lips disproved the theory going around the office that she didn't know how to type when her boss had her produce a memo that Harvey Fineman had been let go for "conflicts of interest" (although she did leave out the 'l' in 'conflicts' spelling it 'confix') and Harvey was not to be allowed back in the doors, not even to collect any of his personal things, should they exist. Reading the memo, Celeste couldn't have cared less. Just one less competitor, and not a serious one, at that.

Church Dickens, however, was another matter. Philby hadn't said anything about Dickens. Getting him out of Los Angeles had been her idea, and she'd done her best to present him in the worst light possible to Alan. The way she talked it up to Philby, Dickens was a suspicious character. He wasn't loyal to Verhu. He had a hidden agenda. It was nothing personal or anything you could put your finger on, but that was because it was hidden; she knew she had great instincts, and she'd been studying his moves. Since the TPL stock mess anybody could see he was just an untrustworthy character. What motivated her to this conclusion was complicated, her private business, she told Philby, leaving him to conclude it was a love affair gone sour. She denied this with just enough emphasis so Alan was sure it was true, and she walked out of his office that morning and left him to stew in his own paranoia.

The simple explanation was the same as always. She wasn't a complicated girl, in her view; she just wanted to be a full financial advisor at Verhu, and Churchie-boy was in her way. But she'd researched Dickens and, mostly from the lack of anything interesting or special, she didn't think he was a real catch; on the other hand, maybe – just maybe – ancient and hopefully wealthy Alan Philby might turn out to be worth the effort. But to do that, she'd have to get Alan to dump Lenora. And gag me with a spoon — as she had said in her childhood — then she'd have a wrinkly old limp dick Alan to deal with on a personal level. Yeah, gag! Still, a girl did what she could to get ahead; when she had suggested to Alan that he might want to send Dickens to Taos, the old fart had gone for it bait, hook, and sinker, however that saying went. But things were moving fast; now Dickens had quit or been fired – nobody was quite sure – and maybe it was because of Harvey, or Harvey's leaving was because of Dickens and nobody was saying because nobody knew for sure except maybe bitchy Annie, and no way anybody was going to get anything out of her.

Bright and early the second Sunday morning in a row Celeste showed up at the deserted Verhu offices. She tried the key from Annie's desk and it did open the door to Dickens' office. She entered his cluttered and windowless room, dim lit under Verhu's weekend energy saving program. She carefully edged her way in past a chunk of giant quartz crystals standing waist high and weighing maybe a half a ton. And there was the pointy yellow splinter he'd more than once suggested she sit on.

Why on earth would anybody pay somebody real money no matter how small an amount to lug stupid rocks up to his office? She sat in his chair, an expensive Herman Miller like Annie's, and looked around. It wasn't that she hadn't been there before, but never alone like this without the gimp hanging around.

Aside from his legal and his geology research books, so much of Church Dickens' stuff was just plain junk – the rock samples and a huge drill bit with traces of oily dirt still on it and pictures of him out in wild country in his old motorized wheelchair that he'd given back to the Wounded Warriors Charity, and the older picture of him with his army buddies, an out-of-place shot of him and some black guy pretending to be some sort of high diving swimmers, and an even more ancient photo – there he was, young college student Church Dickens on a geology field trip, smiling and happy in a treeless, rocky desert somewhere.

There was a big cork board on one wall, but not much there she could use; announcements of upcoming rock collector meetings and hikes and menus for local restaurants; and about a third of it was covered with old scratchers he'd probably bought on a whim here and there, no method to his madness and no ticket over five dollars. Stupid waste of money; he had this ridiculous game going with Harvey – another stupid loser. To her way of thinking, male bonding was all fine and good, until it came down to real life, and then it fell apart.

Still, she believed in hunches; Gimpy Dick was hiding something. For one thing, he traded way too confident for a guy with his limited resources. Her gaze drifted over the documents on his wall. Jesus, on top of his law degree, two simultaneous undergrad degrees, a BA in English and a BS in Geology. What a gimpy grinder! There was his whole sad story on the wall. Tragic if it wasn't so stupid; the guy gets educated, goes to the army, gets himself blown up in Afghanistan, comes back a gimp, gets his law degree, learns day-trading, convinces Alan to sign him on as a full-fledged Verhu financial advisor and in no time at all he claims he's got his own portfolio of clients. That just doesn't happen! Something was missing here!

But after a half hour, she still didn't have a clue and was beginning to feel a little desperate. To go through all the trouble to get him out of town and to give up her Sunday morning when she could be sleeping and then come up with nothing … well, that wasn't supposed to happen. Whatever the answer was, it wasn't obvious.

She was no longer sure what in gimp-boy's goddamn crazy world she might be looking for; something, anything she could use, something that might give her a little edge with Church; the guy who was way more lucky than he deserved. Church-boy, Church-boy, what's your secret, Smurch-boy? She tried going through the drawers on his desk, but they were all locked. Damn, damn, damn, damn! That meant there was stuff in there worth getting at. She went back to her purse and found a chunky Swiss army knife. She pulled open the biggest blade, thinking maybe she could force open the drawers. After all, they were just ordinary office drawers. How hard could that be?

Chapter 43

Jessie picked up a plate of ham and eggs from Chooli. Church Dickens was across the room busy at his computer. He'd been talking to Kate, pointing out something to her on his computer screen.

"He is very handsome man, Jessie," Chooli said. "I think you like him."

"Chooli, don't be silly. I'm a widowed woman with a nearly teenage kid."

"Still, I think so. And, I see the way he look at you." Jessie blushed and turned away, nearly bumping into Kate, who was returning her empty plate to the kitchen.

"What were you two talking about, Kate?"

Kate set down her dinnerware and fumbled for the loose pack of Kools in the pocket of her flannel shirt. "Mr. Big Time Gambler over there was teaching me to be a day trader – not!"

"Huh. I'd like to know how to do that."

"Be careful, silly girl. I don't trust him one bit. I know that type a guy, you just know he's a slickster."

"You think everybody is a crook."

"Nobody is innocent of everything, child."

Child. Kate was only five or six years older than Jessie, and yet Kate played it like she was the Vegas Gal, the one with knowledge of the world, while Jessie was a backwoods bumpkin. Kate was in every Carter face about everything; she'd said her piece often enough – her husband was an idiot, her husband's dad had been a fool to get involved with

151

the cabins in the first place, Billie should be sent away to a boarding school in Santa Fe to get some class, dogs belonged in the barn, not in people-places.

Jessie wondered for the ten-thousandth time (and counting) how Ed put up with his Vegas wife. She had once gotten up enough courage to ask her dad about it. All he said was, he deserved what he'd got. He'd made a huge mistake and he knew it, and it looked like he was going to have to pay for it for the rest of his life.

Jessie walked over to Church's table and eyed his laptop. "Vegas Kate tells me you can teach us to trade stocks...Not!, she says."

"You call her 'Vegas Kate'?"

"That's the nicest thing I call her."

"Have a seat." Church shook his head, "Though, you know, she may be right. You might not be a good day trader."

"Why not?"

"Well, look at you – fiery, impulsive."

"Traders could be like that."

"Right. We who are about to die salute you."

"Who said that?"

"Kamikaze pilots before their last dive."

"You're teasing me — so you definitely don't know me. I bet I could do it!"

"Maybe. But, come on, admit it – maybe you are too impulsive."

Before she could think of a reason to say he was wrong – or even say anything – she remembered the "We who are about to die" line was what gladiators said in the movies — and his

152

computer gave a loud beep-beep-beep warning sound, and Church had to get to it.

From her place on the floor next to Church, Lexi tilted her shaggy head and calmly looked up at him. Bel gave an annoyed snort. She stood and paced around the table on her short legs. That beep was an odd noise, but Lexi felt confident her newly adopted human would know how to fix it. She was right; he pushed something on his machine, the beep went silent and he didn't seem alarmed.

"What's that?" Jessie asked. "Did you just lose a fortune?"

"Nope." He typed in a brief sequence: name, password and code word.

"Somebody is fishing around in my old office back in L.A."

"You can know that?"

"Sure. And they don't know we know they're there."

"But it's the weekend."

"Let's see who it is." He clicked a few keys and a dark and fuzzy picture of his cluttered office came into view on his monitor. He clicked more keys and the screen split and now there were three pictures – the original overview, one of the doorway and one of his desk.

"Someone's sitting at a desk," Jessie said.

"That's my desk. And that's Celeste, sitting in my chair. She's a co-worker, my big rival back at the office, at least she thinks she is. She's almost a lawyer, but she's flunked the California bar twice."

"The lighting's bad but she looks pretty," Jessie said.

"I used to think so."

153

"What's she doing in your office?"

"Well, it was locked, but she might have gotten the key from my secretary's desk. She doesn't believe I resigned, and she wants my job. I think she's looking for any dirt on me she can find."

"Is there any?"

"Everybody has secrets."

"Not the answer I was looking for."

"Everybody," he held her gaze until she blushed and looked away.

There was action on another of the three screens on his monitor and somebody came in the doorway. A man's voice said, "Celeste. What on earth are you doing here?"

"Alan. I could ask you the same thing."

"Did you find his Taos folder?"

"No. I was just about to pry open his desk."

Three states away, Jessie squinted at Church's laptop. "Who is that guy?"

"Alan Philby. The top guy where I work."

"People break into your office and your boss is in on it!" Jessie said. "This is better than a movie."

"You wouldn't say that if it was your office. Well, ex-office."

"What are you going to do about it?"

"Watch," Church said. "She's going to do it to herself."

Celeste slid the blade of her Swiss knife in the thin crack between the drawer and the frame of his desk, and the moment the blade touched the metal lock a low but insistent beeper sounded. Celeste jerked back her knife blade but the beep continued. "Oh my God! We gotta get out of here!"

From the dining room at Carter Cabins Church said, "Yeah, baby, you do!"

He hit a key on his laptop and hundreds of miles away in Church's office in Los Angeles a loud, heavy horn bleeped. "I've got thirty seconds to stop it or that one will bring the cops."

Jessie watched him; he was very calm for a man seeing his office being raided. "Are you really going to?"

"No, probably not. More fuss than it's worth. Look at them, they're like cartoon cops."

Both Celeste and Philby had panicked; she ran into him, pushing him into the nearest book-lined wall as they tried to bolt for the door.

"It's funny, Church but … honest, now – why are those people sneaking around in your office?"

"Good question. I don't know for sure," he said. "But my skullduggery gene gets me suspecting it's got something to do with the lodge next door to here. And maybe even with this place."

"With Carter Cabins?"

"You know I was sent here to see if you'll sell out. Before I quit the company."

"Well, that will never happen. Ed doesn't even want to hear a number."

"I believe you. I'm not going to try."

"Does that mean you're leaving soon?"

"I don't know. I've lost much of my affection for Los Angeles. And I'm done at the Vets' hospital. Or, more correctly, they're done with me. I guess you could say I'm at loose ends. Maybe I'll stay here for a while. I do have an interest in the lodge next door." He closed his laptop. "Do I get to walk the dog today?"

"If you're up to it."

"I think she likes me."

"Are you sure you're ready to be hiking …?" her eyes drifted to the crutches leaning against the table.

"I've been practicing with a cane: an old family relic."

"Well, sentiment aside — I think I've got something better for hiking."

She went to a corner behind the door leading to the front lobby and came back carrying a walking stick. It had the shape of a fairly straight branch, was about as tall as he was, and on the top end was the carved face of an ancient bearded wizard.

"It's made from an Osage orange branch. It's not from around here. From back in Indiana. The branches of the Osage Orange are so straight the Indians used to use them for spear shafts."

"Wow! Perfect! What do I owe you?"

"Some guest left it here. Nobody ever uses it. While you're here, if you walk Lexi every once in a while, we'll call it even."

He smiled and held out his hand. "How about I start this afternoon? I've got to go to town, but it should only take a few hours."

"Deal," she said, taking his hand. "If Chooli has Billie back from town by then, we can all go." Jessie's smile broadened. Again there was that something about the handshake that felt right. Firm and trustworthy and good. And again, for a fleeting moment, she didn't want to let go, and it seemed like maybe he didn't, either.

Chapter 44

Johnny Hunsai was snoozing in one of the chairs lined against the wall in the big waiting room outside the Taos County Clerk's office when the Los Angeles guy limped in with his walking stick, looking all smart-ass and big city in his tailored light wool Southern California suit. Johnny's eyes were nearly closed and he may have looked like he was sleeping but what he thought of as his animal senses were on full alert. He made a snuffling sound like a drowsy buffalo and wiped his nose on one sleeve of his plaid red and white checked wool shirt, allergies acting up again. He squinted around, wondering what was up.

Nope, wasn't a pot dream or some sort of imagined movie scene. There he was, right there, the stranger from Los Angeles standing with his slim black brief case in one hand and his blue mirror sunglasses perched neat on his blond head of hair, totally out of place in a room where ranchers paid land fees and argued about fence lines, crop sprays, and where their goats could chew on whoever's grass. Johnny had been waiting for him, warned by the old fart from that Verhu finance company, and there he was, fit the description, well, sort of – this feller was a bit more healthy than Johnny'd been told, though he did have some sort of cane like they said he might — that or crutches — not that he seemed to need it all that much.

The stranger walked up to the counter and, nobody else in line, he quick as be-Jesus ordered a few documents that Kenny Loran printed out for him, and he paid Kenny in cash money, a hundy that Kenny had to dig around for change.

Johnny hoisted himself to his feet, warning himself to take things a little easy. Wouldn't want to startle the rabbit, you know. "Hey there, City Slicker."

The city boy paused and looked him over. He didn't seem to mind being called out for what he was. "Hey there, Country Bumpkin. How's the frost out on the pumpkin?"

"That there's a country western song."

"Yeah, I know. Cal Smith. Early '90's, maybe."

"Kin I help you?"

"I don't know. What you good at?"

Johnny scratched an itchy place between his shoulder length blond-and-grey hair and his left ear and thought about it. Maybe this wasn't going to be as easy as he'd thought. "My name's Johnny Hunsai, Native American, mental advisor, owner of the Spirit Hut, over near the La Fonda Hotel. We offer all things spiritual. And Southwest silver. Rings, bracelets. We got genuine Pueblo, Navajo, Zuni. Everything for the modern aware mentality. Blankets, dream-catchers, sacred stones." He handed over his business card, the words Spirit Hut big and then a sketch of a long- haired glowing shaman who looked something like a glorified himself, and the address underneath.

"What kind of sacred stones?"

"Rose quartz for meditation; blue-grey angel stone, very powerful; tiger's eye to focus your powers…"

"Huh. Maybe I'll drop over. I could use some power focusing."

"We got stones nobody never heard of: Zebra Stone. Dalmatian Stone. Travelers Rock. Jet Stone. Meteor Stone. Cinder Stone."

"This area, mostly sandstone, right?"

"Well, not all – some igneous infusions."

The city boy nodded and smiled at him, a soft friendly look, but maybe something steel behind it. "So you're an educated spiritualist," he said.

Johnny thought the conversation was going very well. "I see you got the Triple A Indian Country map," he said. "That's a good map. And you got a few docs from Kenny over there and I just thought I might – "

"You might help if I just told you what I was looking for."

"Yes, that."

Dickens laid the Triple A map over the others. Johnny moved closer and moved the maps so he could see the ones the fellow had borrowed from the county files. Dickens didn't move to stop him, but the new maps weren't really land plots; they were topo maps that covered the entire county and didn't tell Johnny anything useful. He was going to have to ask. "Well, whatcha looking for?"

"I don't know," the city fellow said.

That was disappointing. "But you'll know when you find it."

"I don't even know if I'll know then."

"This all used to be our land, you know."

"You don't look like a Native American to me. I mean, the blond hair and all, you have me thinking you're maybe the last hippie survived the dope and the sangria and the rock and roll. Or maybe it was your love-bead parents."

"Look it or not, I am the genuine A-1 model American Indian. Taos Pueblo, Tano-Tigua Tribe. And I got the DNA results to prove it."

"Come on, now…you actually did your DNA?"

"Twice. I didn't believe it the first time."

It was all sort-of true, partly. Johnny Hunsai did know a small smidge of Tano-Tigua dialect, enough not to embarrass himself, and there was a trace of Indian in his DNA (not that that was anything special in these parts).

Johnny pushed the AAA map aside and pointed to one with the Taos ski trails on it. "Our hunting grounds." He indicated a spot on the map where two ski trails merged. "Now that, right there: My great great granddaddy killed a big ugly mean bear right there, shot him dead with an arrow through his eye. What they call it now, Death Drop Ski Run? It's disrespectful. They should call that Bear Kill Hill."

Church took a closer look. "Death Drop. I don't know: Seems to me, that's about right. Least ways, that says it for the bear."

Johnny pointed to his card from the Spirit Hut. "Serious now. I'm offerin' my services. You need any help, call on me."

"Ever get any really good tiger's eye?"

"Huh? Tiger's eye … yeah, some. You interested?"

"Gold or blue?"

"Mostly gold, some blue."

"Hard to find good blue. You run across any, let me know. Church Dickens. Staying at the cabins."

160

"Carter Cabins? That's on our land, too."

"I believe it. It's all your land."

Chapter 45

Alan Philby escorted the freelance security guy he'd hired to Dickens' office, the idea being to debug the place. Annie looked up, startled, automatically on her guard as her old boss walked up to her desk. Alan had always been unpredictable and secretive; but lately he was more and more a loose cannon, and with Dickens gone or fired, she was pretty sure she didn't have much of a future with Verhu.

"Mr. Dickens has been gone a while," she said. "Am I being reassigned?"

"Maybe. We'll see. Haven't made up my mind yet. This here is a security check." Philby blinked, looking around her desk with the corners of his mouth set in their normal downward curve. "This here is Denny Rockson from Ace Security. We have to de-bug Dickens' office."

"His office has bugs?"

"Electronic bugs. Spy cameras."

"What? Does Mr. Dickens know?"

Alan's frown deepened, showing displeasure bordering on anger, "I am the boss of Church Dickens."

"But he's no longer with the firm."

"Rumors are what get people killed, Annie. You been warned of this a time or two." His mood thickened. Annie knew that look.

While they were talking, Celeste showed up carrying a heavy cardboard box full of her office things.

"Can somebody tell me what is happening here?" Annie said.

Celeste tossed her short black wave of hair from her eyes, grinning down at Annie. "Didn't Alan tell you? I'm taking over Church's responsibilities while he's in New Mexico.

"You can't just take over his clients."

"Yes I can. Alan says so. And your clever Mr. Dickens isn't here anymore. I'm going to need a list of names and phone numbers and complete access to their files."

Annie glanced up at Alan, hoping for direction. "Alan, tell her."

Alan looked like he was losing it. Drool appeared at one corner of his mouth. "Some things we'll have to sort out. Look Annie, one thing's sure: Church Dickens is not coming back. I don't think not ever. We have to do what's best for Verhu."

"Okay. But what about my job?" Annie said.

Philby shook his head. "Long term, we'll figure it out. Right now we have to do what makes sense. Dickens is gone; Celeste says her office is too small and cramped and she's probably right. She works here now. You can help her get going."

"What about Church's stuff?"

"Junk," Alan said. "Throw it out."

"Annie, I do want everything I just asked you for," Celeste said. "Client files. Now, with no delays."

"You'll have to ask Mr. Dickens."

Celeste's sleek frame stiffened; to Annie she was like a cheap racing car, high strung, about ready to blow a gasket at any hitch in the speedway.

163

"Annie, I'm telling you to get Church's private files for me. Right now."

Annie smiled like the top rate senior secretary she was. "I'm sorry, Ms. Russo, but those records are in The Cloud, and only Church knows how to fly up there to get them."

"No. That can't be. All I'm asking you for is a list of his clients – "

"I don't have the passwords. I don't even know their names."

Ace Security's man Denny interrupted, pointing to wires dangling from the three video cameras. "You see I got them totally disconnected. I can take them down, cost you an extra hundred and eighty bucks."

"Your call, Alan," Celeste said.

"Who do they belong to? If they were ours, I'd know."

"They're Mr. Dickens'," Annie said.

"Denny, if you want to unscrew 'em and take 'em down for free, you can have them."

"You got a deal, pal," Denny said. "And I debugged the desk. Had to break the locks, though. It was the only way."

"Oh, that's all right," Celeste said. She looked pointedly at Annie. "You people can clear out of my new office now, give me a little space to do some thinking."

Annie gave her a look of poison but didn't say anything more. Celeste closed the door in her face and sat in Church's fancy Herman Miller chair, tapping an impatient little finger roll on the bare desktop. She couldn't wait to get in those drawers and find out who Mister Church Dickens really was.

Denny stopped by Alan's office to pick up his check

"So it was just the three cameras?" Alan blinked twice and squinted in Denny's direction, eyeing him, suspicion clear in his expression. Denny wondered what the hell there was to be suspicious about. He sure was going to be glad to pick up his money and be out of there.

"Yep. And the desk alarms, five in all, one per drawer. Completely routine, Mister Philby. Amateur hour, really. You could get that stuff at Best Buy. Probably installed it his self."

"And there's no chance there's anything more?"

"Not a chance in the world."

Of course Philby wasn't buying that. He knew there was a chance. There always was a chance, always something new, something hidden, something inert and undiscoverable until it was activated. But Denny was doing this job free-lance, and he knew his business; pick up the check, write out the receipt and get out of there. He didn't suggest that Church Dickens may have bugged his own office. Or may have bugged other offices at the firm. After all, old Philby had grumbled and complained until he had worn down Denny's fee to almost not worth the effort. Denny was just the hired help. No way he had to be the grouchy old cheapster's keeper.

Chapter 46

Dickens was back from his morning at the County Clerk's office. He finished off a Diet Coke while listening to Kate's non-stop kidding over his loss of $300 on a tech stock that had decided to go south at the last minute. He finally held up a hand. "Kate. Stop. Look, you know I work for Verhu Financial – at least I used to. You saw it on my credit card when I signed in for the cabin."

The wind went out of her like a punctured balloon. "Well, I…"

"And you hang around because you want to know what I'm doing here in Taos."

"No, I don't care what you –"

"Kate. Stop. You're embarrassing yourself. Look, it's no secret. I am a day trader. I'm also a lawyer, specializing in land rights. And every adult in your family and the neighborhood, probably, has figured out I worked for Verhu Financial, and before I quit they sent me here to find out if the Carters have any interest at all in selling their land."

"Well, nobody told me. I don't know what you're talking about. My husband Ed handles all our financial affairs."

"And you don't know anybody at the Los Angeles firm known as Verhu Financial?"

"Never heard of them."

"Alan Philby?"

Her lips pushed together in a thin line. "Nope."

"Then how did your signature get next to his on a zoning request over at the county clerk's office?"

"Mister, I want you out of here in an hour! Pack your bags and get out!"

It was bad timing entirely and particularly her bad luck that Jessie walked in at that moment. "Kate, what's all the fuss about?"

Kate, flustered, said the first thing that came to mind, "This pervert just made me an indecent proposal! He can't stay here with us!"

"What sort of proposal?"

"I was just telling Kate here that I work for Verhu Financial."

"Everybody knows that. You wrote it in the ledger when you signed in."

"And that I'm supposed to ask if there's any way you Carters would entertain a serious offer on your property."

"Everybody's already figured that one out, too. And we all told you no way. What's wrong with you, Kate?"

"This man's a crooked shyster, Jessie! I want him out of that cabin right now!"

And, like a scene from a movie, Ed poked his head in the front door, "Hey what's going on? Even the neighbors can hear you."

Kate screamed in frustration. "Nothing! Nothing's going on! Nothing at all!" She slammed the palm of her open hand on the nearest table, sending catsup and salt and pepper shakers flying, and left the room. Things were out of control. She was going to have to do something, and fast!

But in the ordinary world, the one outside of Kate's newfound panic, Jessie grinned at Dickens as he closed his laptop and slid it into his slim blue day-hike backpack.

"Okay now — time for that hike, Big Time," Jessie said.

"Big Time. You've been talking to Kate."

"Day Trader has a nice ring to it … like mafia boss or double-oh-seven. I think I like it."

"You like anything that riles Las Vegas Kate."

She gave him a conspiratorial grin. "True enough. Beyond that, you camping out here is like having a professional gambler hanging around. I don't know what you said to set off Kate, but you should wear a black suit and carry a hide-out derringer pistol."

"Maybe day trading is a little bit like gambling, only the odds aren't always against you."

"And they are in the casinos?"

"Why you think there are so many of them?"

"Point well taken. Come on, Dickens, we're gonna hike the hills. Don't forget your walking stick."

"Where's Billie?"

"After school activity. Girls' basketball season starting soon. Chooli's going to stay and pick her up."

Kate called from the kitchen door, "I'm warning you, Jessie. Don't be a fool. You shouldn't go hiking with him."

"Kate, even at your age, it's never too late to learn to mind your own business. Come on, Lexi." The big dog got to her feet and stretched, looking at Church. He gave her a friendly pat on the head and nodded. "Yeah, girl. We're going."

And the three of them went out the door, leaving Kate standing there with a tight look on her thin face, angry and worried. She lit up a smoke, took a deep drag that ended in a coughing fit. When she got herself calmed down she took out her phone and, after making sure she was alone, hit speed dial. "Johnny, I got bad news here, that goddamn bastard knows!"

"Whoa there Nellie, what you talking about?"

"Damn it, Johnnie, this ain't Nellie, it's Kate, and that damn snoop from California knows I signed papers with Alan Philby on our property."

"Hmmm .... Has he talked to anybody yet?"

"I don't think so."

"Where's Ed now?"

"He took an ATV, went trailing."

"Exactly where?"

"Hiking trail near Death Drop. He says lodge people been dumping garbage on our property."

There was a pause and then Johnny's drawl came back on the line. "Well, that's not good. Just calm down a mite, Katie, let me see maybe we can do something."

"Like what? Like exactly what can get me out of this mess?" But the connection was broken, and she was yelling at nothing and nobody.

Chapter 47

Celeste came storming back from lunch, passed Annie's desk without saying a word, went into Dickens' office and slammed the door. There was only one or two explanations that fit: Either Harvey and Annie were dumb as bricks about gimp-boy's affairs or it was on purpose that they hadn't revealed anything she could use. Harvey hadn't even come in to work, and now Alan was saying he was fired. She'd taken over Dickens' office, bulldozing Alan on the idea she needed the space as her headquarters for the Taos Pines Lodge project. TPLP, she was calling it now. Old Alan had blinked at her a couple of times and, after a long and awkward pause, given his okay, but what the hell did that actually get her? This was her golden opportunity to push out Dickens – but crap, with both him and Harvey already gone and crazy old Blinky-boy tight-lipped as a clam – and giving her suspicious looks, to boot – she didn't know what to do next. Maybe it was time to start peddling her own resume around town.

She settled back in gimp-boy's cool steel mesh chair, convinced by now that if her office switch was only temporary, she would roll his chair on down to her old space. If the gimp ever got back from New Mexico and got his office back nobody would remember who sat in what chair and just let bad-back boy try to move it around all by himself.

It was really unfortunate for her plans that he'd taken his laptop, and worse that he didn't have any backups lying around. The one she'd borrowed from him (and later sold on E-bay) had nothing on it. In Celeste's mind that was clear proof he'd been hiding something. And devious Annie took her laptop with her wherever she went; the lying bitch swore she had none of Dickens' files, and maybe that was true and maybe it wasn't. As for Harvey, as best she could figure out, Harvey had been using an old desktop Dell as well as his own laptop, but one quick look convinced Celeste he didn't have anything on it remotely connected with TPLP except that one assignment he'd done for Dickens, and that was just to review stuff everybody knew and to give his opinion. His opinion! Here was a kid just got his MA a year ago and gimp boy was asking his opinion!

Celeste gazed around the room. She was more than a little tempted to take a handful of the gimp-boy's stupid rocks and chuck them at his stupid pictures on the wall. She stared at a color snapshot of him with his buddies in some steep-mountain place, probably Afghanistan. He looked so carefree and happy and – innocent, the bright and eager young warrior gone off to adventuring in his war. A glimpse of the guy he used to be before he caught his lunch on a bomb or whatever; looking at it, she got a little aroused, imagining the two of them in some sort of Turkish Kasbah together, the smell of incense and sight of a crescent moon though veiled curtains. Church, Church, Church-ie, too damn bad you blew yourself up before we even met. We could have been a serious number for the long haul … or at least a couple serious rolls in the hay.

Her gaze drifted to the pinned up scatter of lotto scratchers on his cork board, and something about the cheap little cards brought all her frustration to a boiling point. She found herself yelling out loud. "Loser! Gimp-boy, you fricking big-time loser!"

Anger getting the best of her, she reached for the nearest rock on his desk, a glittery chunk of something heavy and threw it at the board – unthinking, full of rage, threw it as hard as she could. The fist sized specimen hit the wall and broke into a bunch of pieces that fell to the floor, leaving a gouge mark where it had slammed into the pin up board. Oh crap! That was all she needed, gimp boy coming back and pouting about a busted rock and a dent in his precious cork board! She pushed herself up from the comfort of the Herman Miller chair to see if she might re-pin a scratcher or two to cover the dent or at least make it less obvious. She was up close and that was when she saw the one card was different from the others. It wasn't an original. It was a color Xerox on heavy paper, the same size as the rest of the colored flock of scratchers, but different all the same. She went numb, her brain full of white noise. She unpinned the card and wandered back to his chair and plopped down for a while until she was certain what she was looking at. And then another surge of angry emotion overcame her.

"You bastard," she said to his presence in the empty room. "You dirty rotten son of a bitch! You win two million dollars and you don't tell the girl you love?!"

She was out of control. She pulled open the drawers on his desk and grabbed staplers and compact clocks and other junk and started throwing them around the room. And that was when her frantic gaze settled on the small dark maroon velvet box in one corner of his center desk drawer. She opened it and there it was, the ornate silvery ring with the giant glittery diamond, she figured probably worth a hundred grand, at least. She could hardly contain her mixture of joy, frustration and rage.

The dear stupid moron sweetie-pie gimp hits the big jackpot and then he was going to propose to her… and she dumps him before he gets the chance! Talk about rotten timing. Now just how bad did her life suck!

Chapter 48

It was one of those days in the Northern New Mexico highlands when the puffy clouds seemed low enough you could reach out and grab a couple and stuff them in your pockets. Dickens had on a light shell hiking jacket, his small backpack and a woollen cap Jessie loaned him, a purple and gold number with a picture of a flaming basketball and a big knit golden colored ball on the top. The sun was out but the temperature was around 50 and the wind was brisk. He was thinking What a great day for a hike in the mountains with a pretty girl! "Thanks for the funny cap. My self-image has taken a nose-dive but my ears are grateful."

Jessie reached inside her jacket and pulled on her own cap, a red-and-white striped woolly cap with a picture of a mean bird on the front and its own billiard-ball-sized knit red ball on top.

"You should see yourself," Church said.

"Oh, yeah? You should see yourself, Mister Big Time L.A."

She gave him a playful light shove in the right direction and they started along the trail behind his cabin that ran upstream with Lexi staying close, sniffing out things of dog interest, first five yards ahead and then five behind, but always close to Church and Jessie. At the last minute Bel had decided to stay behind, her time for giving birth to her new litter getting very close.

"Did you know that Lexi started her training as a service dog?" Jessie said.

"I did not know that; though I suspected something of the sort."

"Mrs. Anderson's husband – Colonel Anderson – had her in training before he died."

"Hounds — Bassets especially, with due respect to Bel — have a great sense of smell. The Brit soldiers have lots of them. Us Yankees prefer German shepherds. And sometimes we like labs."

The trail was an easy one, a sand-and gravel path that followed the winding stream along one side of the Carter property. They had gone a mile when Dickens stumbled. Jessie caught his arm, and Lexi was right there, on his other side.

He was embarrassed, his face red. "Sorry. I'm not that out of shape. It's just that my legs – "

"I know. You'll be all right, Church. Let's just catch our breath here for a minute."

He looked off into the distance, trying to think of something to say, anything to change the subject. "Pretty scene around here. Your dad own all of this?"

"All of it, to way up there, and maybe a mile or so past what you see." She pointed to the distant brown hills.

"I can see what looks like a bit of a dig out there. Ed's old mine, maybe."

"You've got good eyesight."

"Just ordinary, but I did have a course in geomorphology, long time ago. There's a talus pile that's down slope from what looks like a dig in the side of the hill. It stands out like an old scar on the skin of Mother Earth, as the Indians like to say."

"Yep. That's the remainders of our old gold mine. Kate calls it Ed's Folly."

"That woman's got a wicked tongue."

"There was some gold, one time. Quite a bit, actually. Paid for the timber to build the cabins. But not anymore."

"Too bad. Price of gold's way up."

He was going to say more, but Lexi gave a big yip and charged back along the path the way they'd come.

"Lexi! Heel!" Dickens' sharp command was so sudden and unexpected it startled Jessie, coming from such a quiet-mannered man. Lexi wasn't expecting it either, and it stopped her in her tracks.

"Heel!" Church said again. This time he used an arm gesture and it was effective; Lexi trotted back to their side, looking up at him with an expectant look on her face.

"Down!" he said, and Lexi settled down beside them. Dickens gave her an approving pat on the head and scratched behind her ears. "She really has been well trained."

"I think she saw a skunk," Jessie said. "That could have been bad."

"Yeah. Once a dog gets sprayed you have to wash 'em down with lemon juice, get rid of the smell."

"I heard tomato juice."

"Either way, it's awful," Church said

"Wow. You're a dog person. Who would have thought a day trading city slickster from the big city —"

"I thought you knew I had a dog. In the army."

"No, I didn't…What happened to her?"

"Him. Tucker, a German Shepherd. He saved my life. But …well, it cost him his …."

176

He frowned, troubled by the memory. He wanted to stop talking but he found he couldn't stop and the story came spilling out. "Tucker was trained to find explosives. Charges, shells, improv bombs, anything. Then came that one day he didn't listen to me. Or more likely he heard me and he just overruled my command to save me."

"They're trained to do that?"

"No. What Tucker did for me was something above and beyond the call of duty ... You have to call it unconditional love. That's what I believe."

"I believe in that. Unconditional love. True love, love beyond anything."

"Yes. It is. Tucker overruled my absolute command, and he did it to save my life. We were out in the field, no formation, just single file, a bunch of tired army guys straggling along the side of a gravel road maybe twenty-five kilometers northwest of Kabul. Starts to get hilly, the road narrows. Tucker runs right in front of me, actually jumps on me, knocks me back ... spun me around, knocked me down ...."

Jessie wondered if she'd already heard too much, already too deep into his private life, but she had to ask. "And ...?"

"And he took the full force of the blast."

"And ...?"

"My buddy Tucker died in that horrible flash, gone just like that."

"You don't have to tell me any more if you don't want to."

"I haven't talked about this with anybody. I guess it's healthy to talk about it. At least that's what my doctors say."

"But you don't have to."

"Seems right, somehow. It's all from another life, in a way. I caught some shrapnel, metal bits in my lower back, got lucky, shipped out within a few hours; lucky twice, some genius surgeons in Germany on their way east, decided to stop off for Weiner schnitzel and beer. They heard about my condition and agreed to a stopover, agreed to put me back together and catch the next plane. After that, a couple years rehab got me back on my feet … and they say I'm maybe gonna be 100% someday, or close to it … and I owe it to Tucker. My life. Everything. "

"And to yourself for working hard, for the rehab part. And to the people who love you."

"There's only just me and my twin brother Ruger. My parents were older, Mom couldn't believe it, pregnant at nearly fifty, and twins, to boot. They loved us, though. The most precious flowers bloom in Autumn, my mom used to say. Late Autumn, she'd add with a secret little smile."

"She sounds like a special mom."

"She certainly did love Ruger and me. She said we were her treasures, the only riches she really cared about."

"Maybe we should head back."

"Yeah. Far enough for today."

She smiled up at him, took his arm as they walked back to the cabins. They both were feeling right about each other.

Chapter 49

When Chooli came back from Morely's, the Range Rover loaded down with groceries, she found the side road back to the kitchen area in the main house was blocked with a square-ish, odd-looking little car, green colored like an avocado. There was a driver hunched over the steering wheel, but when she sounded a little honk nothing happened. She got out of the Rover and marched over to see what was going on, and she was surprised with what she saw. Sleeping in the middle of the day! A man was sleeping, hunched over the wheel! How irritating was that!

In spite of the cold weather – past noon now and still barely fifty five degrees – the window was rolled down. She reached in the open window and gave him a little nudge, thinking to get him awake so he could move out of the way.

"Hey! You can't just park here!," she said.

And then, too late, she saw the dried blood on his shirt. His eyes opened, and he groaned. He focused on her and the look of pain was replaced with something else, something she would come to recognize as wonder.

"Hey you ..." His voice reached her, barely more than a whisper. In spite of the blood, she was struck by the look of him. She thought his face was perfect, dark complexion, a hawk nose, dark curly hair with a reddish tint. A Navajo warrior sent from heaven? No, it couldn't be.

"What you say to me?" she asked. Not believing what she'd heard.

"Hyy youuu…" he repeated.

Chooli would never forget that moment. What she heard was Ayoo. The Navajo word for beloved.

Overcome with a sense of her own wonder, a sense of some unknown magic in the air, she looked down at him and whispered "Ayoo, back at you, Ayoo."

Papers on the seat next to him had Church Dickens' name on them. This had to be Dickens' friend, and Church was nice to her, treating her with respect and friendship. His friend was her friend. It was the Navajo way.

Chooli's personal journey had taken her far from the under-age girl who was kidnapped off the reservation and driven to Las Vegas in the trunk of a rumbly old automobile with a missing muffler. In the here and now she was a grown person; her mind was already made up; the Great Spirit ordered all things, and Coyote played tricks for new things to happen. She had an instant strong feeling, the idea that this man was, in some strange way, part of her fate.

"Ayoo. Come now. You are safe with me." She shook the wounded stranger semi-awake, helped him out of his car and half-carried him to Dickens's cabin, putting him in the guest bedroom. Then she slid behind the wheel of the stranger's strange-looking car and drove it into one of the larger stalls at the back of the barn, and threw some horse blankets over it. Not a problem. She had seen wounded people before, and she knew what to do next.

Before Vegas, when she was not even a teen, Chooli's brother had been shot by a white man in a bar in Gallup. Even though Bertran had been the one who was shot, a Gallup sheriff and a tribal policeman had come for him as if somehow he was the bad guy. But by the time the officials got to their Hogan, her brother was no longer there; he was safely up north in Utah on the remote back end of the reservation. A medicine lady named Sally Freedom took care of him with prayers and plant medicines, and he herded sheep for the season; and by the time Bertran came back south, everything had died down, and the white men were no longer looking for him.

"Ayoo...ayoo...ayoo... rest and I will be back for you." Chooli didn't want to go; still, she had to leave him for a while, she had to get back to work. Temperamental Kate would be having one of her hissy fits. The Navajo girl looked down at her sleeping wounded warrior – wounded just as his friend Dickens had been. She found herself wondering if Ayoo's little green car could make it on the unpaved back paths, thinking how best to get him to the safety of the far reaches of the reservation. And if so, could she convince the tribal elders to protect him? She smiled grimly and went about her daily chores. Only one way to find out.

Chapter 50

Jessie and Dickens were retracing their steps back to the cabins, having gone less than a hundred yards when Ed pulled up on his custom-painted dragon flamed ATV.

"Where you been, Daddy?" Jessie said.

"Back side. Near the property line. Them damn lodge people been dumping garbage on our side again!"

"They will do that." She gave her father a closer look. "What else? You look a little excited."

"Well, I am! Coming back, a boulder bounced across the trail in front of me, nearly squashed me and the bike!"

"That doesn't happen but every once in a while …. In fact it never happens, not since I can remember. You think somebody set one loose?"

"I know they did! I seen 'em do it! Two teenage kids out looking for mischief!"

"They could have killed you, Daddy!"

Well, they won't be trying that again. I shot a few wild rounds in their general direction with pa's old blaster!" Ed grinned and pulled out his army-issue officer's .45 automatic. "I missed by a mile, but them teen age punks took off fast!"

"Probably a good thing they did, Ed," Church said.

"They wasn't in no trouble. You're an army vet, so you know there's no way anybody can hit anybody with a short gun at a hundred fifty yards, Church. But city folks don't know that."

Dickens didn't replay to that but he did a stretch and something made the familiar popping sound in his backside. "I guess I better head home." He paused, looking at Ed. "Hey, want to see something?"

"Sure. What you got?"

Dickens opened his backpack and took out his laptop. "A map you might like to see."

"Hell, I lived here all my life, Church. I think I know where I am."

"Maybe you haven't seen a map like this."

That had Ed curious enough to climb off his ATV. Church set the laptop on the big ATV double seat. He put the screen on ultra-bright to compensate for the sunlight and a colorful map lit the frame.

"Looks like Halloween candy," Jessie said.

Dickens carefully positioned the screen so it was in shadow. "It's a geologic map of pretty much right here. And this is a topographic overlay." He clicked more buttons and new data, mostly elevation lines and site markings overlaid the geologic map without obscuring it. He drew with his finger. "See, there's your property lines. Right there's your old mine shaft opening."

"I kind of get that …. But what's that tell us?"

"Well, Ed, it tells me you and your dad were mining a pretty big old pot of placer gold."

"A pot of placer gold. What's that mean?"

Church traced his finger along a dotted line in the direction the old tunnel had taken. "Here's your old dig. See, you were still in sediments. Makes sense; you're close to the streambed, the one where you were panning and finding color.

"But – there's nothing like an actual vein of gold? I'm telling you, I was there, I saw it."

"Right. If it was a goodly bit of gold – and I'm assuming it had to be considerable for your dad to be able to fund your cabins – and if it was laid down in a kind-of thin layer like sometimes happens, it could look a lot like a glittery vein. But that's actually good news. That means, when the earthquake came, it didn't cut you off from your main source. The vein was never there."

"Well then … where is it?"

"Well, we don't know that." Church drew another line with his finger, tracking upstream from the mine. "Probably somewhere up there. Maybe even under the really steep peaks way out there. Or maybe even right over there." He pointed toward Death Drop.

Following the stream toward the bigger hills, the geologic map changed colors, from tans and browns to cherry red and lilac purple. Ed was frowning. "And that could be somebody else's property. Or yours. Or government's."

"Huh. That part on your map looks like raspberry licorice," Jessie said. "Tasty."

"Could be really juicy. Or not." Dickens pointed to a corner on his computer screen. "That formation is an igneous intrusion, a place where a last gasp of old magma might be chock-full with exciting stuff."

"Magma …" Ed said, turning the word over on his tongue. "What exactly would that look like?"

"Imagine a curving layer of cloudy white quartz, here and there threaded with actual veins of gold or silver."

184

"Why don't we go looking for that?" Jessie said, looking over to Church

"It isn't that simple. You know firsthand that people have been scurrying around in these hills for decades. If it was easy like that, they would have found it already." Dickens eyed Ed, who had gone quiet. Ed was squinting as he ran his own finger along his property line next to the Taos Pines Lodge land. Easy to see that at the near end the red-and-purple area on Carter property crossed the line and dipped into Lodge property just about where they had opened their new Death Drop ski run.

"Oh well ..." Ed said. "I guess somebody else is gonna get rich." He shook his head and smiled, a sad look of regret on his face. Then he mounted his ATV and took off, the wheels kicking up dust and gravel in his wake. Dickens and Jessie watched until he disappeared around the nearest bend and then they made their way back to the main house with plenty to think about, with Lexi walking along calm between them.

"He took that easier than I thought he would," Dickens said.

"Yeah. Too easy. He's the Never-Give-Up Man." Jessie patted Dickens on the shoulder, "Tomorrow we go maybe a hundred yards further."

"Deal," he said. "I can do that."

Jessie walked away to her room with an unfamiliar lightness in her step. In spite of Dickens' dubious Los Angeles connections and his assignment to buy Carter Cabins, she was feeling good about him; there was a growing trust, something she hadn't felt for anybody outside her

185

family in a long time. Dickens said he could do a hundred yards more – she had the feeling he could.

She reminded herself she was going to have to watch herself around this one. She'd once fallen hard for a guy, loved him, married him, had his daughter – and then he'd gone off and died in a fiery crash half way around the world. Never again, she told herself. Never, ever, ever again.

But still, she couldn't help wondering what it might be like.

Chapter 51

Taos Sheriff Joey Johnson, acting on an anonymous but interesting tip from Los Angeles, drove up to Carter Cabins where Kate Carter, sensing trouble for Church Dickens, was happy to point out the cabin her daughter-in-law had leased Church for the month. She even gave the sheriff a key and he had walked on over there and was about to enter when Dickens himself showed up, wondering what was going on.

This Church Dickens fellow was so mild-mannered and polite with his handshake and all — and him walking with a cane — that Sheriff Joey was sure he wasn't going to be any trouble. "I'm looking for a desperado from Los Angeles," he said.

"Well, I'm one such," Church said, grinning at him and looking not at all impressed.

"You Harvey Fineman?"

"Nope. I am not. What is that notorious felon wanted for?"

"Attempted robbery and assault."

"Huh. And you think he's hanging out with me?"

"I hear he works for you."

"No, he works for Verhu Financial. At least he used to. He has done some assignments for me, but I'm not a senior partner at Verhu or even an executive. I don't get a full time assistant. Didn't, that is. I don't work there anymore, either."

"Okay, but maybe I can just come in and look around a bit?"

187

"Nope. You cannot."

"Nobody here to stop me."

"You got a search warrant?"

So this wasn't going to be so easy after all. Sheriff Johnson's face flushed and his blue eyes took on a frosty glitter. "Mister, don't play that game with me."

Dickens took a wallet out of his pocket, showed his ID, a lawyer, right there on the paper. Flashed it, stuck it away again and stood there, somehow on the ready. And Dickens steady gaze was full in his face, no longer as harmless and gentle as the officer of the law had thought. "No game, sheriff. Come back with a warrant."

Sheriff Joey was a big guy. He had been a bar-rouser hired on as a bouncer and before that a high school brawler; in spite of himself and the reservations dictated by his law enforcement position, he was tempted more than a little to rear back and let go at this cripple with a roundhouse punch. Thing that stopped him much as anything else, the certainty that blow would never land. This lawyer fellow was casual, relaxed, but his right arm was in just the right place – the wrong place, actually – to block a big left-handed incoming.

"You got no idea," Sheriff Joey said, his voice thick-loaded with promise.

"Come back with a warrant," Dickens repeated.

The sheriff turned to walk back to his squad car. "You ain't heard the last of me."

"Thanks for the warning," Dickens said; I take it, You'll be back; well drop that key off at the front desk or they'll have to charge you for it."

Johnson threw the key on the ground and walked away, steam in his step, vengeance on his mind.

Dickens watched the sheriff get in his black-and-white and drive away. He picked up the key — careful of his balance — and opened the door to his cabin, found Harvey had been there and gone. In his place, a bloody sheet and a rambling note scrawled in His handwriting:

Dicks – Philby shot me! In the shoulder. I'm fixed, okay I think, got plenty antibiotics. Celeste called my cell phone, looking for you, says Alan is gone crazy, coming after us. Everything is upside down. There's this amazing Indian girl saved me. She thinks I'm her warrior prince or something. She's pretty. We're going to a safe place. I'm leaving my cell phone. Watch your back, Hot Shooter! - Harv

Dickens checked his own phone and found Celeste had tried to call him eight times. He sat on a corner of the bed. He clicked on the first message and there was the smooth voice of the old Celeste he'd known before she went cold on him:

Church, I know we've had our differences of late, but it's all my fault, I've been under horrible pressure at the office, and with my dad dying, ahh ... you know, of stomach cancer ... or maybe I didn't tell you. Anyway, not important right now. Point is, I really haven't been myself. Sorry about that. But I want you to know I am your true friend, and so much more. Here's the thing, I think you are in trouble: Alan fired Harvey and Alan says crazy Harvey went after him and attacked him and Alan was forced to shoot him to defend himself. Alan thinks Harvey is heading your way and he's alerted the authorities. Alan also says you have screwed up the Carter Cabins buy. He took his airplane somewhere, left from Santa Monica Airport, they wouldn't say where he was headed. I think he is going to Taos, not sure about that. Love you, Dickey-boy, your Celeste.

Dickens went through the other seven messages. They were all more or less the same, though with increasing panic in her voice. He went to the refrigerator and got a diet Coke and sat at the small kitchenette table to think it through:

He decided Celeste was living in one of her alternate universes where her ambition was colliding with reality and reality was losing; also easy to see something major must have happened to switch her back from his rival to his friend and almost-lover. It couldn't be Philby, himself; even Celeste had to know he was borderline demented. And she wouldn't care if Philby threw Harvey out a window or boiled him in oil: there goes another potential rival. Something else had flipped her. Dickens thought he knew what it was. There could only be one other thing: Celeste had been in his office. She must have seen the scratchers puzzle he'd tacked to his corkboard for Harvey, must have figured out the made-up trick that Harvey never had, must now be off on the new toot that her discarded boyfriend was more than the sad, loser gimp-boy she'd made him out to be. That had to be it. Now she was thinking he had won the big scratch and was a bachelor multi-millionaire. Celeste would do anything for that kind of money. But instead of scooping him in, she had turned him loose, booted him out of her life, called him a bunch of mean names. Bad luck on her part, but good luck for him. He shook his head, feeling a little something for her, not anything like love but a little sympathy, knowing right now she must be grinding her teeth, pouting her full lips and kicking herself in her own sweet, greedy butt. It had to be hard, being Celeste.

And at the same time he was feeling a huge wave of relief that she had herself moved those few steps away from his personal life. He was thinking getting tied down to her would have made the rest of his days a slow and agonizing train wreck and he was glad she'd helped him figure it out before they were stuck on that track together. As for her father dying of cancer, she'd once told him she never knew her father. Even her mother was never sure who her father was, Celeste had said. Church could still respect Celeste's plucky single mom, but not Celeste.

Chapter 52

Jay Bornton squatted on a grey granite outcropping on a hillside above the Taos Pines Lodge. He rested his back against the rough trunk of a big pine tree; from this spot he could see most of the Carter Cabins main house and the first two of the individual log cabins, one that now housed that pesky lawyer and a prize Irish Wolfhound soon to give birth to a litter of very expensive puppies. The Basset hound's location he wasn't sure of. She was somewhere in the complex, maybe still in the barn. Jay had parked his black van across the street and a few houses downhill from the lodge, and hiked back up to the ski lift where the operator eyed him skeptically, "Hey, dude, you ain't got any skis."

Jay wasn't feeling all that great, but he forced a grin, "And you ain't got any real snow."

"Man-made's good enough to run part way."

"Yeah, like you're real busy, sold that lame story to lots of folks today." Jay threw a thumb in the direction of the empty lifts, then showed the binoculars strapped around his neck. "I hear there's a bald eagle nest up there. Five bucks to you, let me ride up so I can take a look-see." Of course the fool went for his story. Easy peasy. Nothing quite like human greed. When Jay got to the top the only snow was the man-made and there was just a short hike to the pines. He found a place where he could settle in and see what he could see.

God dang it, if there was just some way he could get his hands on those pups! He didn't really

192

have a plan. At least, that's what he told himself. But things were slow back at his place and that had started a red-hot anger gnawing at him again. He felt cheated out of what was rightfully his; first pick of the litter had always been in his contracts, his regular clients took it for granted. Feeling sorry for a sick old lady, this one time he forgets the paperwork, and that's what it gets him. Life really was not fair.

He wasn't settled in but a few minutes when he saw way down below that buttinski lawyer come limping back down the trail with sweet-ass Jessie. They didn't kiss or hold hands or nothing, so there didn't seem to be any of that going on. Jesus, if he'd brought a hunting rifle, he could take out both of them! In the next moment, he had a sobering moment, wondering where that idea came from. Hell, he wasn't a killer; he was the best damn dog breeder in New Mexico, and maybe Arizona and West Texas, for that matter. Still, he held on the image of the lawyer guy chugging along with his walking stick, tracking steady in the binocs. In his mind's eye Jay could see the guy's arms and legs fling out in a sudden scarecrow move. He flies back, lands heavy, blood everywhere. Wow, that would be great!

Chapter 53

Alan Philby, in his weaker moments, admitted to himself he was older now, maybe even a little deteriorated and some slight degree maybe a little more careless. He'd certainly blown the Harvey Fineman set-up – in the old days that would have been a turkey-shoot. Alan knew himself, at least knew what he'd once been capable of; he knew Harvey had been dog meat and he, Alan, had blown the kill. And knowing you were less than in your prime, he told himself, you compensated.

Another way to describe how he felt: he was falling apart maybe just a little bit, he could feel the annoying beginnings of internal disintegration, but he wasn't sure how fast, how bad, how much. Half of him was screaming cash in, cash out (however that went) and head for Central America, South America, Belize – wherever might be safe. The other half – and he knew this was the ego self – was saying he could handle things and the big kill was just around the corner. I won't take any chances and I'll be okay so long as I think twice before I pull the trigger. Think twice and shoot once. Still, that hadn't worked so good with that nosey young punk Harvey. Harvey, Harvey, Harvey, better get in all the joy you can out of your miserable little life, about one more week and you're a dead man!

Still, Alan had to admit it was time to close down the Los Angeles office and get his new plan in motion. Hell, the Verhu building was ready for the torch, all he had to do was have his clean-up man fire it up. Or do it himself; that would be more fun. It could be messy, but if they did it careful there would be the insurance money. And like that screw-head accountant had advised, he could get six figures for selling his old airplane. He found his mind wandering, himself dreaming about a bright and wonderful future. Clean up all his messes, old and new and move on. It could be done, and then he could get on with life, with this next phase in the land of the Spanish conquistadores. The next phase, not his ultima thule. That final heaven, well, that might be below the equator, or it might not. Maybe Thailand. He'd have to see. Somewhere in there he made up his mind what to do about Celeste. Tricky Celeste, who had been digging into his past, just like Harvey and Dickens. That bad little gold digger had to go.

Setting aside his dreams, he took the elevator down one floor and gave instructions to Annie in the voice, that way he knew he had that said Do it – or else you have no tomorrow. First the threat, and then Mister Sweety Pie. It was his way with Annie – hell, with all his women – and it had always worked. "You just have to get her up to the penthouse," he said. "Get back out yourself. You're not doing anything wrong. Nothing bad will happen to her. I'll have the plane. I'll be back from Taos in a few days. I just need to talk to her and I can't have her snooping around and causing trouble while I'm away. Understand?"

Annie held her shaking hands to still them, held them out of sight under her desk, and she felt the throbbing beat of her own sinking heart. She had been making her own escape plans, and she had been so close to actually getting away!

Alan, already walking away from her desk, came back, reached in one jacket pocket, pulled out a small revolver with a worn walnut grip and set it on the edge of her desk. She was startled, and she visibly cringed when she saw it, thinking for the moment he was going to shoot her. But it was something else.

"Here's another little job for you," he said. "This here, one of my old pistols from my cop days, been acting up not right anymore. I don't want to dump it around here. Too many prying eyes. Garbage pickup is by your house tomorrow, right?"

Annie shuddered again inside, trying her best to show nothing in her expression. Alan always knew too much about every phase of her private life. He even knew when her garbage truck took its weekly drive down the street where she lived. "Yes, it does. First thing tomorrow morning."

"Put this in a paper lunch bag and dump it in there. Best way, no mess, no fuss. You can do this for me, right?"

She knew he wasn't really asking, so much as ordering. She picked up the ugly little thing by its short dark-grey metal barrel and said she would.

A little later, Alan gave the doomed Celeste some meaningless assignments, little crap to keep her occupied. A last check on his to-do list: he texted one of his clean up men, a tall, skinny fellow named Jake Smoles, to see if the Jake-ster and one or two of his guys would be free for a few assignments. Jake was a wanna-be Hemingway, a

Nam vet who loved to tell far-fetched stories of his crazy times in Southeast Asia. He was tall and thin, graceful like some wild creature – a mongoose or a snake – is graceful. He was known as the Shiv Killer, but nobody was sure if his claiming that deadly skill was true or just another one of his stories.

Alan met with Jake at the coffee shop in the lobby and made plans for him to be free to drive out to Taos in the silver-grey Bentley that Alan had inherited from his second wife. Alan himself would fly out Bella, his trusty old DC-3. That way he'd have both the plane and the car so he could get around, do the stuff he had to do. Things were about to happen and he didn't want to be anywhere near West LA when, as the guys in his cop unit back in Chicago used to say, the fit hit the shan.

Chapter 54

Church Dickens woke with a start, instantly awake, aware of another presence in the room. My fault, I kissed his cheek. It was me, Lexi. I needed his attention.

He reached up and scratched my ear. "What's up, girl?" he said. I could see he wasn't mad or anything. The middle of the night and he's right there for me, that calm voice of his coming at me, wondering what he can do, what I might need, how he can help. You gotta love a guy like that. I really lucked out when I met Church Dickens.

I had his attention and that was a good thing if he wanted to be there when my pups came out, which was about to happen.

Unconditional love, Dickens was thinking. He shook his head, clearing his mind. Something was up. "Come on, dear girl," he said. He led me back to the spare bedroom and my big bed of blankets and comforters. He got out his cell phone. "Lexi's telling us something," he said.

"Be right there." It was Jessie's voice, sleepy and with a yawn, and yet colored with a note of anticipation.

Ten minutes later three generations of Carters – Ed, Jessie, and Billie – showed up; by that time Church had his newly arrived espresso machine hissing and bubbling away.

"All I know how to make is lattes," he said. "It's coffee and you put hot milk in."

"Lattes is good," Ed said.

Billie ran to the big cabin and came back with a half empty plastic squeeze bottle of caramel syrup, and my first puppy arrived about then and they forgot about the lattes to marvel at the wet little bundle of new life. Tan fur, it looked like, though Jessie said she guessed you couldn't be sure, sometimes they changed color in the first month. .

Nothing more happened for another hour. Ed left us and went back to the main house and Billie fell asleep on the sofa in the living room and then my second puppy arrived, this one maybe gray.

Another hour, a third pup. And then at three in the morning, the fourth. And finally, when everybody thought all the excitement was over, at five in the morning when it seemed like I was finished, I managed to squeeze out a fifth one, this one a very little guy, the runt of the litter, making his appearance. And he wasn't moving or breathing. I licked him, but nothing happened. I didn't know what to do.

"Oh no," Jessie said.

"What's wrong, Mom?" Billie's voice rose to a panic note; she had never seen a still birth before.

"Doesn't look like number five made it..." She set the puppy aside.

"No. Give him to me," my master said, holding out his hands.

Jessie was going to tell him it was hopeless, nature, a part of life, but when she saw the look in his eyes she said nothing and handed him the silent little body.

He squeezed it gently once, twice, three times. When the little creature remained still in his hands he placed its muzzle in his mouth. He carefully sucked in while squeezing once again. My last little pup shuddered once and Church spat out a glob of greenish goo.

Jessie and Billie stared, not knowing what to think, as he gently kneaded the puppy in his hands.

"Cardio," he said. "Artificial heart massage. Five minutes went by, and then ten. Finally, Jessie shook her head and reached out for the pup. "No, Church. The little one is gone."

And a miracle happened. There was a little squeak and the pup shuddered and gasped and came to life. Church handed him to Jessie, who gently set him down next to the rest of the litter.

"No," Dickens said. "Give him to Billie. Hold the baby for a while, Billie. Next to your heart. He needs a hug."

"Church…where did you learn how to do that?" Jessie said.

"In a war zone. In the middle of a fire fight. On a human baby. It doesn't always work." Dickens rubbed one arm across his eyes and turned away. Jessie saw the haunted expression on his face. Something thawed in her own heart, feelings stirring that until that moment she had been sure were gone forever.

"Tucker," Dickens said. "I want to call him Tucker. If it's okay with you guys."

"You've got it, Church," Jessie said. "We christen thee Tucker Alexander the First."

Billie happily cuddled the new puppy, holding him in her arms, close next to her heart like Dickens told her to do. This one was a light gray color like Lexi, and soon he was feisty and mewling around, hungry and looking for food. For my part, I was bone tired; my first job was finished, and the feeding cycle was beginning for me.

Billie finally handed over the puppy and Jessie and Billie left. Church sat tirelessly watching as I fed my new litter. We shared a quiet happiness through the rest of the night.

Chapter 55

Jessie's mid-morning call to Lexi's owner did not go as planned.

"Jus' who am I speaking?" It was the Hispanic maid on the other end of the line.

"This is Jessie Carter. I need to talk to Mrs. Anderson."

"Jus' who am I speaking?" the voice repeated.

Someone took the phone from the maid, and it was Mrs. Morganfeld on the line, her voice a rough rasp in Jessie's ear, "Hello, Jessie? Sorry to relay bad news so sudden. Mrs. Anderson died two days ago. Sorry we didn't get back to you, things have been hectic around here as you can imagine."

"Oh. That is so very sad. I was calling to tell her Lexi had her babies. Five beautiful pups. Mrs. Anderson would have liked to know."

"Yes ... yes, she would have loved that." There was a pause and then the lady lawyer cleared her throat and spoke again. "Mrs. Anderson. She knew she was dying. Unfortunate, but she had no close relatives ... nobody she liked, nobody she trusted."

"I'm sorry to hear that."

"Yes, well, she liked you. Before she died, one of the very last things, she wrote an addendum to her will, leaving the dogs in your name ... except one pup, the pick of the litter, that one goes to Mr. Dickens, that nice young man who rescued us all from the greedy clutches of that bad fellow Jay Bornton."

"What about Bel, the Basset hound? It looks like she's due in a couple of days."

"Well, if you can continue our arrangement until her owners return from Europe?"

Jessie agreed to continue caring for the low-slung Basset hound and her new brood after they arrived. She clicked off the phone and sighed, sad that Mrs. Anderson didn't have a chance to see Lexi's new litter. After a while she smiled. She was sure Church would want a dog, and she knew which puppy was going to be his choice.

Chapter 56

To Harvey the night rolled by in a blur, a bewildering jumble all around as his square little urban car crawled and bumped over unpaved paths and gravel roads, performing wilderness feats he wouldn't have imagined possible, bouncing through barren landscapes, images of dark buttes against a star lit sky, a crescent moon lighting sagebrush fields with endless emptiness stretching into the distance.

A giant creature loomed in front of them; Chooli swerved off the gravel road and the creature complained, making a moo-noise at them.

"Yeao!" Harvey said, braced himself for a fender bender, but it never happened.

"Stupid cow," Chooli said, rocketing his car back on the bumpy road and on through the night. "You don't worry, Ayoo, I got this one."

He didn't know how long it went on; he was exhausted and spent from lack of sleep and loss of blood, and at some point he went out like a light, like somebody clicked him off for the rest of the journey.

Harvey woke to total darkness. City guy that he was, it was like sudden blindness and the absolute silence of the deaf, or maybe – he wasn't thinking clearly for that moment – maybe he was dead.

"What? Where? Where am I?"

"Hush, Ayoo! You are safe, here with me," Chooli said. "In my grandfather's Hogan. Old man and me, we carry you from car. We whisper now because grandfather sleeps."

"I feel better … I guess." He winced as he moved, the wound in his shoulder giving him sudden, darting jabs of pain.

"We travel all night to get here. I drive your shoebox car. I remember the way from when I was a girl."

"You drove here from memory?"

"Yes. 'Course. It is the Navajo way … updated."

"But where are we?"

"We are in the far corner of my people's reservation. Utah, maybe even. Your enemy will not find you here. No. No way they can find you. We make sure of that."

Recent memories hit Harvey like buckets of cold water: Philby suckering him into his office with the check and the old man waking up and blinking through his thick reading glasses like he didn't know where he was and then pointing his deadly little revolver straight at him and actually shooting him, and then his desperate retreat from the Verhu offices, the incredible stabbing pain from the bleeding hole in his shoulder, then patched up by the cheap strip-mall doctor, his long drive to Flagstaff and then on to Taos where by grace of God he'd met incredible pretty young Chooli, a little crazy herself, Chooli, who called him her warrior and helped him escape yet again from the vengeful arm of crazy old Philby, Chooli, with whom he suspected he was falling in love.

"Chooli, my friend Dickens is in real danger. I've got to talk with him."

205

Harvey sat up on his wood frame bed, feeling woozy even as he was seeing more clearly now by the dim light coming from a doorway. He looked around. He was in an octagonal room with a low wooden ceiling. "What is this place?"

"This my home. Where I was born. It is what white man calls a Hogan. A Navajo home."

There didn't seem to be any electricity. Harvey reached around himself in a panic. "My phone. Where's my phone?"

"You left it behind. You said your enemies could find you if you kept it. Don't worry. Mary Yazzie has internet." Oddly out-of-place as that sounded, Harvey accepted it, as well as a bowl of warm soup Chooli placed in his hands. "Drink this, then we gather strength, go talk with Mary."

The doorway of the low-walled Hogan faced east and, as Harvey pushed a woollen blanket that covered the opening aside, he was greeted by an orange sun rising above the corner of a starkly beautiful mesa, and by a wide desert landscape that spread out away from them to the south and west. Their Hogan was near the protective brow of a reddish sandstone cliff. Harvey could hardly believe the strange beauty of this place he was seeing. Wild and primitive, he thought, and wonderful!

Mary Yazzie lived a hundred yards away in a rusty old trailer covered with peeling light green paint and without tires, the metal structure resting on flat slabs of rust colored sandstone rock. Harvey's spirits lifted as he saw the roof was covered with a small bank of solar panels.

"Ya ta hey," Chooli said.

"Ta hey." Mary grinned, friendly and happy to see another tribesperson in this isolated place. She wore faded jeans and a Phoenix Suns hoodie. She was deeply tanned, with the wrinkled look of a person who had lived her fifty or so years outdoors. She handed Harvey an old flip phone, "No GPS, Red-Hair Warrior," she said. "Chooli tell me all about you. Not worry. Not nobody find you here."

"But no bars," he said.

"We have to go over there," Mary said, twitching her lips in the direction of the sheer cliff.

"Nooo," Chooli said. "He not strong enough."

"Sure, yes I am," Harvey said. "It's the warrior's way, right?"

It was a slow climb and over an hour before they were high enough so the old phone showed three bars.

Dickens came on the line on the first ring.

Harvey's chuckle was little more than a gasp for air, but his spirits were high. "See, this member of your squad is still alive, Hot Shooter."

"Harvey! We were so worried – "

"I'm better now, Dicks. You were right; Alan fooled me and then he shot me. He's crazy! Nuts in the head! I think I'm maybe gonna be okay with him far away. Chooli is taking care of me. She's really something special –"

"Yes, she is, Harvey. Meanwhile, Old Blinky is telling the world you tried to kill him."

"What? Me, him? What the hell is going on?"

"We're not sure, but we know it's something worth killing for."

"We've got to find out before he gets to us."

"You're hired, Harvey."

"You sure you can afford me? I got to help pay grandma's rent."

"Harvey, I'm starting my own company. We will get through this thing, and you don't worry about granny's rent."

For a moment there was a hint of the old Fineman fire. "Hey, well then okay! I'm in on that!"

On that note, Harvey's voice started to break up. The last thing Church heard was "… all we gotta do is stay alive."

The connection was broken. Church tried to call him back, but there was no answer.

Chapter 57

Celeste wanted to be sure everybody was long gone from the Verhu offices. She waited after hours until she figured no one was around. That was the thing about Verhu; cheap about paying overtime, they discouraged long hours, and everybody from research to marketing to analysis and sales hit the elevators, got in their cars and hit the freeways home, mostly to the San Fernando Valley or east to the high desert where the houses were both newer and more affordable.

This time Celeste wasn't in it for a general snooping raid; she knew she needed something hard and factual to convince Church she was right there with him. Whatever that might be. Maybe if she could locate some bad crap on old fart Alan himself, or something about the important but still mysterious Taos Pines project she could use, anything that might get her back in Church's good graces. She saw nothing wrong with switching allegiances back and forth. It was a dog-eat-dog world. If the truth were told, she would have to admit she preferred gimpy Dickens to moldy old Alan. That old man gave her the creeps.

She played Candy Crush and nursed a Carmel Macchiato in the lobby coffee shop for an hour, then took the elevator up to Church's floor; and found out she wasn't entirely alone. Annie frowned up at her from her desk. "What are you doing here?"

"What do you care, Annie? You don't have a boss any more, now that Dickens quit." She walked past Annie and peered in Church's office. It was empty. All the rock specimens, the pictures of Church in the wilderness and diving through air in his bathing suit and in his desert fatigues at war, all the shelves of law and geology books, everything gone. "What's going on, Annie?"

"What do you expect? Church resigned. You know that. Everybody does."

"Yeah, but I don't know why."

Annie saw Celeste was carrying the small velvet box in one hand. "What are you doing with Harvey's ring?"

"Don't be crazy. It's my ring."

"No, it isn't. Harvey got it from his grandma. He gave it to Church to research it."

Celeste, a wild look in her eyes, frantic as a person trapped in an episode of Twilight Zone, Celeste looking in that surrealistic moment like she'd showed up in some strange alternate reality. "What? What? What? Harvey's ring? No, that's impossible!"

"No, of course it isn't. Church told me what to look for. I did the printouts. Here."

She handed Celeste a few pages of print outs. "It's not a diamond. It's quartz. Back in that time it was the poor man's diamond."

Celeste grimaced and got ready to throw the little box away.

"No. Don't do that. Here. Give it to me."

"Why?"

"Bad karma. I have his grandma's address. I'll get it back to her." Annie shrugged, her plain features not revealing any emotion, but inside she felt a flash of disgust: "Be honest, girl. What do you care, anyway? You're only in it for yourself."

Celeste set the small velvet box on the corner of Annie's desk and gave the older woman a hardened look. "Annie, this is the financial business. Nobody's in it for love and kisses."

"Tell me about it. Alan didn't want me around anymore because he figured I'd gotten too old to …." She didn't finish the sentence. She saw Celeste's incredulous look. "Yeah, I know. Hey, I was young once. At least younger than I am now."

"But he never – "

"That evil man would stick it in a warm cow pie. He's just been too busy to get around to you."

Celeste waved both arms wide, "I don't get it."

"You never did, and won't. If I were you, I'd walk down the hall and get on that elevator and never come back."

"Annie, we both know that's not going to happen."

There was a moment when the older woman seemed uncertain, like she was fighting some inner struggle. Then she pinched her thin lips together and stared at Celeste. "Okay, then. I'll tell you everything you want to know. Come on."

Annie groaned as she got to her feet, feeling old and frightened. It seemed she was damned if she did what Alan was demanding of her and damned if she didn't. Damned to hell forever. She picked up her heavy leather purse and started down the corridor. "Follow me."

The elevator with the two of them in it went up to Alan's floor and stopped with a gentle lurch.

Annie motioned she was not to get out. "Wait for a minute." Annie selected a small key from her key chain, inserted it in an unmarked keyhole in the wall and pressed the up button. There was another lurch and they went up one more floor. "Penthouse. Boardroom floor," Annie said. "Nobody ever comes here. Not ever."

"Not ever?" Celeste was feeling a little timid, something she hadn't felt since she was a teen age girl.

"Not for a long time. Follow me." They hadn't taken ten steps when the elevator door slid shut behind them.

Dim overheads came on as they walked down the silent hallway, went out again as they passed. Desks were covered with shrouds of dusty green canvas. Annie led Celeste into a large conference room. A musty smell hung in the air, as if the place hadn't been used for years and still there was something more, some ancient bad aroma, like they were in an old black and white movie, entering an old Egyptian tomb. The hallway was chilly and Celeste envied Annie her heavy woollen Cardigan, wishing she'd brought her own overcoat.

They entered a big boardroom. Everything looked deserted, unused, dusty. Annie waved, inviting Celeste to take a seat; she placed her own purse on the table and sat nearby. "What do you want to know?"

"Everything, Annie. Please. Everything."

"Okay, girl. From the start. Remember, you asked for this: Alan's real name is Phillip Alan Philby. Summing up the vile man in one sentence – he is a vicious, immoral, evil creature of the devil, and I am scared to death of him. He uses everybody and then throws them aside like dirty laundry. That said, I will tell you his big weakness – he isn't any good with money. Any of this sound wrong? Listen up: In his early days our Alan was in the army. Korea. He did what soldiers do."

"Which was?"

"Celeste. Soldiers in war kill people. That's what Alan did, and unlike most guys, he liked it. And talked about it to anyone who would listen, including me, when I was his secretary and his captive audience. After Korea, he was a cop, a hard-driving young police lieutenant, a detective in Chicago in one of those precincts where the cops were also the robbers. Fraud division — which is ironic. He was a good looking guy back then, charismatic, you know? He married up, way up – a wealthy socialite – but then he got unhappy with her for a variety of reasons including the fact she was nearly twenty years his senior, and she died under mysterious circumstances. Then Alan got really unhappy when he found out his widow wasn't wealthy after all and – "

"But – "

Annie looked annoyed and impatient. "Shh. Long story, no interruptions. So Alan comes out to Los Angeles, gets a degree from somewhere, Loyola Marymount I think, in Finance, doesn't help much, he's still terrible with money. He marries a second aging wealthy socialite, starts Verhu Finance, takes off like a rocket."

"Sort of a come-back ...."

"Okay, so you're not reading between the lines. Yet. That's about the time when I come into the

213

picture. Annie, the loyal secretary. He does me a big favor that I only find out about later. You see I was married to a bad guy who socked me around a lot, and Alan finds out about it, and suddenly I'm not married anymore. My bad guy disappears. Mister Sweetie Pie Alan is right there. First he … well, he sort-of rapes me, but then he says he couldn't help himself. Remember, my husband's gone, I got no backup, nowhere to turn. I really need my job or I'm out on the street. And right there, Alan promises his undying faithful love and that he'll be true forever, and idiot that I was, I believe him."

"And?"

"Again, his second wife – like the first – wasn't as rich as Alan had hoped, and add to that he wasn't nearly the investment genius he'd convinced himself and other people he was. I tell you, Celeste, I was there when Verhu started sliding, slowly sliding. The outcome was obvious. Is obvious."

"But Alan is the envy of the West Coast business community. Hell, his investors enjoy whopping dividends, our reputation is – "

Annie held up a hand, palm out, "It's all sleight of hand, Celeste."

"But the other senior partners – "

"Signed on when things were rosy. You ever met any of them?"

"No …."

"Unbelievable as it sounds, every one of them disappeared, one by one."

"Disappeared…"

"Yes. Disappeared. They lived in different places. Tokyo. Bollywood. Singapore. They went missing, there were accidents, family men, boo-hoo.

214

Anyone present at the creation of the firm either disappeared under the radar on their own, or got disappeared. And as for Verhu – Verhu Financial is nothing more than a Ponzi scheme. And it's been feeding on itself for years now."

"But Taos Pines Lodge – "

"Is the only semi-solid asset left. I'm not sure why Alan hangs on to it. He should have sold out and left the country." Annie stood and stretched her back. She picked up her purse. "Like I'm going to."

"But what can I – ?"

"You can't do anything, Celeste. You should have asked me whatever happened to Alan's second wife."

By now Annie was moving toward the wooden panel on the wall on the other side of the table from Celeste. "That's her over there." Annie indicated a silent, canvas covered mound in a far corner of the room.

"What …?" Celeste's mouth dropped open. She was again out of her element; now nearly frozen in fear, but she couldn't resist. Step by step she had to move to that canvas and pick up one corner. When she saw the horror underneath she gave out a small wail of terror and dropped the canvas. It was the mummified remains of a woman, teeth grinning, skin tight over a skull topped with a bleached blond beehive head of hair.

She turned to Annie, but Dickens' secretary was no longer in her chair at the conference table. She had moved to the far wall.

"What? Annie? Wait!" Celeste said.

But Annie wasn't waiting for anything or anybody. She pushed the heavy oak wall panel closest behind her. A rectangular segment of the wall creaked open and she disappeared through it. She closed the secret panel from the other side. There was the sound of a deadbolt and then Annie's footsteps descending on a hidden staircase. The lights in the conference room clicked off and Celeste was alone in the dark. Alone, that is, except for the dry mummified remains of Alan's second wife.

Chapter 58

Later that night, Annie woke in her own bed in her own room in her apartment over the garage of the home she owned, her bungalow up front in Santa Monica that she rented out for a good profit while she lived over the garage in back. She was alone and nothing unusual about that, but something very bad was going on in her life and she was unexpectedly frightened; she found herself gasping for air.

The moment took her by surprise, this wasn't right, she never woke at night. When she realized what it was, the sudden impact of her awareness was almost more than she could stand: she didn't want to die. She couldn't die. If she died right now she would go to burning hell, and hell was forever.

Once death had seemed so very far away that it didn't really matter. Manning her desk at Verhu in the early years with Philby, and then later with Dickens, she was the other Annie; the self-assured one, crisp and efficient, the problem solver. Even suspecting Philby's involvement in the death of her own husband …well, Annie told herself she wasn't responsible for that. Her husband had been a vicious, mean, cruel, sadistic person, and there never really was any solid proof Philby was responsible for his disappearance. Don't go looking for trouble, she told herself – or checking too closely a gift-horse's teeth. Look the other way. And that's what she did for all those years.

Other times, even when not in the office, she was okay as well. Life was good, nothing to worry about. In the daytime when she was with her sister or their kids, she was the fun aunt, the one who suggested miniature golf and Sno-cones on the way home from school. But that was all gone now. Alan Philby had taken all that away, finally finding a way to replace her cool coast through life with a wrenching guilt. She was no longer an onlooker to evil; she was, no matter how unwilling, a participant. Now she herself, first hand, was going to be responsible for another person's death. Sure, Celeste was a bitch, but that didn't make it any better.

Annie glanced over at her bedside clock. She felt alone, utterly lonely. The hands on the clock showed midnight plus five minutes. A cold bluish glow from the street light lay across her room, her one room apartment above the two car garage in the back yard of the house she had legally inherited a few years after her husband disappeared. The house she earned income on, thanks to Church Dickens's advice, and the apartment that would also help provide for her in the years after she moved into her dream life, retirement on a tropical isle, palm trees and beaches, margaritas and – dare she dream? – maybe even a middle-aged but still presentable beachcomber bum who would treat her like a princess. Soon now. Soon.

But that was the that and the then of a dream and this was the here and now and she was gasping in dark menacing air that was heavy and thick as black cherry Jell-O. What was it? What was the nightmare that had scared her awake? Images came

218

rushing back to her and she wished she hadn't asked. She saw Celeste alone, thinner and thinner, locked in the penthouse where nobody ever went, saw Celeste a player in the same doomed play that had taken Alan's second wife, Celeste in a few weeks or months lying under a shroud in the conference room on the penthouse floor of the Verhu building next to the mummy that had been Alan's second wife.

Annie had been so close, so close to actually breaking free. She was already packed. The consignment papers had been signed; her house was in the hands of a real estate manager. She had her ticket to Miami, Delta, one way, first class. And another ticket, this one on a Princess Cruise liner, this voyage the one she now suspected she would never complete. She had hoped to lose herself among the hundreds of tropical islands south of Florida and once she was there, Alan would never find her.

And yet she now had to ask herself – what sort of life would that be if she was responsible for the horrible death of Celeste? A life of fear, of guilt and shame. And after death, eternal hellfire. No coming back from murder. Sure, Celeste was easy to dislike, even to loath, for the way she treated people, particularly Church Dickens, who was nice to everybody. The problem was Annie took her religion seriously. Bottom line here, God didn't say it was okay to help murder people you didn't like. "Thou shalt not kill." Period.

And yet Annie was sure she couldn't go back there to help Celeste. She couldn't. Alan would know. Alan was the devil. He knew everything. He would know she had set Celeste free. He would come for her. But, but, but … but if she did nothing, this nightmare horror would be with her for the rest of her life. This would be her life, waking up night after night, drowning in her own guilt. And she would go to hell, forever. With that grimmest of thoughts she made up her mind, picked up her phone and punched in the one number she'd learned by heart.

The phone rang and rang and rang. She found herself whispering to herself, "I really need your help. Come on, come on, answer the phone. Church? Church Dickens, are you there …?"

And finally, when she had all but given up, his sleepy voice came on the line.

"Hello. What's up?"

"Church, please. Please help me. Tell me what to do."

"Annie? Annie, is that you?"

"Church, please help me. Alan made me trick Celeste up to the penthouse. She's locked up there now. I'm sure he's going to kill her like he did all the others. I don't know what to do. He'll kill me if I do anything."

"Annie, you know how dangerous he is. I thought you were supposed to leave for Miami. We agreed."

"I was. But Alan found out about it, and he upgraded me to first class. My reward, he said, for being a good girl. But I just had to do this one more thing for him. I knew I had to, or he'd kill me."

"Where is he now?"

"I don't know for sure. New Mexico, he said. He's got a driver taking me to the airport in the

220

morning in a limo, you know, I get the Verhu V.I.P. treatment." There was a lengthy silence on the phone. "Church? You still there?"

"I'm here, Annie. And I'm pretty sure we both know what the Verhu V.I.P. treatment means. Look, here's what you do: Drive somewhere you can catch a cab; park your car on the street and get over to my place. Take your purse and your wallet, that's all; pay cash. My house key is under the geranium pot left of the door. Pink geraniums, full bloom, you can't miss it. Go through the house to the utility room and find the keypad; the code is 666911. My car is in the garage, the key — a classic mechanical key — is in the glove compartment. Drive to Houston, catch a cruise ship from there, he won't expect that."

"But my tickets – "

"That's all gone money, Annie, and so is your car and everything else. We're talking about your life here. I'll send you for the tickets. For me it's a write-off, business travel expenses. Leave the Porsche someplace; when you get someplace far away, text me where and I'll take care of it."

"You don't think I'm being paranoid?"

"Annie, the man kills people. He's a cold-blooded serial killer. You just said so. He thought of something else. "Hey. I just had a bad thought: What if Alan isn't into high-tech tracking and just has one of Jake's goons watching your place? Go out down the alley, walk to a Starbucks or a Carl's, Jr. and call Uber from there."

"Church, I'm afraid. Maybe he'll find me even if I go to the islands. He'll find me and invent some secret way to disappear me, just like the others. I don't know where to go. I don't know what to do!"

"Annie, no panicking now. You have come this far; don't let me down. You get my car, just like I said. Drive to Houston or New Orleans or Tampa, you decide."

"He'll kill you, too, Church."

"Annie. We're teammates. I can take care of myself. But you have to buck up. I need you strong."

"I'm not sure I –"

"Well, I'm sure. Just do it. Go. Now. Get my car and drive on out of there. You can do this. You have to do this."

Annie said her goodbyes and then sat there in the darkness, trying to decide what to do. She was chilly in her underwear so she pulled on sweat pants and a hoodie jacket. After a while there was a knock at the door. A gruff voice said, "Hey, sweetheart, it's Tug. Alan Philby sent me. Alan asked me to shoot on over, make sure, see how you are doin', if everything is okay. "

She didn't say anything. She knew about Tug Augustino. He was more than Alan's driver, he was one of his clean-up men. There was a pause; then the door shook, Tug testing it. "Annie? You in there?"

She stood and picked up her purse, crossed the room and silently stepped over a knee-high ledge out the open back window and onto the garage roof. She was careful to close the window behind her until she heard the automatic lock click. She was committed now; no way she could get back in. There was a vine trellis on the far side of the garage.

It was strong and like a hidden ladder, probably strong enough to hold her. Probably would have to do. She slung her purse by the long strap around her shoulder and carefully moved toward the edge of the roof, reaching over the shaky lip of the gutter for the top wooden bar on the trellis. Her escape route! After all those years working for Alan, it would be crazy to think any other way.

Chapter 59

Church's brother answered on the second ring. "Dickens Industries, here."

"Wow, very prompt response. You guys don't dick around, do you?"

"Actually, we dick around a lot. What's up, bro?"

"Did you go back East?"

"No, I was sky-falling in the Mojave, met some Hollywood dudes, I got a part in their movie!"

"How'd that happen?"

"Guy's chute failed. Opportunity knocked.

"Okay, big time, but I need your help. Seriously."

"Hey, I'm free, bro. Movie finished yesterday. Last night actually. Free fall in the dark. What a rush!

"I'm not fooling around, Ruger. I really need you."

"It's what brothers are for."

"You think you could rescue a lady in distress?"

"James Bond, at your majesty's service."

Chapter 60

Celeste sat still as she had when she was a little girl in big trouble, when bad old Horace, her mother's provider, locked her in a closet and started beating on the poor Mom, at that time a swiftly aging drug addict already hopelessly lost in the downward spiral of her life.

Now, alone in the penthouse on top of the Verhu building, Celeste heard the ragged sounds of herself breathing, and she fought to hold down her growing panic. It was night and there was nothing but dim emergency lighting on the entire floor. The hallway was dark except for light stealing in from the window at the end of the corridor, a dim glow having made its way from the windows, themselves shuttered with old fashioned blinds, the slats turned closed and further darkened with the curled concrete ornamentation meant to keep out the too bright Southern California daylight. She couldn't stay still. Couldn't. Couldn't. Couldn't. She had to do something. But what?

After her quick glance at the still outline on the floor under the old canvas tarp – a mistake, seeing that mummified horror, that poor woman in her crumbling gown of pink gone to grey, wearing a sad necklace with the gemstones plucked out – after one look at that, Celeste had shuffled in a numb and shocked state across the room, then panicked and ran down the hall to the elevator. She jabbed the down button, slammed her fist on it over and over but the door didn't open. Of course not, there was another little keyhole on the panel right next to the down button. And only Annie had that little key, and maybe the guard below, and he worked for Old Blinky.

Water! Would they have shut off the plumbing? The toilet facilities were on the same configuration on every floor in the building. Would the penthouse be any different? Celeste flung open the door to the men's room and managed to get to the sinks before the automatic door closed behind her, plunging her into total darkness. Fighting back panic, she groped for the faucets in the closest sink and turned them on. There was a gasp of air and finally a burst of water. Probably rusty as hell, but she wasn't going to die of thirst. Still … what to do? Keep busy, keep thinking, go forward, she told herself. She stubbed her foot on the wastebasket on her blind way to the door, managed to keep from falling, get the door open and make her way down the hall. What could she possibly do to save herself? She had to escape. She had to get out of here!

What if somebody other than Annie knew she was here? Where the hell was Alan? Had he really gone to Taos? Why?

Her thoughts were running wild: What if the guard in the lobby had been alerted? No, she decided, maybe not. But maybe. For sure, somebody would come to finish her off. Verhu owned the building, but the guards wore those generic security company outfits, halfway between an airline pilot's suit and a police officer's uniform. They were lightweights. So it wouldn't be one of the guards. Probably not. But somebody. Alan would send some professionals. And soon.

Celeste pulled some dusty canvas tarps from a pile in a far corner and dragged them to the receptionist's desk nearest the elevators. She built herself a small tent in a corner behind the desk. She had a few minutes of twilight left and her curiosity out-voted her fear, at least for the moment. She left her makeshift tent and moved carefully down the hallway, deciding to see what she could see.

She could use answers to some unfilled blanks that had been bothering her since she started working for Verhu. It couldn't hurt to know things. Information – anything that might save her life. Everybody knew the company had five senior directors; there was Alan Philby, and there were the other four who had those difficult foreign sounding names – two supposed East Indians, one Chinese and one Japanese.

They were on the corporate stationary: Joseph Ahuja. Mohatmud Pawar. Louis Zhang. Miko Takahashi. But in the year and a half since Celeste had been there, nobody ever saw them, related to them, typed up their memos, corresponded with them, talked about them. They were like non-people. Now as she walked down the hallway, their names were still there, each one on a little bronze plaque outside an office door. The secretarial desks had the normal work-a-day things – rulers, tape, pencils and so on – but they were just left behinds, and anybody could see the place hadn't been active, not in use for years. Old fashioned electric typewriters instead of computers. Older style office phones. No sign of computers. Even the small lunch room had an old-style Mr. Coffee coffeemaker.

The doors were all locked, but she jammed her shoulder hard against the one farthest from the elevators and it popped open. There was a dust-covered desk, but the drawers were totally empty. There was a framed print on the wall, something famous, a little boat in dangerous seas with a snow-covered mountain in the background. There was a long wooden filing cabinet against the wall, as empty as if it had never been used. On the cabinet was a glass case presenting a curved sword that was mounted on two wooden blocks lying on an ornate silk robe. Mr. Miko Takahashi was long gone … if he'd ever actually been there (or existed). But his sword now … maybe it was just a phony antique, but who cared? It was some sort of weapon. Not as good as a gun, but better than a sharp stick. Getting it out of the locked case was no problem. She pushed it onto the floor. The brittle clear plastic shattered and she took the sword in her hand. It was shorter than she figured, and heavier, but beggars couldn't be choosers. She took it with her and made her way back to her low, sagging make-shift tent.

It was then Celeste realized she'd left her designer brief-pack behind in the conference room. Until that moment she'd been so rattled she'd forgotten everything. You couldn't trust anyone, ever, at Verhu; out of sheer unthinking habit she had brought her shoulder strap leather pack with her when she foolishly got on the elevator with Annie. But then, what? She couldn't remember. Had Annie taken it when she slipped out that secret door? Celeste forced herself to return to the conference room, every step of the way fighting her revulsion over the mummified body lying there like a curse from a movie, like the victim of some ancient Egyptian deity come real. Thank God! The leather case was on the floor where she'd left it! She breathed a sigh of relief, but then her spirits began to sag again.

She was feeling real despair for the first time since she couldn't remember when. Awareness of her pending doom rushed over her; she was going to end up like the lady mummy. How could she avoid it? She had no friends, nobody thinking about her, wondering where she was. Worse, she realized, she had no real friends, period, and no family. Her battered and broken mother was long dead, there was (or had been) a father she never knew, and there were no brothers, no sisters, no relatives she knew of.

Her only hope had to be Church Dickens. She had to talk to him. He would fly back to L.A. and rescue her. That was her only hope. Church would come. He would get her out of this mess. She opened her laptop – and remembered with a sinking heart that Verhu routinely blocked all regular web service on all the company floors. The only reception she could get was the company's employee-to-employee internal use. And Church Dickens, resigned in disgrace from the company, was erased from the site. And everybody else hated her. Well, disliked her, and for good reason, she now saw; in her unrelenting climb to make junior partner she had stepped on anybody she thought was in her way. That just about included everybody but the janitors. And the few times she saw janitors, she hadn't been nice to them.

Chapter 61

When Alan Philby showed up at the Spirit Hut in Taos, Johnny Hunsai gave him the showy little blessing bow with folded hands and motioned he was to enter the meeting room to one side of the big rocks n' rings n' things showroom. But Philby gave a narrow-eyed glance around the dark and shadowy room with the smoking sticks and funny burning smells and said he needed some fresh air so could they take a little walk maybe to that coffee café down the street. He didn't trust this bleached blond long-haired sort-of-white man with his pretend-injun ways, didn't trust him for a second. It was fundamentally wrong bad casting, Roy Rogers pretending to be Tonto, John Wayne gone to seed as Chief Sitting Bull. But right now the man from Verhu needed the fake voodoo Spirit man, so there had to be a truce going on.

"I'll call the Pueblo guys," Johnny pulled his cell phone from his beaded man-bag, a big pouch with a blazing sand painting design popularized in the Santa Fe Railroad heyday over a half century ago.

Philby gave him a skeptical look. "Them the guys who worked any of your last fool-proof ideas?"

"It ain't my fault," Johnny said. "I told Kate Carter she was pitchin' stupid ideas. You talk to that woman, she don't listen."

"All women is useless. Did you know the cabins are in the Carter family trust? And Kate Carter isn't."

Johnny puffed out his cheeks, let out a half whistle of exasperation. "What exactly does that mean?"

"What in holy hell do you think it means?"

"Still, she's our spy in the enemy camp ...."

"Yeah. Pig-headed, stupid, greedy ... some spy."

Philby seemed in worse humor than usual. "Okay Spirit-man — You say you got a great idea for me. Let's hear it."

"Well, yeah, I do. I call it our injun bones move."

Philby looked like he wanted to spit on the nearest display, a bunch of polished cloudy blue rocks that claimed (the small cardboard banner claimed) they were ten times more powerful in gathering blessings from a higher dimension. "It better not involve Dumb and Dumber doing anything complicated" he said. "Come on, let's get out of here."

They were ordering coffee and sweet rolls when Jeb and Arty did show up, and in spite of the fact that the Pueblo brothers were an integral part of the new plan, Johnny assured Philby it was sure-fire and simple, simple, simple. Not even an idiot could muckle it up. All it involved was a backhoe and a midnight run to a local church cemetery, and these guys had worked with construction equipment and knew their beans. It did sound easy-peasy and yet so far-out crazy that Alan found himself thinking it just might work, and the next thing he knew he was peeling off ten one-hundred dollar bills from his thick front pocket pants roll and somewhat reluctantly putting them down and then pushing the hundies across the table.

Chapter 62

Celeste huddled outside her makeshift tent, darkness settling over her. The day had been cloudy and damp. A chill was settling in. Maybe nobody was coming to kill her, at least not for a while, at least not until they — he? — figured out what to do with her. Maybe they would never come, just leave her to wilt and wither and die like that shriveled up old-lady corpse in the conference room. Was that really one of Philby's wives? Celeste had to admit it probably was. Once Annie had trapped her, there was no reason for her to fib about stuff like that.

Celeste crawled inside the low canvas hut she'd built and wrapped her shoulders in a dusty old woollen sweater she'd found on the back of one of the secretary's chairs. She clicked on her laptop and tried to send Church an email. No luck. No luck. No luck. Crap, why was she even trying?

Running out of ideas, she started searches, researching the senior directors of Verhu. And ran into a brick wall.

The four names were all there, glittering bright and clear in the internal Verhu ether, all listed as giants of the financial industry, captains of commerce, directors at Verhu Financial. But aside from these bare details, nothing more. She finally moved to the nearest window and got a faint and intermittent reception from god-only-knew where. No email capability, but she was able to Google Alan Philby and read he was a giant of the financial industry, a captain of commerce, a director at Verhu

Financial, a Delaware corporation based in West Los Angeles. One other thing struck her as odd, but maybe significant. The Google references to all the Verhu directors went to Wikipedia, and all of them were so similar they could have been input by the same public relations firm at the same time, probably by the same person. As were their obituaries. All of the actual directors but Alan had died. One in a car crash in Singapore, one while swimming alone at night in a hotel swimming pool, one in a bar fight in Tijuana, and one of a sudden heart attack. Their surviving family members mourned their loss. Below the level of directors, nothing until the boiler plate talked about the Verhu agents, building them up as mighty hunters of the market, the point of the spear on the cutting edge of the battlefield of financial enterprise, and so on like that.

All of this resolved itself into unwelcome clarity of a sort. Celeste hadn't been born paranoid, but she had been a loner from early on, the lone unhappy child of a sad single mother who had sold her affections for money that she shot on the short-term solace of drugs. Mom even had a typed-out menu, quick and easy hand jobs were so much, the full treatment was so much, and so on. In her own sad way Mom was proud of herself, of what she saw as her business sense. So it was that, after seeing the way the world treated her mom, Trust nobody became Celeste's motto. She herself took up hooking at an early age, charged a lot, avoided pimps and the more dangerous drugs, saved her money, had a knife, knew how to use it (used it twice, actually, though she didn't think she'd ever

234

killed anybody), went for education, hooked her way through the educational system. After college and law school, an application for a junior research spot at Verhu had presented itself. She applied, promoted herself the right way with human resources, and nailed the job. The salary wasn't that great, but it had seemed like a great first step in the direction of the big money, a place to wring stepping stones dry, learn what they knew about a business where the action was and where fortunes were made every day, and maybe even have a happy ending and land a rich guy. All that and she ends up locked away in a place where somebody was going to find her dusty bones in a decade or two! That wasn't fair at all.

She could see clearly now, too late, that Alan was an unpredictably dangerous man, disintegrating, falling apart, but still vicious – a stone killer – and these other four corporate directors weren't active players at all; they were the ghosts of dead men: they were conjured-up fronts for dark money, but in actuality they were real dead men. Alan probably personally killed them, too, or had it done. Just like he had his wife.

Celeste realized she should have done more digging before she signed on. She should have listened to Annie, who was clearly frightened of the man. What the hell had she been thinking? She had gotten sloppy; there was no easy street anywhere in the world. She should have known. She should have known. She should have known.

And cursing her fate like that, Celeste fell asleep over her laptop. It ran another half hour before the battery began to dim and finally went dead.

Chapter 63

Celeste was jarred awake by the sound of the opening elevator doors. She shook her head, trying to clear her mind as somebody rushed past yelling her name. She didn't know the voice; it wasn't Church. Somebody else, come for her! Come to kill her! Well, they weren't going to finish her off without a scrap! She scooped up her leather brief, grabbed the heavy Japanese sword and dashed for the elevator.

She hit the down button, but nothing happened. Damn, damn, damn! Whoever it was, a man's urgent steps. No time, no movement from the elevator. She set down her bag and gripped the sword with both hands, ready to impale and slice open the fool who would dare come after her.

A big man rounded the corner and dodged just in time to avoid the weapon, buried and quivering in the side of the elevator. A huge man, she saw. And black. And gorgeous.

"Don't kill me," she said.

"Kill you?! You've got the knife!"

"Who are you?"

"The other Dickens. Church's brother. Ruger Dickens. At your service."

"You are not!"

"Am, too. Don't argue identity with me. I don't like it."

"Get me out of here! There's a dead body back there!"

"You sure?"

"I know dead when I see it!"

"Show me."

For a moment she felt like killing him. Screaming. Opening him with the katana — now the word came to her! — anything. She let out an exasperated breath, took his arm and pulled him along the hall toward the conference room, lifted the edge of the canvas shroud to show him the mummy.

"Wheeou. That's really, really long-time dead."

"You idiot! Get us out of here!"

They were staring at each other like creatures from warring planets in a Star Trek episode. And then there was something more, a mutual heat stirring and they reached for each other and who knows where the moment might have led, but at that same moment a popping noise sounded from the elevator shaft and Ruger was on the alert. He'd seen too many movies not to know that sound. "Oh, oh. Somebody firing the place. We go Now!" He grabbed her by the waist and half pulled, half dragged her back from the conference room into the corridor of the penthouse.

"The elevator is our only way," she said.

"No. We have to find something else. They're torching the building. Elevators go first."

"What, you wrote the arson manual?"

"No, but I could. Shut up, woman!"

Ruger was a caged beast, looking for options. He thought he saw one. He pulled the nearest desk into the corridor. "You help. We push this thing that way!" He pointed to the long narrow window on the far side past the elevators. "Push with me. Get it going. Fast enough! We have to – "

He said no more as they crashed the desk into the window, starring it into a thousand fragments that were held together with a clear inner sheet. "Damn it! Shatterproof!"

"It's no use," she said.

"You a quitter?!"

"You shut up, asshole! The sword!"

She ran back to the elevators, returned with the curved Japanese sword and started hacking a hole in the shattered glass. After a few strokes the entire splintered mess let loose of the window frame and went crashing down out of sight. She stared after it.

"Wooh. Long way down. Eleven floors…"

"Nothing to it. Plenty of hand holds," he said, taking her hand and helping her find good grips on the curled cement façade. "Praise the lord for artsy-fartsy architects. Just don't look down."

Ruger was right on both counts. The curled ornamental cement that some creative architect had thought up to keep out the Southern California heat provided good if not great handholds, and looking down was something Celeste only tried once.

Chapter 64

When they reached the ground level they were at a back corner of the building. The top four or five floors were already engulfed in roaring flames. Fire trucks and police cars were arriving and a crowd was gathering, milling around, shouting, looking up and pointing. A helicopter from Channel 7 Action News circled low overhead and the odd thing was nobody gave them a second look.

"This way." Ruger took her hand and led her down the street away from the madness. "You ever been sky-diving?"

"What? Isn't that what we were just doing?"

"Not exactly. I've got another three days on a condo next to an airport out on the Mojave. You wear a neoprene suit, something like a flying squirrel."

"Doesn't sound all that appealing to me. Just get me out of here!"

Moments later they were at his car, a shiny new red Ferrari. "Well, I can let you off wherever you'd like. Airport. Your place. Wherever."

Things were moving too fast and her mind was still in a twirl from their climb down the outside of the Verhu building. Did she really want to go back to her apartment where Philby would probably have one of his goons waiting? She flicked a sideways glance at the handsome and dashing fellow who had rescued her and now was proposing some outrageous plan to jump out of airplanes for fun. And it wasn't a Mustang or some SUV pretending to be a survival car – it was a hot red Ferrari, beckoning with the sort of adventures she only dreamed of but never expected to actually happen in real life. She tossed her dark hair and gave him a prim little smile.

"I have a better idea," she said. "Philby's place is only a few miles away – and the devious old asshole is out of town."

"You sure, girl?"

"Call me girl ever again — or even "gal" or "woman," and I'll kill you. My name is Celeste. Celeste.

"How about Ce-Ce?"

"Ce-Ce will do."

"Let's go then."

Chapter 65

"Spooky house," Ruger said, looking up at the shabby Queen Anne. "And three blocks from the beach. You'd think they'd tear it down, put up a big high rise."

The way temperature was climbing between them as they eyed each other, it was a toss-up whether they'd get inside before they started tearing off each other's clothes and rolling around on the closely clipped grass on the front lawn. They did make it inside, ran up the stairs to the closest bedroom and managed to get mostly naked and ended up on a shag rug next to the big 4-poster bed. After some exploratory kisses and an extended period of wild thrashing about on the floor, there were exclamations of ecstasy followed by some time to pause and catch their breath. It was when Celeste got to her feet and sat on the edge of the mattress to pull her Spanx back on that Ruger suddenly grabbed her foot and yanked her back off the bed.

"Yeao!" She yelled. "What the f – !"

She didn't have time for proper outrage as some dark thing, huge and dangerous, brushed past her head. After she saw what it was, her anger was replaced with a fear that had her quivering. Crazy old Philby had rigged a tall, heavy wooden credenza to tip over and crush anybody foolish enough to slip under the covers in his bed. Coming to Philby's place had been a terrible idea! They had to get out of there! She dressed as fast as she could, snapping at Ruger to get his act together. She was only half dressed when they ran out of the room and started down the stairway.

After it was all over, forward in the times to come, there would be moments while sipping a scotch or two in a lonely bar somewhere, something like that, and Ruger would admit to himself breaking into Philby's place had been a dumb idea, but at the time it seemed like the right thing to do – or maybe the two of them, wrapped together in the moment, just weren't thinking at all. They hadn't thought enough about Philby, hadn't realized what years of living a secret life could do to a person inclined to paranoia and lacking normal inhibitions. Philby was psycho, so it was easy to get in the front door of his house, but hard to get out, or to get out while still alive. Back in the moment, Ruger and Celeste panicked and ran. Neither of them felt the trip wire, but they both saw the twin barrels of the sawed off shotgun wired to the chandelier as it swiveled toward them.

Something happened to Celeste in that moment, something new for her. They were at the top of the steep stairway, staring directly into the wide twin mouth of the shotgun. But instead of cursing her fate and diving to save herself, she pushed Ruger out of the way. And he in turn grabbed her and they both fell down the carpeted stairs, nearly saving each other as the blast went off … nearly out of the destruction except for the leather boot on Celeste's left foot, that disappeared in a bloody spray.

They tumbled down the stairs together, lay in a stunned heap on the floor by the front door.

"You okay, Ce-Ce?"

"No, I'm not okay!" She looked at him in shock glazed astonishment.

"What?"

"That asshole ruined my best pair of boots!"

Worse than that. He saw her dark maroon leather boot, with her foot still in it, lying next to the door. Moving on instinct, he stopped the blood pumping from the bottom of her leg with one of his shoelaces. He picked her up, his thought to carry her over his shoulder to his car.

"My shoe, Ruger!"

She was in shock; not registering that her severed foot was still in the shoe. He shoved it in her hands.

"You have to carry it."

Then they were out the door, Ruger desperately afraid for this dynamo of a woman he knew so well and yet barely knew at all. Ce-Ce. The woman who had saved both their lives.

"Stay with me, Ce-Ce," Ruger shouted. Long minutes up Santa Monica Boulevard through light traffic, him yelling at her to stay with him.

"No," she said in an alarmingly sleepy voice. "No. I don't want to live my life like gimpy boy."

"You have to stay with me!"

"No, I don't. Nothing to live for. Life is just a joke."

"No joke, Ce-Ce. Dicks says you love money. I'll give you a hundred thousand dollars. Your own account. No strings attached."

"A hundred thou is nothing. Gimpy boy won – 2 million! In the Lottery."

"No! He didn't! That was just a gag on his pal Harvey Fineman."

"Don't believe it. Even worse, I do believe it. What a joke, the story of my life …."

"Two hundred thou. I'll put it in your own account. Two hundred, you get to show what you can do. You think you're smart. Here's your shot, Ce-Ce!"

Arguing like that, Ruger urgent and Celeste drifting further and further from him, they pulled up in front of emergency at St. John's Hospital. Tougher than she sounded, she hung in there and went into surgery a half hour later, and six hours later she had her foot sewn back on and was still alive.

Chapter 66

Annie breathed easier once she was in Dickens's Porsche and rumbling down the road toward the freeway, now only a half mile away. She had to make one last stop at the mailbox, to send off the package with Harvey's Herkimer diamond ring. She checked and it was still there, in her big purse. She'd slapped on enough postage to send it to Mars, she figured – certainly enough to get to the Taos Lodge – and if it wasn't enough Harvey would be glad to take care of any postage due to get his precious heirloom back.

But the box was just too big to fit in the narrow slot for the outside drop off, so she left the engine running and dashed into the post office lobby, open all day and all night but deserted at this late hour.

And on her way back to the car, her heart sank because a black Dodge Challenger had pulled close up behind it, nobody inside but the engine still on, grumbling away, headlights on park but bright enough to see she was no longer alone.

And there he was: Tug, Philby's bad ass clean up man, leaning on the Porsche, grinning at her like the Cheshire Cat from Alice in Wonderland. He was tall and fat, with crooked yellow teeth and a big gut that hung out over his belt. His shirt was missing a bottom button so his belly button actually showed. How gross was that? Her fear had her thinking wild, crazy stuff. Where were all the sexy hit men like in the movies? No, she gets a chubby loser with his belly button sticking out like a cherry cough drop.

The loser raised his raspy voice, "Hey, Babes, what's the deal here? Me, myself and I was supposed to take you to the airport. You're not runnin' out on us ... ?"

Annie felt the color drain from her face. Would she never, ever, ever get away from these people?

"I had to drop off a package for Alan," she said.

"Okay. You done that, so let's go."

"You see I already have a ride."

"Two rides. I say now you come with me."

"I don't have any choice, do I?"

"No, you don't, Annie."

"You sure I can't change your mind?"

"No, Annie, you can't."

"How about I write you a check for a thousand dollars?"

"No, Annie."

"Ten thousand?"

"No amount, Annie. Your money's no good here."

"You're going to kill me."

He shrugged. " 'Course, maybe. But not right here. Get in my car. Maybe you can talk me out of it." He gave her a crooked-tooth come-on smile as he took her arm and tried to push her toward his car.

"I wouldn't even try," she said

"Try to what?"

"Talk you out of it." She surprised him, stronger than he figured, turning toward him and talking in a calm and sensible way. "Tug, let's be reasonable about this, two people just talking things over. Look at this situation from the poor, doomed woman's point of view. Listen to me sharp now, Tug. Get this, say to yourself it's just the poor doomed woman's way of looking at her hopeless situation."

"Yeah, yeah, yeah. I'm all ears. Shoot, baby."

"I want to shoot, believe me. I'm holding one of Alan's police specials right here, but my hand is in my purse and I don't want to pull the trigger because this is a good purse, it would put a hole in the leather. "

"Sure you do."

"So come on, Tug – let me go, and I'll let you go. No harm, no foul for either of us."

"Nice try, babes. Now get in the car."

She lifted her hand, the one holding Alan's dark wood handled police special, and pointed the gun across her body directly at his stomach.

"Hey, wait – " He managed to say. She shot him in the belly button, knew it because his shirt flaps flew open to show it. He grunted once. "Just a .32, huh?" And she fired again, this one a few inches to the left, a small hole in his pink belly. And he grunted again, and actually grinned, showing more of his yellow teeth, one of the front ones framed in gold. "Give it up, sweet cakes. You know I'm going to kill you."

She aimed higher and fired again, hitting him in the forehead. This time his head flew back, and he gave out a loud, involuntary cry like a startled bird, Akk! The muscles in his body froze for a moment and then he sagged and fell backward to the sidewalk.

Annie sucked in a deep breath, looking down at Tug's quivering body. He wasn't going to force anyone into his car ever again. She took a small packet of Cottonelles from her purse, stripped off two of the moist little light blue towels and carefully wiped the pistol, like she'd seen people do on the CSI TV shows, and then she placed it on Tug's chest.

The post office parking lot was deserted. Annie took a last look around to be sure she was alone, then hurried back to Dickens' car and drove away.

She felt numb, outside of her real self. Jesus, she was thinking, Jesus Christ, listen to me, help me out here a little bit: you would not call it murder if you shot Judas if he had a gun and was going to shoot you? Would you? But then she remembered Judas had betrayed the Lord and Jesus had just turned the other cheek, so maybe that was a bad example. Still, betrayal wasn't the same as cut-and-dried murder, as if Judas had pulled out a knife or something and said he was going to cut Jesus' throat. No, that didn't quite work, either. There was a lot to think about and with a little time she could probably come up with a better example, but Annie was certain that, if she had to, she'd do the same thing all over again. Actually, maybe shoot stupid Tug in his fat face first thing. Get it over with, and wipe that goddamn smirk off his face.

Chapter 67

Ruger was reluctant to call Church, put it off while he waited in a coffee shop near St. John's. He told himself he was waiting for the latest update report on Celeste, but that came and went and she was all right, hanging in there, and he still didn't call his brother.

Finally Church called him, and he had to answer as best he could the questions that came pouring out of the phone at him.

"No, no, no, Church, she's okay. I got her out."

"I saw on the internet, they torched the building."

"That they did. We had to climb down the side on those fancy concrete drape things. It was very heroic."

"You are superhero material."

"Yeah, well, not all that great …. So much happened — let me start at the beginning. Unbelievable. I bribe the guard, costs me a cool thou, I get a key to the top floor, I get up there and guess what — Ce-Ce shows me a mummy! What's-his-name, Philby, has stored his dead wife's body up there!"

"Wooh…"

"Yeah. Ce-Ce says —"

"You call her 'Ce-Ce'?"

"Yeah, like the letter 'C'. You mind?"

"No, I do not mind – what happened next?"

"Well, you know somebody torched the building. You should put in a crime-stoppers report to the cops, see if any mummy bones survived the conflagration, as they say.

"How is Celeste holding up in all this?"

This was the part Ruger was dreading. "Well Church, we did a dumb thing … we went over to Philby's house, which seemed like a good idea at the time, but which turned out to be booby trapped."

"Oh, no …."

"He'd rigged a shotgun. Nearly killed us both."

"But you're okay?"

"Well, the good news, Ce-Ce is probably not going to lose her foot. They stitched it back on, and we think they saved it."

Silence from Church's end of the line. Ruger continued, "Maybe she'll limp a little."

"What are you going to do?"

"Me? I don't know. She's kinda in a black mood. Suicidal, maybe. Doesn't want to be a gimp like you, she says."

"Same old Celeste. And how do you feel about her?"

"I dunno, bro. I know she's got a witchy streak a mile wide, but I kind of like her. She's not your girl or anything like that?"

"No, Ruger, she is definitely not."

Church could hear the relief in his brother's voice, "She saved my life, you know. That is probably why she lost her damn foot. She could have just done a dive out of the way, let me catch the buckshot."

"Well, okay, Ruger, but that's no reason to …."

"I know, I know, you're saying it's the wounded bird syndrome."

"Well, what if it is?"

251

"Yeah, but ... I'm thinking maybe it's something more. I'm not sure; being serious about somebody is not my area of expertise, but to tell it true, it's come on sudden—"

"No shit, Ruger!"

" — but we've had a moment or two. Intense, you know? So maybe I've got something kind of special here."

"You know," Church said slowly, "you're always trying to get me to move back to D.C., help with the family business. Maybe you need an assistant back there. Give her a real challenge."

"She's good at business?"

"She's good at business; you'll have trouble trusting her and you'll have trouble keeping up. From the other side, her challenge would be surviving with you. Your record for fidelity is a D-minus."

"Okay, but what if we were meant for each other?"

"That is a most unusual sentiment, coming from you."

"Love changes people," Ruger said.

"Sometimes," Church said, "Sometimes even for life.... Sometimes."

Chapter 68

Harvey Fineman woke in the warm confines of the low walled Hogan and saw by the dim illumination thrown from a coal burning Franklin stove in the center that he, and Chooli sitting on the bedding at his side, were not alone. Three very old Navajo men sat quietly on mats on the floor while a fourth chanted in a low voice. When they saw he was awake, the three nodded, but said nothing. And the other one continued his song, or prayer, whatever it was.

Chooli sat up and spoke in Navajo, talking back and forth, asking questions and listening to measured answers. The tone of the conversation was friendly, but Harvey had the feeling the subject was the two of them, and he was right.

"You and I are greatly honored," she told him. "We have received the blessing from the head of this branch of the Dine, the Dine, that is us, the Navajo people."

"The blessing! What does this mean?"

"Well ... I hope maybe you will understand, beloved Ayoo, and I hope with all my heart that it does not displease you ... we are to receive the honor of our wedding ceremony."

"Wedding?!" Astounded, he said the first thing that came to mind. "But I'm Jewish!"

This started an animated round of conversation between the old men. They came to a nodding agreement, spoke to Chooli, and she in turn smiled at Harvey. "This is an additional honor, Ayoo

Harvey. You are already a Dine, a member of the Navajo people."

"I am?"

"Oldest man — him over there — say Navajo belief we people are from a lost tribe of Israel."

She studied him, trying to read what was on his mind. "What? You don't want to marry me?"

Reviewing his options, Harvey realized for sure that he wanted to be with this beautiful wild-woman who had rescued him and risked everything for him. As for his grandmother, well, he was going to have to explain the lost tribes thing and that was going to have to be okay with her.

"No … I mean, yes, I do, very much. In return, could you do something for me …. Chooli, would you agree to have a ceremony with my family? I mean, back in Los Angeles, when we get there, so my mom and grandma and uncles and aunts could give us their blessing, as well …."

"Yes," and then, "Of course!"

The old men, who knew more English than they were saying, nodded and smiled. Bowls of special food were brought in and the ceremony began.

Chapter 69

"Don't cut my finger off, dumb ass!" Jeb Pico said. He looked like he was going to drop the big Yale lock and run off like a toddler.

"Why the fart would I do that, idiot child?" Arty said in his lazy drawl, comfortable with his younger brother's usual drama-queen ways. Younger brother, but Jesus, he was already almost thirty! Kid couldn't even roll a rock downhill! When was he going to grow up?

It was ungodly late, three in the morning, and they were behind a busted down old adobe church abandoned on a bald little hillock on the deserted outskirts of Taos; uncomfortable highland weather, ice-cold and a cutting wind, a hint of snow in the air. Jeb held the lock as steady as he could in his freezing hands; Arty snapped it with one quick snip, the heavy bolt cutter making easy business of it, and nobody's fingers were in any danger at all.

The church was not in use but the old Indian graveyard itself wasn't really abandoned – the diocese wouldn't do that, or rather, they couldn't – how do you keep order if you have to move hundreds of remains that had been buried over the centuries – but decades ago, before the chapel roof had rotted and finally fallen in, and before the living parish itself had been moved. The over two-hundred-year old cemetery was simply fenced off, allowing sand and sagebrush to sift and gather and grow between the tombstones still jutting like broken teeth from the dry ground. Now, the hillside was only visited by an occasional coyote, and now and then a grave robber slipping in under the fence, and that rare these days since the place had been combed over by experts looking for turquoise beads and silver belts and bracelets ornamenting the long dead ancestors.

Old Dyna, the rusty yellow Dynahoe 190 the brothers borrowed from the construction company owned by their Uncle Henry – Sure, boys just fill the tank with diesel when you're done foolin' around – Old Dyna was standing there, already off the back end ramp of their truck-hauler, muttering and ready to go.

Jeb pulled the wide cyclone fence gate open so the massive backhoe could squeeze on through and get inside. "Where we go now, bro?"

Arty scratched his head under his faded Make America Great Again baseball cap and squinted around in the darkness to get his bearings. "Shoot, man. Everything looks different by the light of the silvery moon."

"High poetry, but there ain't no moon out tonight, idiot bro."

"Granpappy Idris's bones over this way … I think."

"Let's bring the hoe, so we don't gots to come back for it."

That seemed like a good idea, so Jeb got in the cab while Arty stood on a fender, banging on the roof and pointing the way. The ten-ton backhoe lumbered across the cemetery by fits and starts, knocking over a tombstone here and there. When they got to Granpappy Idris's grave, it had already been robbed – they had suspected that – but worse,

256

there was nothing left but a sunken depression in the ground.

"Oh crappers," Jeb wailed. "Shoot. Piss. Crap. Rats. What we gonna do now? We come back with no bones, Spirit Man not gonna pay us a dime."

"Hell, just dig up next one over. Everybody's a Pueblo around here – it's a redskin graveyard. How's anybody gonna tell the difference?"

They talked it over and argued a bit and then Arty traded places with Jeb. He had been on more jobs with the Dynahoe 190 and had developed a better technique with the back scooper, picking-and-lifting rather than simple scraping, and using his skills, in a half hour or so they had savaged a dozen old gravesites and managed three fourths of a scoop of savers, lots of leg and arm bones, something that might have been a pelvis or maybe part of a cow, lots of dirt – that couldn't be avoided, them being in a hurry and all – and most important, three grinning human skulls that gave them both the shivers but was exactly what Johnny the Spirit Hut Man said was the main ticket.

"I guess back then there was no wooden coffins. Looks like they just wrapped them in wool blankets, put 'em right like that in the ground."

"Makes it easier for us," Arty said. "But you do notice there ain't even one scrap of turquoise."

"Yeah. Dirty filthy rotten bastard grave robbers been here before us."

They managed to reload Uncle Henry's Dynahoe back on the hauler, only spilling half their precious load of bones the one time that needed a pickup by hand. Jeb didn't want to do it – not that he was afraid of ghosts or nothing like that – but

Arty glared him something fierce and no choice he put on a pair of thin rubber gloves he'd lifted from his sister the nurse and gingerly replaced the skulls and several long bones back in the big shovel scoop, holding them far out from his body as he did it. Finished, he grimaced and threw the gloves on the ground, got in the hauler next to Arty and, as a few light flakes of snow began to fall, he signed himself with the cross and they drove off into the night without bothering to close up the gate behind them.

Chapter 70

Jessie came running in the dining room in the main cabin. "I just heard from Chooli! Chooli and your pal Harvey got married!"

Dickens was sitting at his usual table, trying to make an honest — or legal anyway — thousand or two with his day-trading skills. He greeted the news with a huge grin. "Wow, things move fast in Indian country. I guess that means the boy is recovering! What else did he say?"

"He needs to talk to you. He's remembering more about when that Philby person shot him."

Kate had been gathering breakfast dishes in a cart, doing Chooli's work and not very happy about it. "He says Philby shot him. That doesn't mean it actually happened that way."

"Shut up, Kate," Jessie said, an automatic response, not much heat to it.

"Come on, Church; time for our walk." Jessie, Lexi and Dickens's hike was becoming a daily ritual they looked forward to. Jessie could feel the bond growing between her and Church Dickens, even as she realized she knew very little about him, realized it more than ever because Kate kept harping at her that he was a scoundrel with bad intentions. Jessier liked his quiet confidence, but today, she promised herself, today we really talk, talk about ... stuff. Actually what stuff? She had to ask that of herself. Everything, she answered. I want to know him, have to know him, who he is, what makes him tick.

The day was overcast, a bitter wind up coming in from the West Coast, the local weather people on both KTAOS Solar Radio and KXMT promising as they had for weeks that the first serious winter storm could possibly arrive soon. Lexi, happy to be freed from the constant chore of feeding her pups, was charging around, circling the humans in her pack and then darting after a rabbit that disappeared behind a screen of dry tumbleweed. Jessie took in a breath and plunged in with what was on her mind. "So, tell me about yourself, Church."

"Sure. What do you want to know?"

"I was thinking since our last walk. I don't really know anything about you. I mean, I like you, you know, sort of as a friend, I mean, we are friends, but I don't really know you."

Her words came to a stumbling halt and he looked at her and the silence lengthened between them. And then he smiled, and she felt a sense of relief and believed everything was going to be okay.

"Yes. And I've been meaning to talk to you. There is a lot," he admitted. "But there's a lot I don't know, and frankly I'm stumped at the moment. Let me start in, and I'll try to be open, and you ask me anything as we go along, and I'll try to explain."

"I promise."

"My brother Ruger and I were – are from the Dickens family. We're from Virginia, go way back to before the American Revolution. We're the last of the bunch, heirs to the tattered remains of the Dickens plantation. There's the old place and some land and a small fund. In the world of business it's not a huge pile, but it is quiet money, safe, and

Ruger mostly handles it. Me, I got my education in earth sciences, went to the army, got shot and got out, got a law degree, got signed on by Verhu to help with land use ventures; Verhu seemed like a good fit at the time."

"And are they?"

"Well, no; they are absolutely not. I got out of there, too. I resigned even before I found out what a really bad guy the head boss is."

"How bad is he?"

Dickens shook his head. "Unbelievable, a psychopath — or maybe it's sociopath — and that's just the little we know. He's a man to stay away from."

"Seriously?"

"Seriously. Look, I'm not a secretive guy, not normally, and I've tried to keep you out of most of this, but the truth is your Carter Cabins is involved in whatever is going on."

"So what is going on?"

"I don't really know, but you and Ed might be in trouble, if not real physical danger, and maybe both."

"No … how can that be?"

"Because this company I used to work for – Verhu Financial – is run by this really bad guy I'm telling you about: he is a tricky and dangerous old man, and he has a history I'm just learning."

"You mean Alan Philby? Kate has had some contact with him."

"I think more than you realize. And that's totally not good."

"What do you mean?"

"Kate thinks that, as Ed's wife, she can represent Carter Cabins."

"But — ?"

"She can't. Not legally. There's a family trust, and she isn't on it. But your mother-in-law doesn't seem to be aware of the law."

Jessie frowned. "Isn't that supposed to be private? How do you know about us?"

"I'm a lawyer. I paid some bucks, looked it up."

"So we're not in any trouble?"

"That, I don't know. Alan Philby is a conniver – and worse – and he's in deep financial trouble, and he's got some plan to dig himself out of it and it involves the lodge next door as well as your land. He really wants to take you over … but he's been forced to take some financial risks that maybe he shouldn't have."

"What risks?"

"Verhu's situation was hopeless even before his headquarters got torched. Philby's bankrupt even if he won't admit it. He'll do anything, and his investors stand to lose everything. He doesn't know it yet, but he's lost control of the lodge."

"Lost it? To who?"

Dickens was shaping the words to tell her when they were interrupted by a yell from the distance. It was Ed, and he was in a bad mood.

"Goldang interlopers! Nobody got no respect for property anymore!" He came skidding up to them on his sporty ATV with the custom flame paint job, one hand off the steering, fist pumping air. "Some damn fool slid a backhoe into Backwash Ravine on Carter land, over near the old mine!"

Chapter 71

Ed was usually a quiet and level headed man, but his anger over the stranded backhoe increased to thundering fury as Jessie and Church got another ATV and followed after him. They approached the fenced off old mine area where Ed had his second unpleasant surprise of the day – a crowd of people who had no dang business on his private property, milling around a small area some fool had roped off with yellow plastic tape! And he heard the slow beat of a pow wow drum and there, right in the middle of all that nonsense was Johnny Hunsai – of all people – and the fake spiritual man was chanting some sort of crazy fool blessing or curse, in a language – if it was one – that Ed doubted anybody there really knew or had ever heard of. The idiot numbskulls gathered around looked like hikers or maybe they were skiers bored waiting at the lodge with the promise of the winter snows that never seemed to come.

Sheriff Joey and his deputy, an affable fellow named Fred, were hustling about, keeping onlookers from getting too close to what they were telling anybody who would listen was a treasured find.

Dickens, seeing the commotion, began clicking away with his cell phone camera. The sheriff tried to warn him off, "You can't do that, son."

"What, take pictures on private property?"

"This is a historical site, claimed by a branch of the Pueblo Indian tribe."

"Where's the paperwork on that?"

"Well, it's all verbal so far – but you see the bones!"

"Right. Tell me when you've got something actual and real."

"Like what?"

"How about DNA? Or how about that scoop of dirt doesn't match anything else on this talus pile and in fact looks like it was dumped there since that little half inch of snow fell last night."

Shirley Treskee, local TV news reporter, rushed up to Ed and stuck a mike in his face, and he found himself staring into the round shiny black circle of a video camera. He tried to wave it away, but that didn't work. Bright lights glared in his face and the lady with the frizzy hair was pushing at him with her mike, insisting on his answer, whatever it was, just give her some reaction.

"What do you think?" Shirley said.

"About what?"

"All this," she waved an enthusiastic hand at the crowd gathered around Johnny Hunsai. "What a great find! An actual Pueblo burial grounds right here on your land!"

Ed took another look inside the newly taped off area in the talus from his mine shaft.

"I can't believe somebody who makes their living doing the news can ask me something so stupid."

"You don't insult me on the air!"

"Sorry, Shirls, girl – I ain't used to this. Lookie here: I ain't worked this mine for over a decade, and you can see shrubs and live oak growing everywhere except in that one little bitty pile of foreign tan dirt with them few bones and that grinning skull sticking out."

"And that means?"

"Well, Shirley – you don't mind I call you Shirley? We are on live television right now?"

"I think we're way past that, Ed."

"Okay. This, what you see here," Ed turned and pointed across the yellow tape barrier, "this is a scoop of old bones from a local cemetery somewhere. See these big tire tracks right here? Make sure your camera guy gets a shot of them. Important evidence, you know."

"Get that, Charley!" Shirley directed, her voice taking on an excited edge.

Ed nodded and pointed off in the distance. "Them tracks was made by a Dynahoe 190, the same backholer what dug up these bones and carted them over here."

"Wait a minute, Ed. How do you know any of that?" Sheriff Joey pushed his way into the shot and held up a hand to block the camera. Charley the cameraman deftly avoided him by stepping back and widening the shot.

Ed couldn't hold back his smile. "Look for yourself, Sheriff Joey. You rightfully are the detective here. These tracks right here lead right over there to my gravel road, and you can follow them a hundred yards or so, still on my property and you'll find that same rusty old backhoe digger I'm talking about – and it is not my machine – stuck on its side down there in my ravine. Come on, Sheriff Joey Johnson, you'll want to see this, like, it's real evidence of a real crime scene."

265

The sheriff had the feeling he was way behind this whole event, maybe he was even being made out to be a fool, but he had an election coming up and he didn't want to be looking bad in what might turn out to be a story with a different ending than the one he'd been fed by Johnny and that blinky old man from California. He started after Shirley, who was already trotting down the gravel road with her cameraman panting to keep up. The Action News truck caught up and they piled in, except for Sheriff Joey who was too late; he cursed and picked up his pace, risking a heart attack by trotting faster than he had in a decade or so.

By this time, Johnny Hunsai had caught the scent that something off-script was in the air. He stopped his chanting, and motioned the drummer and the steady beat faltered and then fell silent. After a brief whispering conversation they quietly moved off, heading back toward the lodge side of the property line.

The small group in the Action News truck piled out at the edge of the ravine, the sheriff and a few stragglers caught up and everybody gathered at the edge, looking down at the end of the hauler cab bumper stuck between two boulders in a nearly dry stream bed, the backhoe itself tipped over sideways on the rocky ground.

Shirley saw they had no clear story here; something wasn't adding up, but they really had no idea who had done what. But she also knew that didn't really matter. They had clear proof something very interesting and maybe even of significance had happened; they had footage of drums and chanting and great shots of ancient human bones – two or three grinning skulls even! Maybe she was just local news, Santa Fe and Albuquerque spilling over into West Texas, but she knew her job; above all she knew they were on live television and that meant they plowed forward, no matter what.

"So just what does this all mean?" she said, again motioning to Charley the cameraman and pointing her mike in Ed's face.

Ed in turn put his arm around the sheriff's shoulder.

"I don't know, Sheriff Joey Johnson," Ed said. "Looks to me like a clear attempt to poach my land with some fake injun burial grounds scheme. What do you think?"

Sheriff Joey, trapped for his opinion on the local nightly news, frowned, cleared his throat, tried for on air presence, "Well, clearly now, Miz Shirley, we have a matter here that demands more investigation …"

"I'll say," Ed agreed, giving Joey a healthy slap on the back. "And you, Sheriff Joey Johnson, are just the man for the job!"

Ed, as a long-time resident of Taos, knew as well as his old pal Joey that those elections were coming up.

Chapter 72

Chooli returned to the Carter Cabins as Mrs. Harvey Fineman, radiant and beautiful, wearing a necklace of sky blue sleeping beauty turquoise and an ornate belt of silver studded with turquoise that seemed to glow in its black spider web matrix. The new couple showed up in the big dining room and Jessie had the Hispanic girls bring them breakfast. Billie stared at the new bride in wide-eyed wonder, and the girls looked on with just a bit of envy. Ed announced her trip to the reservation was with pay, his wedding gift to the new couple, plus she got the rest of the week off. Kate hissed her disapproval and left the room in a huff.

Harvey was looking much better than when he first arrived. Dickens gave him a knowing once-over, top to bottom, the way he would have looked over one of his troopers after a night recon. "You heal fast, Harv."

"I'm getting there. Look what I've got." He handed over a small grey bullet. "A medicine lady pinched it out of my back."

".32 caliber. Got you high and to the right. Save it. The police are going to want to see it."

"Something I been meaning to talk to you about that whole mess. I know, you warned me, but … I mean, it happened so fast –"

"Sure. Combat time; it all goes by like lightning but you play it back it later in slo-mo. Tell me what you remember."

Harvey nodded. "You really do understand: My remembering of that moment, when Alan Philby aimed his revolver at me and actually pulled the trigger, it's like a photograph in my mind. And I'm seeing details – little, big – everything, like it's burned in my brain."

Jessie held up both hands, as if she was stemming the tide of an unpleasant subject. "Maybe we should save this for some other time. I mean, it's your celebration breakfast."

"Just one thing," Harvey said. "Only take a minute, but it might be important."

Jessie and Chooli exchanged a knowing glance, both shrugging at the same time and then smiling at Billie, who grinned back, delighted to be in on big people's stuff.

Harvey leaned back in his chair, his eyes narrowing as he thought back to the terrifying moment when Philby shook himself awake and pointed the short barrel of that little gun at him. But when he spoke, the conversation took an unexpected turn. "I never took the old guy for an intellectual type, but he had books all over his office."

"Books?" Jessie said.

"What sort of books?" Dickens shook his head. "That's not the Philby I'd expect."

"Well, books a-plenty, they were there. History books. Spanish history in the New World. Coronado. Fabulous Inca gold. One of his books actually saved my life. No, honest – it was a big, thick sucker; The Complete History of the Spanish in the Southwestern United States, some long title like that. Man, I was desperate. He'd already shot

269

me in the shoulder. I grabbed that heavy thick old book and held it out in front of me and that second shot slammed right into it, knocked me backwards out the door."

"History was your friend," Dickens said. "Saved your life."

"And I'm remembering something else. He had written right on his wall in big black letters with a magic marker, Siete Cuidades de Oro. On his wall, for God's sake."

One of the Hispanic girls pursed her lips, amused, "Seven Cities of Gold. That old legend again."

Chooli sighed. "People such fools for gold. Everybody knows that old story. The Spanish hear big rumor from a nutsy old Indian guide –probably a bad liar Pueblo man – story about some fabulous gold city, off in distance, shines in the sunset. Then the Spanish men in their iron helmets get dizzy with greed, have many expeditions, lose many fortunes, many lives lost, but to this day they find nothing."

Harvey nodded, still remembering. "Only Philby had crossed out Cuidades and replaced it with another word – Cueva."

"Cave," one of the girls said. "Cavern. Hole in the ground."

Chooli, who had gone to St. Michael's grammar school near Window Rock, crossed herself, with the same gesture showing both her acquired Christianity and the ancient Navajo fear of underground places.

Dickens nodded, his thoughts moving more to outer space. "Harv, I've got a new assignment for you …; I hear the US Geological Survey has a new batch of satellite survey strips. We should see if there's any of Ed and Jessie's property. And the lodge property next door."

"So you think it's maybe something?"

"Who knows? Life is just one big scratcher."

"I'm on it, Hot Shooter."

Dickens pushed a small plain-wrapped package across the table to Harvey. "We're forgetting this; one more thing. You've done it backwards, Harvey. It's supposed to be first you give her the ring, then she says yes, and then the wedding."

Harvey didn't have to open the package. He knew what was inside. And the look of pure delight on his face was something The Hot Shooter would never forget.

Chapter 73

"Wahooiebirds," Jake Smoles said. "Pretty car! That's a classic! Same color Steve McQueen had!"

He was sitting with Johnny Hunsai and Alan Philby on the patio in front of the Taos Pines Lodge as Church Dickens' dark-grey Porsche sportster flashed on by. Johnny was dressed like an Alaskan Eskimo in a heavy hooded overcoat, and Philby had scarves and a plaid wool jacket, but the third guy in the group, Jake, was a Southern California dude; he didn't come prepared for winter. The patio gas lamp heaters were glowing, but there was a stiff wind, weather coming in, and Jake wondered why the old fart had them sitting outside when they could be comfortable on the other side of plate glass not twenty feet away. Jake didn't know it, but Philby recognized the pretty car he was referring to; and the last Philby had heard, his man Tug had been tailing Annie, who had somehow gotten her hands on it. But Annie was supposed to be at the bottom of L.A. Harbor, a cement cinderblock duct-taped firmly between her legs.

"I know that car," Philby said. "God damn that Dickens! Get on it; find out what's up."

Jake sighed and frowned, tired of the constant drama, the Life with Philby Show; he grunted as he pulled up the collar of his light shell jacket and hoisted himself out of his chair.

"What did you say?" Philby said.

"Nothing. Too cold this morning."

It took thirty seconds to get out to the street and then he saw the car had pulled to a stop in front of the Carter Cabins next door. He trotted over, but the fellow behind the wheel of the Porsche didn't know anything; he was just a driver, one of those for-hire car transport guys. Jake offered him a ten-spot to look at the paperwork; big surprise, the job was paid for with Philby's credit card, the name Alan Philby printed out right there on the receipt.

When he heard, Alan went wide-eyed, blinking and red-faced and he sputtered his orange juice in his oatmeal.

Jake gave him a What now boss? look. "Want me to go do something?"

Alan shook his head no, but his mind was racing. If Dickens's Porsche was here, if getting it here was paid for with a Verhu credit card – and Dickens didn't have one any more – then it had to be Annie ... but it couldn't be Annie, unless ... Philby made a snap decision, pulled out his cell phone and called Tug back in LA and a voice answered right away, "Hello. Who is this?"

"No. Who is this? I'm calling for Tug Augustino. Put him on the phone – right now."

"Who is this?" a male voice on the other end of the line repeated, raising his tone from impatience to anger. The guy sounded pompous. Arrogant. In control. Used to giving orders, not taking them. Like a cop.

Philby frowned and clicked him off. Damn! He shouldn't have made that call. Something had gone bad wrong, he was sure of it. No way to tell exactly what had happened. But one thing he was sure of – Annie had gotten away, and that was just one more little bug from his past he was going to have to track down and squash. You had to handle the important things personally; that was the only sure way.

Chapter 74

Ruger sat in the uncomfortable chair next to Celeste's hospital bed doing his day trader thing on his shiny black notepad. He'd come every day even after they'd moved her from the hospital to the rehab home, and now it was a month later and she couldn't figure out what his game was, and she was feeling in the dumps, she had nothing to give him, nothing to give anybody, nothing, nothing, nothing.

As for the total black mood she was in now, that was her fate, she had earned it, and she more or less accepted it. Bad karma, the romance novels called it. The horrible, rotten, bleak future she'd earned for all the crap she'd dumped on Church Dickens, back when they were competitors at Verhu. So be it; Church wasn't the only one she'd stepped on, and she could accept bad Karma, but she didn't have to like it.

"You didn't have to come see me, you know. You don't have to. I'm not going to be anybody's charity." She was in the blackest mood of her life. In the past, she'd always felt there was some little ray of hope for her, some path to the light, no matter what: Her mother had been a doper-whore, so what? that wasn't the daughter. Okay, so she herself had hooked her way through college, but who was going to judge her? Nobody got hurt, and she got just as good grades as those amateurs who gave head to the profs for their A's and B's. She hadn't passed the bar exam like goddamn Church, but so what, she'd pass it next time. But with her lame, even with the foot sewed back on – now she was a gimp, too, a poor loser in as bad shape as gimp-boy Church who at least had two good feet to stand on.

"Might want to check up on your 200 g's," Ruger said. She dismissed the idea of his stupid game with a wave of her hand.

"There is no 200 g's." She knew what was going on; that was just another fantasy Ruger had conjured up to keep her alive. The three of them were in some make-believe market trading competition he'd invented. There was a monthly prize, winner got free breakfast at a coffee house, loser bought dinners somewhere.

"Well, you're right. I think you earned about eight dollars yesterday. I made three grand on Amazon. Even Churchie-boy made six hundred." Ruger tapped the bright red laptop on her over-bed table. "Aren't you even going to look?"

She frowned and pushed the laptop away a few inches. "Why are you doing this?"

"Don't know," he admitted. He gave her an intense look. "I see something I like here. Something in you. Buried way deep in there, under all the crap. Not sure what it is. But I'd like to find out."

"There is nothing here. If I ever had anything to give to anybody, it's gone."

"Maybe I see something you don't. You got a lot to offer, Ce-Ce, and I think we work good together. I think you're something special."

"I'm not special," she insisted.

"You gotta admit there's a certain attraction." She didn't say anything. "Like I mean you got the hots for me, baby. You're just keeping it a secret, deep inside."

"You are a smug, egotistical man and not worth punching out."

"You were right to fall for me, Ce-Ce. I got what my director calls the black Nordic look. It's very desirable in show biz right now."

"You don't have a director."

"Well, I did. Principal photography finished just in time before I rescued you from that burning building."

"Liar! You're telling me you're in a movie."

"Yes, I am. And if you treat me right I'll take you to the world premiere."

"Yeah, sure, can you see it? Me, hopping down the red carpet on one foot."

"You'll barely have a limp by that time. I can see it. You'll be wearing one of those sexy long silk pants ensembles. Nobody'll even know about your foot."

Her resistance crumbled, her lower lip trembled and then she started sobbing.

"Come on, Ce-Ce? Talk to me. Talk to me, baby."

"You don't want me! I'm p-p-pretty sure I'm p-p-pregnant!"

"Well then, you're gonna have to seriously consider marrying me. This is Hollywood, you know. They say they don't let nobody but honorable women walk down that red carpet."

It was one of those unexpectedly topsy-turvy moments. Ruger was on his knees by the side of her bed, his head close next to hers. He was holding a small box in his hands, a box with a carved platinum ring with a huge glittering stone in it. She was stunned, the last thing she'd expected, flying at her out of an unknown future. Even in her dark mood, Celeste could see she was going to have to re-evaluate her notions of karma.

Chapter 75

Three weeks later Belinda Royale's overdue litter dropped eight tiny pups off at the Carter Cabins. It looked like her owners were never coming back from Portugal, and Billie was hoping she could sell off most of the pups for her college fund and still keep one for herself. The many-times promised big snow had yet to drop down out of the sky and many were thinking it wasn't coming at all this winter. Still, something was in the air: Maybe it was Lexi's adopted human's excitement: Church Dickens was wound up over the coming TPL annual stockholders meeting and Lexi herself sensed something big was about to happen.

Philby was in the area, but he was staying out of sight; Dickens had spotted his classic old Bentley at the lodge next door a time or two, but he wasn't there much – and Bella, his DC-3, was parked at the Taos airport.

Philby had mailed all the TPL stockholders and declared this year's annual stockholders meeting would be a "virtual meeting," no need to show up in person, he wrote, as he was claiming Verhu was the majority stockholder, and that would make any dissenting votes irrelevant. Dickens re-counted his shares and checked with the lodge reservations; sure enough, Philby had to know he wasn't telling the truth; he had at some point made and then recently cancelled a reservation on a small conference room. Dickens reserved the room in his own name and texted Philby a short reply: TPL meeting's back on. Same place, same time.

The morning of the off-again, on-again stockholders meeting, Jessie had a Parent-Teacher's conference and so Church was alone as he took Lexi for their walk, their usual meandering amble on the seldom-used path along the creek behind the cabins.

Lexi went frisking on ahead, but then came back and stood in Dickens way, blocking him from moving forward.

"What is it, girl?" he said, patting her head and trying to move around her.

These days the friendly wolfhound hardly left Dickens' side except to be with her pups, who now were growing big as regular size poodles and eating the Carter Cabins out of all the premium kibble they could stock. Church scratched behind her ears, looking over her to the path ahead … and saw why Lexi was holding him back.

There was a tan string across the path, nearly invisible on the sandy ground, only slightly visible where it merged with dusty scrub brush on the creek side of the path. Church went on full alert.

"Lexi, sit!" he said. "Stay!"

The big dog obeyed, watching calmly to see what he would do next. The tan string was taut; two ways it could go – either kick it or cut it, the result might be the same. Church's gaze carefully followed the string to the creek side of the path and realized it was rigged to trigger what looked like a rusty old World War II pineapple grenade.

The problem was, if he left to get help, someone else might come down this same path and set off the grenade. He studied the area, pondering what best to do. They were in a natural depression, the small brook on one side and a hill on the other. And there were some big boulders twenty yards or so downstream.

"Lexi," he said. "What if we throw a rock at it?"

He made up his mind; he commanded Lexi to stay close at his side while they retreated the way they'd come and then pushed through the brush down to the stream. Once he was sure Lexi was safe behind the biggest boulder, he started chucking baseball sized stones at the bush where the grenade was. It took longer than he'd supposed. He'd throw a rock but had to duck before it landed, so he was never sure how close he was. Finally, on the fifth or sixth toss, he was rewarded with his explosion. He missed seeing the ball of flame, but there was a fierce cloud of black smoke and a brief hailstorm of falling rocks, and a chunk torn out of where the trail had been.

He gave Lexi a big hug, not letting go of her broad shoulders until his jitters calmed and he was himself again. His shaggy friend seemed to understand, patiently sitting next to him. It was one of those mornings when there didn't seem to be anybody around. He'd have thought, with an explosion like that, somebody would have come running. He couldn't wait to hear what Ed would have to say about the section missing from the old path.

After a while, Lexi had enough of his hugs. She stood and yawned and looked at him and he gave her a treat and they started back the way they'd come.

"Thanks, old girl," he said. "Maybe that's enough of a hike for today."

Chapter 76

At the stockholders meeting Alan Philby did show up, blinking furiously as he took one of the twenty seats set up facing a makeshift table. And when Church Dickens called the roll, Verhu Financial did have a sizeable amount of stock, in fact enough to assure Philby could have a place on the board of directors. However, the controlling interest went to RC Industries, an investment firm based in Washington, D.C.

"What?!" Philby said. "Nobody ever heard of RC Industries!"

"Nevertheless, the paperwork is right here," Dickens said. "All dated, signed, legal. Want to see?"

"No, I do not want to see your phony, trumped up papers!"

Philby lurched to his feet and for a moment it was clear to Dickens he was thinking of the hide out pistol in his leg holster. The old man was in the back of the room; he'd made a commotion getting up and now everybody in the small room turned around and was staring at him.

Philby saw the scene as a storyboard of his own mistakes: There was Church Dickens, who was supposed to be dead; Harvey Fineman, also supposed to be dead, very much alive with some Indian woman at his side; and that damn persistent Ed Carter and his stubborn daughter; and a tall black man with devious Celeste: the vixen in a wheelchair, her leg in a cast for reasons Alan was aware of (having heard from the agent who managed his house), though by rights she should be dead; the Flaggs, managers at the lodge, not important, would do anything he said; and Johnny Hunsai, showed up because he had a hundred shares of TPL Alan had found it necessary to give him at some point or other. Well, damn it, he couldn't kill them all, not enough bullets, and that was crazy thinking anyway, no way to get away with a public shootout like that.

The thought of his own soon-to-unfold plan was what saved him, the thought of how he was going to best this entire mob of fools. Sure, TPL was a lost cause, but that had never been the heart of his planning, and now his real work was well in motion, nearly finished, in point of fact – and in a few days he could finish loading up Bella, take off, and fly away from all this stupidity and petty crap. He cast a quick look around the room, the scorn plain on his face. These people were idiots. They had no idea! Alan Philby was ready for his phase three.

Chapter 77

Billie didn't like it much when her best pal and nemesis Jimmy Flagg called her a chicken livered snot-face, so she hopped on her board and navigated down slope through the wet snow, dodging around the bare rock spots until she stood next to him, taking a breather and looking back up the way they'd come. They were under the deep and foreboding brow of the Death Drop, the only place they could find where the sun hadn't melted what little natural snow there was.

"If she knew I was here, Mom would kill me," she said.

Jimmy grinned at her and shrugged. "I dunno – it isn't technically the Drop; you'd have to start way up at the top of the ridge, and then the air leap. That's the Death Drop."

"You ever see anybody air it?"

"Nope. Not since that pro-am guy broke his neck trying."

"Professional amateur fool is what he was."

They'd picked up their boards and were about to start on a faint trail they knew that would take them down to the valley floor when they heard a rustling noise and turned to see a small rush of gravel that stopped at their feet.

"Hey," Billie said. "Somebody's up there."

"Not possible. That rock face is straight up and down."

"Can't be. Wanna go see?"

"Ahh, I don't know. Back up there?"

"Who's the snot-face chicken-liver now?"

"Dork-brain."

"Potato-head."

They grinned at each other and started in the new direction, eager to see what was up there on the ledge under the Death Drop.

Chapter 78

I knew – the way all dogs know the important things – that an emergency had come up, that something was vitally wrong in our pack. This one was easy for me: the young girl Billie was late, had not come home, her mother Jessie was fretting, everyone in the cabins was throwing on heavy clothing and rushing outside. What was more, the darkness of early evening was settling over the cabins, the wind was up and the first real storm of winter was coming in. I got up on all fours and stretched. I knew my pups would be okay here. Nobody was going to leave me behind.

"Is Jimmy at your place?" Amy, Jimmy Flagg's mom, called from the lodge; Jimmy hadn't come home either, and he'd said something to one of his friends about there being a little patch of snow under the drop.

"Billie is forbidden from going anywhere near Death Drop," I heard Jessie say.

"Right. Forbidden," Kate said.

"Shut up, Kate," Ed said. "You're right, but now ain't the time."

Jessie told Amy they'd keep in touch. She was already reaching for her winter boots.

It only took a few minutes to get bundled up, and then Jessie and Ed and I started for the back door, the way to where the ATVs were parked. Chooli and Harvey came in, saw what was happening, and decided to join us. Church Dickens, my special human, had been distracted, glaring at the bright screen on his laptop computer all afternoon; while the others were getting ready to go out, he absent-mindedly strapped on his heavy back brace and the closest outdoor clothing that was handy, a woollen scarf and an oversized shell jacket belonging to Ed.

"I'm coming," he called after us. "Don't leave without me."

There was already over two inches of new snow on the ground, with no sign it would let up any time soon. The icy wind was coming in gusts, burning the humans' cheeks, pushing the fallen snow around and starting little drifts where it would.

Carter Cabins had four ATVs that were ready to go, and soon all four were off in different directions, Ed on his flame-striped number headed for the lodge ski lift, Chooli starting down slope toward Taos with Harvey clinging on behind her, and Dickens and Jessie set to ride singles toward Death Drop, hoping to pick up the two kids on the way before they got there.

I had been pacing restlessly back and forth in front of the barn, waiting for Dickens and Jessie, nodding and impatient for us to be on our way.

"I think Lexi's telling us Death Drop Ridge," Jessie said. "Let's just follow her lead."

"Okay. You know the trail better than I do. You go after her, I'll follow," Church said. He wrapped the woollen scarf around his ears. I could see my human was already regretting not putting on a warmer sweater as he mounted the remaining ATV.

"Snow's getting worse," Jessie squinted up at the darkening sky. She didn't hesitate, she gunned her machine away from the barn and we all were speeding away from the cabins with me leading the way. They stayed close behind me, leaving tracks in the new snow as we hurried along the trail past Ed's old mine on our way to Death Drop Ridge.

***

From a ridge across the valley, Jay Bornton watched through his heavy old Bushnell Sporting binoculars. "Son of a bitch," he muttered to himself. "Talk about finally catching a bit of luck! Nobody at the cabins but my gal Kate." He started down the steep path toward the cabins, unaware that he was being watched by Alan Philby from the warmth of an enclosed booth next to the ski lift. Philby set down his empty coffee cup and passed a twenty dollar bill across a small table to the lift operator. He grimaced as he stood, the pain in his aging legs giving him trouble. There was a moment when his mind stutter-stepped and he had to think twice what he was doing. Then he remembered, blinked twice and started for the door. "Mum's the word now, pal. I never was here."

"It's like you never was," the young kid wearing the Sponge Bob Squarepants hoodie agreed. What did he care? Hey, twenty bucks from an old fart he would never see again for doing exactly nothing. Beat working for a living.

Chapter 79

As Philby limped toward the main Carter Cabin entrance, he saw Bornton Breeder's van parked outside, the motor running and the side door open. He'd met Jay Bornton one time on the hill overlooking the cabins, and he figured he knew everything he needed about Jay; he was a sneaky fellow, not to be trusted. But no reason to whack him – you never knew; the enemy of your enemy could be your helper, even if he didn't know it.

The hour being what it was, Philby guessed it was an animal pickup, and knowing some little bits of the rumors flying about the bad blood between the Carters and Jay Bornton, he pretty much could guess some heavyweight dog thievery was about to go down. Not that he cared one way or the other – the devious little breeder being there might help, but he also might complicate things.

More out of habit than with any real plan, Alan retrieved his replacement .32 from his leg holster and carried it at his side as he entered the cabin. This little number had a pearl handle. A fancy-pantsy sidearm, way too fancy for his tastes, but it could do the job, would have to do. Years ago, when he was still back in Chicago, he'd swiped an even dozen .32s , one by one, from the evidence lockers, and he was now down to his last two or three revolvers. Probably didn't matter; once he got out of the States, he might never need another one.

Philby moved carefully in through the wide front doors of the main cabin and quietly made his way into the open dining/recreation area. He saw the place was deserted. Nothing of interest except – wonder of wonders – there was a laptop that looked like the one Church Dickens' owned, sitting right there on one of the tables!

Alan's enthusiasm dimmed as he saw the flash drive port was empty – he knew Dickens used smart sticks for just the reason that somebody might come along, like now, and would want to take a look. But maybe Dickey-boy had left too much in a hurry, left something up – and that proved to be the case. Alan pulled up a chair, absent-mindedly set his revolver on the table and lifted the monitor. He clicked the computer back on and his face clouded in anger. Dickens had been looking at a geologic map! Alan couldn't be sure. Yes? No? He couldn't make sense of all the colors and swirls of different rock deposits – whatever they were – but he was pretty sure what he was looking at was from the Death Drop area. Whatever, the goddamn gimp was getting too close with his snooping around!

"I got to get rid of this guy," Philby said to himself.

And a voice behind him said, "What's up, honey?" He whirled around and it was Kate Carter – the blasted sneaky woman had crept up at his side while he was adjusting the zoom on Dickens' monitor to see if he could get a better idea of just what he'd found! The woman had no sense at all! In the next moment almost as if to prove his point Kate picked up his pistol like it was a toy gun, looking in the barrel and then admiring the look of it, like it was a piece of jewelry. "Hey, we got a nice pearl handle, here. This thing real?"

291

"Put that down," he said. "And I'm not anybody's "honey".

"Could have fooled me, Alan; last month at the Howard Johnson's in Albuquerque."

"Oh, shut up! And stop it! That thing's got a hair trigger."

The timing was all wrong; there was a scuffle from the adjoining hallway and some yelps; a moment of thrashing around and then Jay Bornton burst in the room with all of Lexi's pups on tangled leashes. It was dinnertime and more dog energy than Jay had expected, and he was barely in control as the young dogs lurched about. Jay turned away, pulled by the dogs, and Kate had no idea what was going on. Acting on instinct rather than common sense, she pointed Alan's revolver at the commotion and the gun went off with a loud bang.

Jay yelled "Ow!" and sprawled over a table. The young wolfhounds ran everywhere.

"Scoot! Scoot!" Alan got to his feet too fast, paused for a moment to regain his balance, and then chased them back down the hallway to the nearest empty room, closing the door so they would stay away.

"Kate! You shot me!" the dog breeder wailed.

"It was an accident, Jay! You know I love you. You don't shoot somebody you care for."

Philby snorted, "You love him? I thought I was your sweetie pie."

"Aw, Alan, grow up. Love is complicated."

Philby ripped the .32 from her hand. It went off again, the bullet smashing a china plate with a blue sketch of a sailing ship that had been displayed on the wall.

292

Alan blinked in dismay. This fuss and bother was too much for him. Nothing more to see here, anyway. He pushed Dickens' laptop onto the floor and stomped on it. He reached down and shoved his pistol in its leg holster and started for the door. His legs were on fire and even the small weight of the pistol made his limp that much worse. He was thinking back on the good old days, better times when he bulled through everything; back then he never even would notice the dragging weight of a leg holster.

His mind got a little fuzzy and he was thinking of Chicago, and then his early days at Verhu. He'd been so close, so near to so many fortunes, opportunities all fizzled away except for this last one. Well, this was going to be the good one, the one that made up for all the rest! He was going to do whatever it took to hang onto this one.

The weight of the grenade in one pocket of his heavy jacket reminded him he had some work to do before he slipped away. He checked his other pocket; yep, the dynamite sticks were still there. He slowly turned completely around to get his bearings, and headed for the back door; he knew which cabin Dickens was renting.

"What about me?" Jay wailed.

"It's just an ass shot," Alan said, dismissing him with a wave of the hand. "Lotsa blood but you'll be okay." And then the old man was out the door.

Jay didn't believe him for a second. He was sure he was dying. "Kate, you gotta get me to a hospital."

She eyed him like a third grade teacher whose bratty kids said they needed to take a whizzer. "Oh, for Christ's sake. Come on."

She roughly pulled him up from the table and gave his butt a closer look. "Say, you are bleeding some, considerable 'some,' I'd say by the look of things."

"Kate, please. Hospital! My van's right outside."

She eyed him like he was an animal exhibit at the county fair, "Why not? But you're gonna owe me."

It was interesting times, but it got even more so. Kate brought out two suitcases while Jay waited, moaning and groaning in the passenger seat of his van.

"Jay, hon, you are truly bleeding to death, but I'm in a bit of a bind. I need cash real bad for a sudden emergency come up."

"But I –"

"Hush now, Jay. You gotta hand over every cent you got right now or I'm gonna have to shove you out right here in the street and get to the bank before it closes."

Jay reluctantly handed over his wallet and his contribution amounted to several hundred dollars and two credit cards. Added to the seven thousand cash she'd managed to set aside from the Cabin's household funds and the twenty-some thou in her secret bank account, she figured it would have to be enough for a new start. Sooner or later Ed was going to figure out she'd thrown in with Alan Philby, for all the nothing that had gained her. As for the divorce, all Ed ever had to do was check with the county clerk back in Vegas, he would see the papers were bogus, there never was no real wedding. Eddy had to be one of the world's biggest fools. Regardless, it was high time for her to cut and run.

A bit later, after gassing up the van, she pulled up in front of Emergency at Holy Cross Hospital. "Jay, get out!"

"I can't! I don't think I can stand!"

"Oh, for Christ's sake!" She put his van in park, ran around to the passenger side and yanked the door open. "Jeez, do I have to do everything for you?"

"Maybe get me one of those stretchers on rollers?"

"Don't be silly!"

She took his arm and pulled him out of the van; surprised he couldn't stand by himself, or maybe he was just kidding around because he rolled to the sidewalk and lay there like a shuddering mess.

"God! Don't bleed on my outfit!"

He stared up at her. "Aren't you going to call someone?"

"I'll beep the horn. And don't worry, I'll let you know where to pick up your dog truck. 'bye now, hon."

What the hell, she was thinking, sure, give him his stupid truck back, not much use to anybody with that big yellow sign on the side advertising his dog place. On the other hand, she knew a guy who knew a guy who cut up vehicles for spare parts, might be worth a phone call, see if he was out of jail yet.

Back in the van, she wasted no time getting on the road to Vegas. After all this time, the gals at the ranch were going to be surprised to see her. And, boy, did she have some stories to tell!

Chapter 80

I know I was impatient. I also knew there wasn't anything I could do to hurry Jessie and Church along. The snow fall was thick and heavy, and the trail along the ridge to where I knew the children were was steep in some places and everywhere slippery for their riding machines. I kept running ahead and then coming back to make sure they were still following. It was now the dark of night. There was no wind, mostly just silence, the falling snow, and the roar of their engines and their single beam lights shining the way, keeping them on the trail.

The main path ran along the top of the ridge. Church and Jessie and I had walked it, but now everything looked different with the dark of night and the new blanket of snow on the ground and in the branches and more coming down in a steady fall of flakes. There was a branch off the main trail. I knew this was a good way to go, but it was a short cut the humans didn't use very much, and Church and Jessie continued on past me down the main trail. I barked and sat on my haunches in the cold. Church saw me – I swear that man knew woof-speak – and after a brief back-and-forth with Jessie they both turned their ATVs around and followed after me.

We stopped at the base of the vertical cliff at the top of the Death Drop run. No skiers or hikers ever came here; it was a dead end, nothing to see and nowhere to go. The occasional daredevil who chanced a leap over the precipice might land a few hundred feet or so downhill from here, or maybe not, but if they came up short, that was disaster and a trip to the hospital with some broken bones; hikers weren't interested in this area either, nothing to see but a bare, impossible outcropping, a cliff face of crumbling granite. Then who used the faint trail that led us here? Bel could've smelled something, but all I could smell was what I needed to smell: the human pups.

The snow was heavier now, large flakes coming down, small drifts beginning to pile up at the base of the grey rock and covering the slope where the daring jumpers and boarders hoped to land, and on down the run to the base of the hill. I stopped again, and looked up the cliff face. Jessie and Dickens climbed off their ATVs and joined me, Dickens puffing on his hands, now whitish blue; he'd forgotten gloves as well as a proper sweater.

"Lexi, you sure?" Jessie said. "I don't see anything."

Well, neither did I! But the smell was there, and now I could hear breathing and a stifled sob.

I barked once, and from fifty feet above and out of sight, we all heard a voice, Billie crying out, "Mom, mom, mom! We're up here! We can't get down!"

"Billie, where are you? We can't see you."

"Mom, Mom, it's me and Jimmy! Some mean old guy said we shouldn't be here. He took away the ladder for a punishment!"

"We don't see a ladder."

Dickens took her arm and pointed to a lightweight ladder that was partly hidden in a nearby shrub-covered crevasse.

"Okay, we got it now!"

"You have to use it a couple times," Billie said. "You do it at the bottom, then pull it up, and more times where it's steeper with no other way, like that to up here!"

"Come on!" Jessie said, extending the ladder and leaning it against the vertical stone wall. Church steadied the ladder for her, and once she reached the next elevation he began to pull up the rope extending down from the bottom.

"My God, how did they ever ..." he said.

"Leave it, Church! Get on up here!" He shrugged and scrambled on after her up the ladder.

They found themselves on a two foot deep shelf, barely enough to pull up the ladder, lean it against the even steeper vertical face and start up again, each time the operation more vertical and less steady than before.

"My God, the kids climbed up here?" Jessie said.

Still, in a few minutes Jessie had scrambled on up to the top as far as they could go and was hugging her daughter. Jimmy cheered Church on as he climbed up after Jessie. Even for Church, who knew geology, this was a rare and unusual place.

"What on earth have we here?" he said.

"Gold mine," Jimmy said, feeling more confident now that adults had showed up. "Look at that." He pointed to several picks and a pile of burlap bags. They were at the mouth of a cave that went back into the dark. Jessie had a mag light; it showed there wasn't much of a cavern, just an indentation that ended up in a wall about fifty yards away. A wall with a thick white streak of quartz running through it. And some glittering threads Church recognized. He stared in wonder. "Philby's cavern of gold ... a quartz intrusion with veins of pure gold!

His amazed surprise lasted for all of ten seconds. He was alerted by Lexi barking from below. But it was too late. Someone had used the dangling rope to pull down the ladder from below. He looked over the edge and Johnny Hunsai grinned and gave him a little wave. Johnny gave the ladder a push and it started down the ski slope like it might keep on going until it got to the bottom.

"See you later, city slicker," Johnny said. "Or maybe not."

The four of them were trapped in the cavern on the side of a steep cliff, imprisoned in one of the Siete Cueva de Oro, the legendary seven caves of gold that had for centuries eluded both Spanish conquistadors and, after them, the hordes of grizzled old miners and new age fortune seekers.

Chapter 81

Trapped in the cave of gold, the seconds seemed like minutes, the minutes like hours, and slowly, real hours went by. There was no relief from the icy cold wind, and now the snow was coming down thick, a white-out in the dimming beam from Jessie's mag light. Billie and Jimmy, Jessie and Church sat huddled together, praying Ed or Chooli would find their ATV tracks before the storm covered them.

More time went by with no sign the snowfall was stopping. The weather turned even colder, and the snowflakes were many but smaller. Jessie knew from her years of experience that a real winter blizzard was setting in.

"We're in big trouble, aren't we?" Billie was looking to Church for some hopeful answer.

"There's always a way," he said. "There is always a way – and we will find it."

He stood looking over the edge into the nothingness at the lip of their cave. "How tall was that ladder?"

"I think about twenty-six feet, extended," Jessie said.

"And we had to drag it up a ways. And then use it again."

"No, Church. No. You can't be thinking –"

"The cliff face is nearly vertical. And there's ten or twenty feet of talus slope before the snow begins. When you think about it, the snow isn't that far out there.

"You can't be thinking of jumping."

"Not jumping. Diving … no, more like flying … sort of …."

"That's suicide," she said. "Church, no. Even if it was possible, with your bad back …."

"We can't let the kids freeze to death, and with that wind puffing right at us, I'm thinking of an idea that might work." Dickens unzipped Ed's big jacket half way down and tucked the bottom in his pants, snugging it tight with his belt. "I used to be a pretty good diver in college."

"But I don't see how –"

"Home-made wing suit. It's not really diving, more like controlled falling. My brother did some out on the desert. All I need is a little lift. Not much; that snow starts only ten feet or so distance out from the base of the cliff."

"I didn't agree –"

"Jessie, don't say any more. Please. I know the odds." He was staring into the falling snow. She saw him in that moment as he must have looked when he was in the army, in combat, calculating the odds, determined in the face of an uncertain future. He turned to her and a softer expression came to his eyes. "If it's not too trite, I mean, you have to take life where you find it … I mean, Jessie Carter, would you kiss me for luck?"

She was numb, staring, she couldn't say no. She'd certainly thought about what that might be like. Their lips met, soft, just for a moment.

"Hey, Sweet Girl. Hold my place in line, would you?" he said.

"There is no line, Church Dickens. You're the only one."

He smiled, their gaze locked, taking each other in for a precious moment, and then he turned away, again facing the icy wind. He took a deep breath. And with one short rush he was gone.

He was falling head-first, on his way, arms spread out, in mid-flight, a projectile. The top of the dive felt okay, but then, he told himself, they always did. The rush of wind, the dark nothingness, he concentrated on that inner sense, finding his balance in the plunge. But he outstretched his arms even further and the wind died or simply wasn't there in the first place and maybe he had miscalculated and killed himself — and then he felt a true moment of panic; there was no lift and he was accelerating, plunging straight down to the jagged rocks below.

And then, at the last moment, nearly almost too late, Ed's big jacket billowed out, blooming like a small parachute, pushing him away from the cliff face. But would it be enough?

Too soon the ground came up and smacked him hard, an unexpected punch in the chest, knocking the wind out of him. Still, it was snow! He'd landed in snow, was rocketing down the steep slope through snow! He stretched his body taut, hoping not to roll or crash into any rocks, and he found himself zipping along on the fresh new layer at what had to be over sixty miles an hour – the speed limit on the Los Angeles freeway, his dazed mind told him. And then he lost it, tumbling over and over to land in an aching mess against a webbed barrier some angel had thought to install to keep skiers from flying off the trail into a clump of fir trees. Moments of silent nothing and falling snow. And flakes of snow falling down on a silent human form

Chapter 82

When I saw my human jump headfirst off that vertical cliff, I knew somehow everything would be all right. After all, he thinks, he is smart, he is my human. He didn't exactly fly until the end, when his jacket puffed out, and he smacked into the snow going very fast. I ran after him, coming to the place where he lay quietly. He couldn't be dead. No, he couldn't be. This was Church, my human. He was a survivor. I leaned down and kissed his silent face.

And his eyes opened and he smiled at me and wrapped his arms around my neck.

"Lexi," he said. He said that one word, my name, and I knew everything would be all right now. Had to be all right now.

Chapter 83

It was minutes before Church dared try to stand, and then only with Lexi's help. He was dizzy, shaken from the fall. But his legs supported him; he wasn't paralyzed! His back ached, but that was nothing new. Probably no bones broken. Probably. The big back brace from Doc Jane, had saved his back. But now, snow all around so thick he had no idea where he was. Uphill, he told himself. Come on Lexi! Let's get ourselves back up the hill.

At the base of the Death Drop, the ladder was gone, but Dickens was thinking in another direction. He was remembering Philby's rock climbing wall in the gym in the Verhu building. And there was something else – the vein with the streaks of gold running through it was incredibly rich, and metallic gold was heavy. How did Alan get it out of the cave? If he could get rope up there, there had to be a way to lower everybody down.

Groping around in the dark, he found his ATV and retrieved a flashlight. It took five minutes to find Philby's secret on the far side below the cave opening; there was a coiled nylon rope with a big canvas bucket attached to it. And, dimly outlined in the vertical cliff face, an irregular line of metal clamps hammered into the stone surface. Dickens knew the risk, but he had no choice. He tied the canvas bag around one shoulder and threaded the end of the thick rope through the first metal clamp. He reached for the next one overhead and pulled himself up, standing carefully on the lowest clamp.

That upper body strength he'd used to compensate for his bad back and weak legs for so long — well, he was thankful for that now, and even grateful for the sadistic rehab therapists at the VA hospitals who made him do all those excruciating exercises.

There were bad moments when his hands felt frozen solid, and once one of the clamps pulled free and went clanging down the cliff, but Billie spotted him coming and Jessie helped pull him over the edge and back into the cave.

It was Billie who found the overhead pulley that saved them all. The cave ceiling was low and they could easily reach it. They threaded the nylon rope through the pulley and Church knotted the big canvas bucket in place.

"You have to go first, Jessie."

"No, the kids first."

"No, you have to so you can use the rope from below."

Once she was down, they lowered Billie and then Jimmie, and finally all three of them were able to lower Church. There would be no one left behind in the no-longer-just-legendary Cave of Gold.

Chapter 84

It was past midnight by the time they'd made their escape. There was nearly six inches of new snow on the ground, but the leading edge of the storm front was past, the clouds breaking up and from time to time showing a nearly full moon.

They drove their ATVs back to the main cabin, dropped Jimmy off with his parents and tucked Billie in her bed.

Ed, Harvey and Chooli returned and everyone pitched in to calm the still-excited young wolfhound brood and clean up the blood spattered here and there, not knowing it was from Jay Bornton's unfortunate butt-wound. They gathered around one of the larger tables like a bunch of amateur detectives to try to piece together what had happened in the cabins while they were looking for the kids. Ed, who had gotten into a six pack of beers, passed around a note from Kate telling him – no big surprise – exactly how she felt:

Eddie

This place is a crazy madhouse. You should have

sold it back when I first told you but you don't listen.

You are a big loser. I am leaving you forever.

I took the cookie jar money. Don't try to get it back.

I earned it, putting up with you.

K.

P.S. Guess what. We never really were married.

Ha Ha, that one's on you.

Ed handed the letter to Dickens and finished off a bottle of beer, adding it to the three empties in front of him. "Church, you're a lawyer. You think it's true?"

"It's true, Ed. I checked the records in Clark County weeks ago. There is nothing there. Nothing at all to indicate any of the three of you were married."

Chooli grinned and shrugged, "White man's papers mean nothing anyway. Important is what is in the heart."

Harvey smiled and nodded his agreement.

"Where's Clark County?" Ed said

"Nevada. Las Vegas."

"And you didn't say nothin'?"

"Of course not. That's your business. The only reason I checked you out in the first place, I wanted to be sure Kate had no claim to Carter Cabins. As for the rest …well, it's your private affair. And would you have believed me?"

Ed thought about it, was slow answering. "No, I guess maybe probably not."

Jessie took her father's hand, "Dad, you know you're better off without her."

"Yeah. I suppose so. It's just that a man hates to be wrong about the one, you know, the one he hands his heart to."

"A good guy like you … give it time, you'll find somebody out there meant for you, Ed, that is, if you want," Church said.

Harvey and Chooli were smiling, lost in their young love. "You'll like my grandma," he said.

"Yes, but will she like me?"

"Sure, once I explain about the lost tribes."

Jessie looked around the room and shook her head, "So just what happened here?"

Ed popped open another beer from his six-pack. "Well, here's part of it: from the choke leashes that were on the pups, we know Jay Bornton was here. They all say RETURN TO BORNTON BREEDERS."

Church reached for the last beer. "I hate to see a man drink alone, Ed. You're right about Bornton. Looks like he came here, was going to steal the pups. But he was interrupted by somebody. Somebody with a small caliber pistol. Since we have Kate's note, I think we can assume it wasn't Kate who got shot, so it had to be Bornton." Dickens gestured to his laptop, lying smashed on the floor. "And that was done on purpose."

"Looks like somebody stomped it," Harvey said. "I got to agree with you, Dicks. That looks like the work of a frustrated person probably suffering from dementia."

"We know somebody like that," Church said. "I wonder what other mischief he's been up to around here."

It was late and everybody, even Ed, got to their feet, yawning all around. Jessie looked at Church. "Thank you. Thank you for everything. I don't know how to –"

He kissed her on the forehead and then the lips. "You are wonderful, Jessie Carter," he said.

Everybody went their separate ways, and though Church was aching all over from his heroic dive and fall, and feeling light-headed from his growing bond with Jessie, he didn't go directly inside his cabin. And that was a good thing, because from outside one of the side windows he spotted the little surprise package Philby had wired to the front door.

Dickens pried open a window with a crowbar he found in the barn. It didn't take him long to dismantle the device. It was a simple enough invention; Philby had tied one of his World War II grenades to the door knob. Opening the door would pull the pin on the grenade, setting it off. The other package Dickens found, the one under his bed, was more complicated. This one had a cell phone wired to ten sticks of very old dynamite. Dickens sighed and set the rig on the bed. There had to be a way to deactivate it, and he knew he'd better figure it out before he went to sleep just in case the crazy old Slammer Bammer decided to give him a call before breakfast.

Chapter 85

A few days later about five in the afternoon Church was sitting in the small waiting room at the Taos airport when Jake Smoles showed up.

"I know you drive the Bentley," Church said. "You fly the DC-3, too?"

"Mostly, Alan does. Me, when he's got the shakes."

"He's a man of many talents. Runway's cleared off; I guess you can take off any time now."

Jake moved to sit next to him, but Dickens held up a hand and motioned him to a nearby seat. "Over there," he said.

"What, I smell bad?"

"You've got a reputation, Shiv Killer Man."

They'd seen Jake Smoles often enough, hanging around in the lobby of the Verhu building, waiting to pick up Philby, drive him around in the Bentley. The rumor, floated around the office mostly by Jake himself when he'd get to talking, was that as a young G.I. trooper he had learned to silently kill with a thin knife he called a shiv or a shiver, a lethal trick he supposedly had picked up from an old French Foreign Legionnaire.

Jake grinned and did as Dickens indicated. He liked his reputation. "What you doing here, anyway, Mister Church Dickens?"

"I heard Philby checked out at the lodge. Thought I'd say goodbye."

"I wouldn't recommend that. After all what you done, he doesn't like you."

"I don't blame him. But don't kid yourself – he doesn't like anybody all that much."

Church eyed Jake for a moment, wondering if the Shiv Killer Man stories were real, wondering if Smoles could leap at him while pulling a long shiny knife hidden from God Only Knows where and stab him in the heart.

"What?" Jake said.

It was memorable conversation, talk across enemy lines, tense but pretend-casual. Church had to think of something, and so he said what came to mind, "You are aware Alan's no good with money. Right?"

"Don't tell me that. We got gold in the hold, man. Pure gold. Strands and chunks and veins of it. Gotta be millions."

"Doesn't matter, Jake. You've been around him a while; you know the history. Sooner or later he's gonna run out. Chances are, probably sooner."

Smoles shrugged his thin shoulders. "Then we'll be back."

"And you're sure that's what you want to do."

"You can count on it." The Shiv Killer looked up, saw Philby gesturing in the distance, irritated, wanting to get going. "Oops. There's the boss now. Gotta fly, do an instrument check. See ya later."

"Yeah. Later days, dude," Church Dickens said.

That evening he and Jessie were sitting together on the heated lodge patio, drinking hot chocolates with miniature marshmallows while they watched the sunset. Lexi was nearby, chewing on a hollow red colored Kong toy stuffed with a big carrot. Dickens saw the speck in the distance before they heard anything. Then the speck grew larger and larger and there was the familiar clattering sound that increased to an engine roar and Philby's DC-3 did a thundering low passover, flying directly over Carter Cabins. It was after dusk, the overhead purple about all drained to night time blue-black, the sky clear, a full moon rising over the mountains. A beautiful night, night skiing on all the runs and – joy of joys! – the weather people were promising another snow storm, an even bigger one, in the seven-day forecast.

As they watched the DC-3, the pilot, probably the Shiv Killer, waggled the wings once. Dickens was thinking it had to be Jake Smoles with his hands on the controls; Philby would be busy with his next move. Dickens was pretty sure he knew what was going on up there, what that next move would be. He could almost see Jake in the pilot's seat and crusty old Alan sitting next to him, the ageing killer intent and thorough as ever, blinking as he gazed down to make sure Bella took on the right bit of distance, all the while impatiently eyeing his cell phone, figuring he would need to make his call while still in direct visual contact with the Cabins. Not too near to be a suspect and not too far as to be out of range.

"You know that's Philby's airplane," Dickens said.

"I did not know that."

"He named it Bella. I'm not sure why."

"Maybe he dreams of a beautiful life."

"That must be it."

"Why did he fly over us?"

313

"To let us know he won and we lost. He's telling us we're the suckers and he got what he wanted."

Jessie frowned. "Got away with our gold, is what you mean."

"He's pretty sure of himself."

It was one of those One-in-a-Million shots like you see in the movies, the vintage DC-3 in a deep blue-black sky crossing in front of a huge full moon at the precise moment when the nose of the plane erupted in a ball of flame. A second or two and Church and Jessie heard the sharp report of the explosion, the sound rolling across the landscape.

Jessie pointed at the sky. "Oh, my God! What happened?"

"Maybe some sort of accident. It's an old plane …."

"Will they get out?"

Church Dickens had seen all sorts of explosions in his decade with the military, and he knew what ten sticks of old but still serviceable dynamite could do; but he wanted to spare Jessie any of that. He paused a moment, considering possibilities, and then said, "I'm sure they'd have parachutes."

She seemed to accept that. "It's going to be raining gold all over Taos," she said.

Bella was falling at a sharp angle, turning on her way down, spinning clockwise like the last autumn leaf set free in the breeze. They watched as the plane disappeared behind a hilly ridge.

Dickens shook his head. "No Spanish gold for Alan Philby. Just fool's gold from that deposit behind your cabins, maybe."

"You're not telling me everything."

"Okay. Here it is: Your dad and I borrowed that Dyna back hoe the other night, you know, the one they used to dump those old Indian bones on your property. We went out to Philby's plane, nobody was out there so we did some trading. Ed's pretty good with machines, promised he'd teach me sometime."

She gave him a quizzical look. "Trading …?"

"Yeah. Real gold for iron pyrite."

"Fool's gold."

"Some call it that."

He put his arm around her shoulder and held her close, looking intent off toward the distant mountain horizon like he was seeing the wonder and freedom of these wide open spaces for the first time.. "We put the real gold under some tarps in the back of your barn. Ed thinks he might like to build another cabin or two on further up the hill. Great views up there, he says. Spectacular, really."

Chapter 86

Resting close to the heat lamp on the patio, I watched as the two beloved members of my pack drew even closer and touched lips tenderly in one of those long and gentle kisses nice humans seem to like. I could sense more snow was on its way and that was good, too; I knew the humans loved to frolic around in the cold stuff as it collected on the ground. My people, my children, my pack – everyone was safe. All was right in the world.

THE END

www.ingramcontent.com/pod-product-compliance
Lightning Source LLC
Chambersburg PA
CBHW051516260626
47170CB00003B/645